The Real Man

Francis Lynde

The Real Man

Copyright © 2020 Bibliotech Press
All rights reserved

The present edition is a reproduction of previous publication of this classic work. Minor typographical errors may have been corrected without note, however, for an authentic reading experience the spelling, punctuation, and capitalization have been retained from the original text.

ISBN: 978-1-64799-676-5

TO

THOSE FRIENDS OF UNACQUAINTANCE
AMONG HIS READERS
WHO FROM TIME TO TIME EXPRESS, THROUGH THE
MEDIUM OF
KINDLY AND HEART-WARMING LETTERS,
THEIR APPRECIATIVE SYMPATHY AND APPROVAL,
THIS BOOK
IS AFFECTIONATELY INSCRIBED,
WITH GRATEFUL ACKNOWLEDGEMENTS FROM
THE AUTHOR

CONTENTS

I: Host and Guest	1
II: Metastasis	6
III: The Hobo	15
IV: The High Hills	25
V: The Specialist	35
VI: The Twig	41
VII: A Notice to Quit	44
VIII: Timanyoni Ditch	52
IX: Relapsings	57
X: The Sick Project	63
XI: When Greek Meets Greek	72
XII: The Rocket and the Stick	77
XIII: The Narrow World	83
XIV: A Reprieve	93
XV: "Sweet Fortune's Minion"	98
XVI: Broken Threads	103
XVII: A Night of Fiascos	110
XVIII: A Chance to Hedge	117
XIX: Two Women	121
XX: Tucker Jibbey	130
XXI: At Any Cost	133
XXII: The Megalomaniac	139
XXIII: The Arrow to the Mark	145
XXIV: A Little Leaven	149
XXV: The Pace-Setter	155
XXVI: The Colonel's "Defi"	159
XXVII: Two Witnesses	166
XXVIII: The Straddler	170
XXIX: The Flesh-Pots of Egypt	173
XXX: A Strong Man Armed	180
XXXI: A Race to the Swift	185
XXXII: Freedom	190
XXXIII: In Sunrise Gulch	198

I
Host and Guest

It is conceivable that, in Noah's time—say, on the day before the heavens opened and the floods descended—a complacent citizenry of Antediluvia might have sat out on its front porches, enjoying the sunset over Mount Ararat and speculating upon the probable results of the next patriarchal election, all unsuspicious of chaotic cataclysms. Under similar conditions—fair skies, a good groundwork of creature comforts, and a total lack of threatening portents—there was no reason why the two men, smoking their after-dinner cigars on the terrace of the Lawrenceville Country Club, should suspect that the end of the world might be lying in wait for either of them just beyond the hour's relaxation.

They had been dining together—Debritt, a salesman for the Aldenguild Engraving Company of New York and the elder of the two, as the guest, and Smith, cashier of the Lawrenceville Bank and Trust, as the host. After banking hours, Smith had taken the engraving company's salesman in his runabout for a drive through the residence district and up the river road; and business, the business of printing a new issue of stock-certificates for the local bank, had been laid aside. The return drive had paused at the Country Club for dinner; and since Debritt's train would not leave until eight o'clock, there was ample leisure for the tobacco burning and for the jocund salesman's appreciative enthusiasm.

"Monty, my son, for solid satisfaction and pure unadulterated enjoyment of the safe-and-sane variety, you fellows in the little cities have us metropolitans backed off the map," he said, after the cigars were fairly alight. "In New York, believe me, you might be the cashier of a bank the size of the Lawrenceville B. and T.—only you wouldn't be at your age—for a thousand years and never get a glimpse out over the top of things; never know the people who lived next door to you. Here you know everybody worth knowing, drive your own motor, have more dinner invitations than you can accept, and by and by—when you get deliberately good and ready—you can marry the prettiest girl in town. Am I right?"

The carefully groomed, athletically muscled younger man in the big wicker lounging-chair laughed easily.

"You are not so far wrong, Boswell," he conceded. "I guess we get all that is coming to us, and I get my share. Since we have only one multimillionaire we can't afford to be very exclusive, and my bank job answers the social purpose well enough."

"I'll bet it does!" the jocose one went on. "I've been piping you off ever since we left the hotel. It's "lo, Monty-boy,' everywhere you go, and I know exactly what that means in a town of this size; a stand-in with all the good people, a plate at anybody's table, the pick of partners at all the social dew-dabs. Tell me if I'm wrong."

Again the younger man laughed.

"You might be reading it out of a book," he confessed. "That is the life here in Lawrenceville, and I live it, like thousands of my kind all over the land. You may scoff at it if you like, but it is pleasant and harmless and exceedingly comfortable. I shouldn't know how to live any other kind."

"I don't know why you should want to live any other kind," was the prompt rejoinder. "To be a rising young business man in a rich little inland city, beloved of the gods and goddesses—especially of the goddesses.... Say, by Jove! here comes one of them, right now. Heavens! isn't she a pomegranate!"

A handsome limousine had rolled silently up to the club carriage entrance, and the young woman in question was descending from it. Only a miser of adjectives—or a Debritt—would have tried to set forth her triumphant charm in a single word. She was magnificent: a brown-eyed blonde of the Olympian type, exuberantly feminine in the many dazzling luxuriances of ripe-lipped, full-figured maidenhood. The salesman saw his companion make a move to rise, but the beauty passed on into the club-house without looking their way.

"You know her, I suppose; you know everybody in town," Debritt said, after the cashier had again settled himself in the lounging-chair.

Smith's nod was expressive of something more than a fellow townsman's degree of intimacy.

"I ought to," he admitted. "She is Miss Verda Richlander, the daughter of our one and only multimillionaire. Also, I may add that she is my very good friend."

Debritt's chuckling laugh proved that his prefigurings had already outrun the mere statement of fact.

"Better and more of it," he commented. "I'm going to congratulate you before you can escape—or is it a bit premature?"

"Some of the Lawrenceville gossips would tell you that it isn't; but it is, just the same. Mr. Josiah Richlander has but one measure for the stature of a man, and the name of it is money. The fellow who asks him for Miss Verda is going to have a chance to show up his bank-account and the contents of his safety-deposit box in short order."

"In that case, I should imagine you'd be lying awake nights trying to study up some get-rich-quick scheme," joked the guest.

"Perhaps I am," was the even-toned rejoinder. "Who knows?"

The round-bodied salesman broke an appreciative cough in the middle and grew suddenly thoughtful.

"Don't do that, Monty," he urged soberly; "try to take any of the short cuts, I mean. It's the curse of the age; and, if you'll take it from me, your chances are too good—and too dangerous."

The good-looking, athletic young cash-keeper planted in the opposite chair met the salesman's earnest gaze level-eyed.

"Having said that much, you can hardly refuse to say more," he suggested.

"I will say more; a little more, anyway. I've been wanting to say it all the afternoon. My job takes me into nearly every bank in the Middle West, as you know, and I can't very well help hearing a good bit of gossip, Montague. I'm not going to insult your intelligence by assuming that you don't thoroughly know the man you are working under."

The cashier withheld his reply until the Olympian young woman, who was coming out, had stepped into her limousine to be driven away townward. Then he said:

"Mr. Dunham—our president? Oh, yes; I know him very well, indeed."

"I'm afraid you don't."

"I ought to know him," was the guarded assumption. "I've been with him six years, and during that time I have served a turn at every job in the bank up to, and now and then including, Mr. Dunham's own desk."

"Then you can hardly help knowing what people say of him."

"I know: they say he is a chance-taker, and some of them add that he is not too scrupulous. That is entirely true; true, not only of Mr. Dunham, but of nine out of every ten business men of to-day who make a success. The chance-taking is in the air, the Lawrenceville air, at any rate, Debritt. We are prosperous. The town is growing by leaps and bounds, and we've got the money."

The ash had grown half an inch longer on the salesman's cigar before he spoke again.

"They say worse things of Mr. Watrous Dunham than that he is a chance-taker, Montague. There are men, good, solid business men, in the neighboring cities and towns who tell some pretty savage stories about the way in which he has sometimes dropped his friends into a hole to save himself."

"And you are a good enough friend of mine to want to give me a tip, Boswell? I appreciate that, but I don't need it. It may be as you say. Possibly Mr. Dunham does carry a knife up his sleeve for emergencies. But I wasn't born yesterday, and I have a few friends of my own here in Lawrenceville. My only present worry is that I'm not making money fast enough."

The salesman waved the subject aside with the half-burned cigar. "Forget it," he said shortly; "the Dunham end of it, I mean. And I don't blame you for wanting to assemble money enough to call Mr. Richlander's hand." Then, with the jocose smile wrinkling again at the corners of his well-buried eyes: "You've got all the rest of it, you know; even to the good half of a distinguished name. 'Mrs. J. Montague Smith.' That fits her down to the ground. If it were just plain 'John,' now, it might be different. Does she, too, call you 'Monty-boy'?"

The young man whose name pointed the jest grinned good-naturedly.

"The 'J' does stand for 'John,'" he admitted. "I was named for my maternal grandfather, John Montague, and had both halves of the good old gentleman's signature wished upon me. I stood for it until I grew old enough to realize that 'John Smith' is practically nothing but an alias, and then I dropped the 'John' part of it, or rather, let it shrink to an initial. I suppose you can count all the Debritts there are in the country on your fingers; but there are millions of indistinguishable Smiths."

The fat salesman was chuckling again when he threw the cigar end away and glanced at his watch.

"I don't blame you for parting your name in the middle," he said; "I'd have done it myself, maybe. But if you should ever happen to need an alias you've got one ready-made. Just drop the 'Montague' and call yourself 'John' and the trick's turned. You might bear that in mind. It'll come in handy if the big ego ever happens to get hold of you."

"The big what?"

"The big ego; the German philosophers' 'Absolute Ego,' you know."

Smith laughed. "I haven't the pleasure of the gentleman's acquaintance. I'm long on commercial arithmetic and the money market; long, again, Lawrenceville will tell you, on the new dancing steps and things of that sort. But I've never dabbled much in the highbrow stuff."

"It's a change," said the salesman, willing to defend himself. "I read a little now and then, just to get away from the commercial grind. The ego theory is interesting. It is based on the idea that no man is altogether the man he thinks he is, or that others think he is; that association, environment, training, taste, inclination, and all those things have developed a personality which might have been altogether different if the constraining conditions had been different. Do you get that?"

"Perfectly. If I'd been brought up some other way I might have been cutting meat in a butcher's shop instead of taking bank chances on more or less doubtful notes of hand. What's the next step?"

"The German hair-splitters go a little farther and ring in what they call the 'Absolute Ego,' by which they mean the ego itself, unshackled by any of these conditions which unite in forming the ordinary personality. They say that if these conditions could be suddenly swept away or changed completely, a new man would emerge, a man no less unrecognizable, perhaps, to his friends than he would be to himself."

"That's rather far-fetched, don't you think?" queried the practical-minded listener. "I can see how a man may be what he is chiefly because his inherited tastes and his surroundings and his opportunities have made him so. But after the metal has once been poured in the mould it's fixed, isn't it?"

Debritt shook his head.

"I'm only a wader in the edges of the pool, myself," he admitted. "I dabble a little for my own amusement. But, as I understand it, the theory presupposes a violent smashing of the mould and a remelting of the metal. Let me ask you something: when you were a boy did you mean to grow up and be a bank cashier?"

Smith laughed. "I fully intended to be a pirate or a stage-robber, as I remember it."

"There you are," drawled the travelling man. "The theory goes on to say that in childhood the veil is thin and the absolute ego shows through. I'm not swallowing the thing whole, you understand. But in my own experience I've seen a good man go hopelessly into the discard, and a bad one turn over a new leaf and pull up, all on account of some sudden earthquake in the conditions. Call it all moonshine, if you like, and let's come down to earth again. How about getting back to town? I'd be glad to stay here forever, but I'm afraid the house might object. When did you say Mr. Dunham would be home?"

"We are looking for him to-morrow, though he may be a day or two late. But you needn't worry about your order, if that is what is troubling you. I happen to know that he intends giving the engraving of the new stock-certificates to your people."

The New York salesman's smile had in it the experience-taught wisdom of all the ages.

"Montague, my son, let me pay for my dinner with a saying that is as old as the hills, and as full of meat as the nuts that ripen on 'em: in this little old round world you have what you have when you have it. This evening we've enjoyed a nice little five-course dinner, well cooked and well served, in a pretty nifty little club, and in a few minutes we'll be chasing along to town in your private buzz-wagon, giving our dust to anybody who wants to take it. Do you get that?"

"I do. But what's the answer?"

"The answer is the other half of it. This time to-morrow we may both be asking for a hand-out, and inquiring, a bit hoarsely, perhaps, if the walking is good. That is just how thin the partitions are. You don't believe it, of course; couldn't even assume it as a working hypothesis. What could possibly happen to you or to me in the next twenty-four hours? Nothing, nothing on top of God's green earth that could pitch either or both of us over the edge, you'd say—or to Mr. Dunham to make him change his mind about the engraving job. Just the same, I'll drop along in the latter part of the week and get his name signed to the order for those stock-certificates. Let's go and crank up the little road-wagon. I mustn't miss that train."

II
Metastasis

It was ten minutes of eight when J. Montague Smith, having picked up the salesman's sample cases at the town hotel, set Debritt down at the railroad station and bade him good-by. Five minutes later he had driven the runabout to its garage and was hastening across to his suite of bachelor apartments in the Kincaid Terrace. There was reason for the haste. Though he had been careful, from purely hospitable motives, to refrain from intimating the fact to Debritt, it was his regular evening for calling upon Miss Verda Richlander, and time pressed.

The New York salesman, enlarging enthusiastically upon the provincial beatitudes, had chosen a fit subject for their illustration in the young cashier of the Lawrenceville Bank and Trust. From his earliest recollections Montague Smith had lived the life of the well-behaved and the conventional. He had his niche in the Lawrenceville social structure, and another in the small-city business world, and he filled both to his own satisfaction and to the admiration of all and sundry. Ambitions, other than to take promotions in the bank as they came to him, and, eventually, to make money enough to satisfy the demands which Josiah Richlander might make upon a prospective son-in-law, had never troubled him. An extremely well-balanced young man his fellow townsmen called him, one of whom it might safely be predicted that he would go straightforwardly on his way to reputable middle life and old age; moderate in all things, impulsive in none.

Even in the affair with Miss Richlander sound common sense and sober second thought had been made to stand in the room of supersentiment. Smith did not know what it was to be violently in love; though he was a charter member of the Lawrenceville Athletic Club and took a certain pride in keeping himself physically fit and up to the mark, it was not his habit to be violent in anything. Lawrenceville expected its young men and young women to marry and "settle down," and J. Montague Smith, figuring in a modest way as a leader in the Lawrenceville younger set, was far too conservative to break with the tradition, even if he had wished to. Miss Richlander was desirable in many respects. Her father's ample fortune had not come early enough or rapidly enough to spoil her. In moments when his feeling for her achieved its nearest approach to sentiment the conservative young man perceived what a graciously resplendent figure she would make as the mistress of her own house and the hostess at her own table.

Arrived at his rooms in the Kincaid, Smith snapped the switch of the electrics and began to lay out his evening clothes, methodically and with a careful eye to the spotlessness of the shirt and the fresh immaculacy of the waistcoat. There were a number of little preliminaries to the change; he made the preparations swiftly but with a certain air of calm deliberation, inserting the buttons in the waistcoat, choosing hose of the proper thinness, rummaging a virgin tie out of its box in the top dressing-case drawer.

It was in the search for the tie that he turned up a mute reminder of his nearest approach to any edge of the real chasm of sentiment: a small glove, somewhat soiled and use-worn, with a tiny rip in one of the fingers. It had been a full year since he had seen the glove or its owner, whom he had met only once, and that entirely by chance. The girl was a visitor from the West, the daughter of a ranchman, he had understood; and she had been stopping over with friends in a neighboring town. Smith had driven over one evening in his runabout to make a call upon the daughters of the house, and had found a lawn-party in progress, with the Western visitor as the guest of honor.

Acquaintance—such an acquaintance as can be achieved in a short social hour—had followed, and the sight of the small glove reminded him forcibly of the sharp little antagonisms that the hour had developed. At all points the bewitching young woman from the barbaric wildernesses, whose dropped glove he had surreptitiously picked up and pocketed, had proved to be a mocking critic of the commonplace conventions, and had been moved to pillory the same in the person of her momentary entertainer. Smith had recalled his first tasting of a certain French liqueur with perfume in it, and the tingling sense of an awakening of some sort running through his veins as an after effect not altogether pleasant, but vivifying to a degree. Some similar thrillings this young person from the wide horizons had stirred in him—which was his only excuse for stealing her glove.

Though he was far enough from recognizing it as such, the theft had been purely sentimental. A week later, when he would have courted a return of the thrills, he had learned that she had gone back to her native wilds. It was altogether for the best, he had told himself at the time, and at other times during the year which now intervened. Perfumed liqueurs are not for those whose tastes and habits are abstemious by choice; and there remained now nothing of the clashing encounter at the lawn-party save the soiled glove, a rather obscure memory of a face too piquant and attractive to be cheapened by the word "pretty"; these and a thing she had said at the moment of parting: "Yes; I am going back home very soon. I don't like your smug Middle-West civilization, Mr. Smith—it smothers me. I don't wonder that it breeds men who live and grow up and die without ever having a chance to find themselves."

He was recalling that last little thrust and smiling reminiscently over it as he replaced the glove among its fellow keepsakes: handkerchief boxes, tie-holders, and what not, given him on birthdays and Christmases by the home-town girls who had known him from boyhood. Some day, perhaps, he would tell Verda Richlander of the sharp-tongued little Western beauty. Verda—and all sensible people—would smile at the idea that he, John Montague Smith, was of those who had not "found" themselves, or that the finding—by which he had understood the Western young woman to mean something radical and upsetting—could in any way be forced upon a man who was old enough and sane enough to know his own lengths and breadths and depths.

He had closed the drawer and was stripping off his coat to dress when he saw that, in entering the room in the dark, he had overlooked two letters which had evidently been thrust under the door during his absence with Debritt. One of the envelopes was plain, with his name scribbled on it in pencil. The other bore a typewritten address with the card of the Westfall Foundries Company in its upper left-hand corner. Smith opened Carter Westfall's letter first and read it with a little twinge of shocked surprise, as one reads the story of a brave battle fought and lost.

"Dear Monty," it ran. "I have been trying to reach you by 'phone off and on ever since the adjournment of our stockholders' meeting at three o'clock. We, of the little inside pool, have got it where the chicken got the axe. Richlander had more proxies up his sleeve than we thought he had, and he has put the steam-roller over us to a finish. He was able to vote fifty-five per cent of the stock straight, and you know what that means: a consolidation with the Richlander foundry trust, and the hearse and white horses for yours truly and the minority stockholders. We're dead—dead and buried.

"Of course, I stand to lose everything, but that isn't all of it. I'm horribly anxious for fear you'll be tangled up personally in some way in the matter of that last loan of $100,000 that I got from the Bank and Trust. You will remember you made the loan while Dunham was away, and I am certain you told me you had his consent to take my Foundries stock as collateral. That part of it is all right, but, as matters stand, the stock isn't worth the paper it is printed on, and—well, to tell the bald truth, I'm scared of Dunham. Brickley, the Chicago lawyer they have brought down here, tells me that your bank is behind the consolidation deal, and if that is so, there is going to be a bank loss to show up on my paper, and Dunham will carefully cover his tracks for the sake of the bank's standing.

"It is a hideous mess, and it has occurred to me that Dunham can put you in bad, if he wants to. When you made that $100,000 loan, you forgot—and I forgot for the moment—that you own ten shares of Westfall Foundries in your own name. If Dunham wants to stand from under, this might be used against you. You must get rid of that stock, Monty, and do it quick. Transfer the ten shares to me, dating the transfer back to Saturday. I still have the stock books in my hands, and I'll make the entry in the record and date it to fit. This may look a little crooked, on the surface, but it's your salvation, and we can't stop to split hairs when we've just been shot full of holes.

"Westfall."

Smith folded the letter mechanically and thrust it into his pocket. Carter Westfall was his good friend, and the cashier had tried, unofficially, to dissuade Westfall from borrowing after he had admitted that he was going to use the money in an attempt to buy up the control of his own company's stock. As Smith took up the second envelope he was not thinking of himself, or of the possible danger hinted at in Westfall's warning. The big bank loss was the chief thing to be considered—that and the hopeless ruin of a good fellow like Carter Westfall. He was thinking of both when he tore the second envelope across and took out the enclosed slip of scratch-paper. It was a note from the president and it was dated within the hour. Mr. Dunham had evidently anticipated his itinerary. At all events, he was back in Lawrenceville, and the note had been written at the bank. It was a curt summons; the cashier was wanted, at once.

At the moment, Smith did not connect the summons with the Westfall cataclysm, or with any other untoward thing. Mr. Watrous Dunham had a habit of dropping in and out unexpectedly. Also, he had the habit of sending for his cashier or any other member of the banking force at whatever hour the notion seized him. Smith went to the telephone and called up the Richlander house. The promptness with which the multimillionaire's daughter came to the 'phone was an intimation that his ring was not entirely unexpected.

"This is Montague," he said, when Miss Richlander's mellifluous "Main four six eight—Mr. Richlander's residence" came over the wire. Then: "What are you going to think of a man who calls you up merely to beg off?" he asked.

Miss Richlander's reply was merciful and he was permitted to go on and explain. "I'm awfully sorry, but it can't very well be helped, you know. Mr. Dunham has returned, and he wants me at the bank. I'll be up a little later on, if I can break away, and you'll let me come.... Thank you, ever so much. Good-by."

Having thus made his peace with Miss Richlander, Smith put on his street coat and hat and went to obey the president's summons. The Lawrenceville Bank and Trust, lately installed in its new marble-veneered quarters in the town's first—seven-storied—sky-scraper, was only four squares distant; two streets down and two across. As he was approaching the sky-scraper corner, Smith saw that there were only two lights in the bank, one in the vault corridor and another in the railed-off open space in front which held the president's desk and his own. Through the big plate-glass windows he could see Mr. Dunham. The president was apparently at work, his portly figure filling the padded swing-chair. He had one elbow on the desk, and the fingers of the uplifted hand were thrust into his thick mop of hair.

Smith had his own keys and he let himself in quietly through the door on the side street. The night-watchman's chair stood in its accustomed place in the vault corridor, but it was empty. To a suspicious person the empty chair might have had its significance; but Montague Smith was not suspicious. The obvious conclusion was that Mr. Dunham had sent the watchman forth upon some errand; and the motive needed not to be tagged as ulterior.

Without meaning to be particularly noiseless, Smith—rubber heels on tiled floor assisting—was unlatching the gate in the counter-railing before his superior officer heard him and looked up. There was an irritable note in the president's greeting.

"Oh, it's you, at last, is it?" he rasped. "You have taken your own good time about coming. It's a half-hour and more since I sent that note to your room."

Smith drew out the chair from the stenographer's table and sat down. Like the cashiers of many little-city banks, he was only a salaried man, and the president rarely allowed him to forget the fact. None the less, his boyish gray eyes were reflecting just a shade of the militant antagonism in Mr. Watrous Dunham's when he said: "I was dining at the Country Club with a friend, and I didn't go to my rooms until a few minutes ago."

The president sat back in the big mahogany swing-chair. His face, with the cold, protrusive eyes, the heavy lips, and the dewlap lower jaw, was the face of a man who shoots to kill.

"I suppose you've heard the news about Westfall?"

Smith nodded.

"Then you also know that the bank stands to lose a cold hundred thousand on that loan you made him?"

The young man in the stenographer's chair knew now very well why the night-watchman had been sent away. He felt in his pocket for a cigar but failed to find one. It was an unconscious effort to gain time for some little readjustment of the conventional point of view. The president's attitude plainly implied accusation, and Smith saw the solid foundations of his small world—the only world he had ever known—crumbling to a threatened dissolution.

"You may remember that I advised against the making of that loan when Westfall first spoke of it," he said, after he had mastered the premonitory chill of panic. "It was a bad risk—for him and for us."

"I suppose you won't deny that the loan was made while I was away in New York," was the challenging rejoinder.

"It was. But you gave your sanction before you went East."

The president twirled his chair to face the objector and brought his palm down with a smack upon the desk-slide.

"No!" he stormed. "What I told you to do was to look up his collateral; and you took a snap judgment and let him have the money! Westfall is your friend, and you are a stockholder in his bankrupt company. You took a chance for your own hand and put the bank in the hole. Now I'd like to ask what you are going to do about it."

Smith looked up quickly. Somewhere inside of him the carefully erected walls of use and custom were tumbling in strange ruins and out of the débris another structure, formless as yet, but obstinately sturdy, was rising.

"I am not going to do what you want me to do, Mr. Dunham—step in and be your convenient scapegoat," he said, wondering a little in his inner recesses how he was finding the sheer brutal man-courage to say such a thing to the president of the Lawrenceville Bank and Trust. "I suppose you have reasons of your own for wishing to shift the responsibility for this particular loss to my shoulders. But whether you have or haven't, I decline to accept it."

The president tilted his chair and locked his hands over one knee.

"It isn't a question of shifting the responsibility, Montague," he said, dropping the bullying weapon to take up another. "The loan was made in my absence. Perhaps you may say that I went away purposely to give you the chance of making it, but, if you do, nobody will believe you. When it comes down to the matter of authorization, it is simply your word against mine—and mine goes. Don't you see what you've done? As the matter stands now, you have let yourself in for a criminal indictment, if the bank directors choose to push it. You have taken the bank's money to bolster up a failing concern in which you are a stockholder. Go to any lawyer in Lawrenceville—the best one you can find—and he'll tell you exactly where you stand."

While the big clock over the vault entrance was slowly ticking off a full half-minute the young man whose future had become so suddenly and so threateningly involved neither moved nor spoke, but his silence was no measure of the turmoil of conflicting emotions and passions that were rending him. When he looked up, the passions, passions which had hitherto been mere names to him, were still under control, but to his dismay his restraining hold upon them seemed to be growing momentarily less certain.

"I may not prove quite the easy mark that your plan seems to prefigure, Mr. Dunham," he returned at length, trying to say it calmly. "But assuming that I am all that you have been counting upon, and that you will carry out your threat and take the matter into the courts, what is the alternative? Just what are you expecting me to do?"

"Now you are talking more like a grown man," was the president's crusty admission. "You are in a pretty bad boat, Montague, and that is why I sent for you to-night. It didn't seem safe to waste any time if you were to be helped out. Of course, there will be a called meeting of the bank board to-morrow, and it will all come out. With the best will in the world to do you a good turn, I shan't be able to stand between you and trouble."

"Well?" said the younger man, still holding the new and utterly incomprehensible passions in check.

"You can see how it will be. If I can say to the directors that you have already resigned—and if you are not where they can too easily lay hands on you—they may not care to push the charge against you. There is a train west at ten o'clock. If I were in your place, I should pack a couple of suitcases and take it. That is the only safe thing for you to do. If you need any ready money——"

It was at this point that J. Montague Smith rose up out of the stenographer's chair and buttoned his coat.

"'If I need any ready money,'" he repeated slowly, advancing a step toward the president's desk. "That is where you gave yourself away, Mr. Dunham. You authorized that loan, and you meant to authorize it. More than that, you did it because you were willing to use the bank's money to put Carter Westfall in the hole so deep that he could never climb out. Now, it seems, you are willing to bribe the only dangerous witness. I don't need money badly enough to sell my good name for it. I shall stay right here in Lawrenceville and fight it out with you!"

The president turned abruptly to his desk and his hand sought the row of electric bell-pushes. With a finger resting upon the one marked "police," he said: "There isn't any room for argument, Montague. You can have one more minute in which to change your mind. If you stay, you'll begin your fight from the inside of the county jail."

Now, as we have seen, there had been nothing in John Montague Smith's well-ordered quarter century of boyhood, youth, and business manhood to tell him how to cope with the crude and savage emergency which he was confronting. But in the granted minute of respite something within him, a thing as primitive and elemental as the crisis with which it was called upon to grapple, shook itself awake. At the peremptory bidding of the newly aroused underman, he stepped quickly across the intervening space and stood under the shaded desk light within arm's reach of the man in the big swing-chair.

"You have it all cut and dried, even to the setting of the police trap, haven't you?" he gritted, hardly recognizing his own voice. "You meant to hang me first and try your own case with the directors afterward. Mr. Dunham, I know you better than you think I do: you are not only a damned crook—you are a yellow-livered coward, as well! You don't dare to press that button!"

While he was saying it, the president had half risen, and the hand which had been hovering over the bell-pushes shot suddenly under the piled papers in the corner of the desk. When it came out it was gripping the weapon which is never very far out of reach in a bank.

Good judges on the working floor of the Lawrenceville Athletic Club had said of the well-muscled young bank cashier that he did not know his own strength. It was the sight of the pistol that maddened him and put the driving force behind the smashing blow that landed upon the big man's chest. Two inches higher or lower, the blow might have been merely breath-cutting. As it was, the lifted pistol dropped from Mr. Watrous Dunham's grasp and he wilted, settling back slowly, first into his chair, and then slipping from the chair to the floor.

In a flash Smith knew what he had done. Once, one evening when he had been induced to put on the gloves with the Athletic Club's trainer, he had contrived to plant a body blow which had sent the wiry little Irishman to the mat, gasping and fighting for the breath of life. "If ever yez'll be givin' a man that heart-punch wid th' bare fisht, Misther Montygue, 'tis you f'r th' fasht thrain widout shtoppin' to buy anny ticket—it'll be murdher in th' first degree," the trainer had said, when he had breath to compass the saying.

With the unheeded warning resurgent and clamoring in his ears, Smith knelt horror-stricken beside the fallen man. On the president's heavy face and in the staring eyes there was a foolish smile, as of one mildly astonished. Smith loosened the collar around the thick neck and laid his ear upon the spot where the blow had fallen. It was as the Irish trainer had told him it would be. The big man's heart had stopped like a smashed clock.

Smith got upon his feet, turned off the electric light, and, from mere force of habit, closed and snap-locked the president's desk. The watchman had not yet returned. Smith saw the empty chair beside the vault door as he passed it on his way to the street. Since the first impulse of the unwilling or unwitting homicide is usually sharply retributive, the cashier's only thought was to go at once to police headquarters and give himself up. Then he remembered how carefully the trap had been set, and how impossible it would be for him to make any reasonable defense. As it would appear, he had first taken the bank's money to help Westfall, and afterward, when exposure had threatened, he had killed the president. No one would ever believe that the blow had been struck in self-defense.

It was at the hesitating instant that Debritt's curiously prophetic words came back to him with an emphasis that was fairly appalling: "To-morrow we may both be asking for a hand-out, and inquiring, a bit hoarsely, perhaps, if the walking is good. That is just how thin the partitions are." With one glance over his shoulder at the darkened front windows of the bank, Smith began to run, not toward the police station, but in the opposite direction—toward the railroad station.

This was at nine o'clock or, perhaps, a few minutes later. Coincident with J. Montague Smith's dash down the poorly lighted cross street, a rather weak-faced young man of the sham black-sheep type of the smaller cities was lounging in the drawing-room of an ornate timber-and-stucco mansion on Maple Street hill and saying to his hostess: "Say—I thought this was Monty's night to climb the hill, Miss Verda. By Jove, I've got it in for Monty, don't y' know. He's comin' here a lot too regular to please me."

"Mr. Smith always puts business before pleasure; haven't you found that out yet, Mr. Jibbey?" was the rather cryptic rejoinder of the Olympian beauty; and after that she talked, and made the imitation rounder talk, pointedly of other things.

III

The Hobo

For J. Montague Smith, slipping from shadow to shadow down the scantily lighted cross street and listening momently for the footfalls of pursuit, a new hour had struck. Psychology to the contrary notwithstanding, the mental mutations are not always, or of necessity, gradual. In one flaming instant the ex-cashier had been projected across the boundary lying between the commonplace and the extraordinary; but for the time he was conscious only of a great confusion, shot through with a sense of his own present inability to cope with the strangenesses.

In the projecting instant, time and the graspable realities had both been annihilated. Was it conceivable that this was the evening of the same day in which he had entertained Boswell Debritt at the Country Club? Was it remotely thinkable that, only an hour or such a matter earlier, he had been getting ready to call upon Verda Richlander?—that, at this very moment, his dress clothes were lying on the bed in his rooms, ready to be put on?

It was all prodigiously incredible; in the collapse of the universe one scene alone stood out clearly cut and vivid: the railed space in the bank, with the shaded drop-light and the open desk, and a fleshy man stretched out upon the floor with his arms flung wide and a foolish smile of mild astonishment fixed, as for all eternity, about the loosened lips and in the staring eyes.

Smith hurried on. The crowding sensations were terrifying, but they were also precious, in their way. Long-forgotten bits of brutality and tyranny on Watrous Dunham's part came up to be remembered and, in this retributive aftermath, to be triumphantly crossed off as items in an account finally settled. On the Smith side the bank cashier's forebears had been plodding farmers, but old John Montague had been the village blacksmith and a soldier—a shrewd smiter in both trades. Blood will tell. Parental implantings may have much to say to the fruit of the womb, but atavism has more. Smith's jaw came up with a snap and the metamorphosis took another forward step. He was no longer an indistinguishable unit in the ranks of the respectable and the well-behaved; he was a man fleeing for his life. What was done was done, and the next thing to do was to avert the consequences.

At the railroad station a few early comers for the westbound passenger-train due at ten o'clock were already gathering, and at the bidding of a certain new and militant craftiness Smith avoided the lighted waiting-rooms as if they held the pestilence. Nor was it safe to pass beyond the building. The May night was fine, and there were strollers on the train platform. Smith took no risks. A string of box cars had been pushed up from the freight unloading platforms, and in the shadow of the cars he worked his way westward to the yard where a night switching crew was making up a train.

Thus far he had struck out no plan. But the sudden shift from the normal to the extraordinary had not shorn him of the ability to think quickly and to the definite end. A placed road-engine, waiting for the conclusion of the car sorting, told him that the next train to leave the yard would be a westbound freight. He would have given much to know its exact leaving time, but he was far too clear-headed to give the pursuers a clew by asking questions.

Keeping to the shadows, he walked back along the line of cars on the make-up track, alertly seeking his opportunity. If worst came to worst, he could select a car with four truss-rods and crawl in on top of the rods after the manner of the professional ride-stealers. But this was a last resort; the risk was large for his inexperience, and he was very well aware that there must be some sort of an apprenticeship, even to the "brake-beamer's" trade.

Half-way down the length of the train he found what he was looking for: a box car with its side-door hasped but not locked. With a bit of stick to lengthen his reach, he unfastened the hasp, and at the switching crew's addition of another car to the "make-up" he took advantage of the noise made by the jangling crash and slid the door. Then he ascertained by groping into the dark interior that the car was empty. With a foot on the truss-rod he climbed in, and at the next coupling crash closed the door.

So far, all was well. Unless the start should be too long delayed, or the trainmen should discover the unhasped door, he was measurably safe. Still cool and collected, he began to cast about for some means of replacing the outside fastening of the door from within. There was loose hay under-foot and it gave him his idea. Groping again, he found a piece of wire, a broken bale-tie. The box car was old and much of its inner sheathing had disappeared. With the help of his pocket-knife he enlarged a crack in the outer sheathing near the door, and a skilful bit of juggling with the bent wire sufficed to lift the hasp into place on the outside and hook it.

Following this clever removal of one of the hazards, he squatted upon the floor near the door and waited. Though he was familiar with the schedules of the passenger-trains serving the home city, he knew nothing of the movements of the freights. Opening the face of his watch, he felt the hands. It was half-past nine, and the thrust and whistle of the air-brakes under the cars gave notice that the road engine had been coupled on. Still the train did not pull out.

After a little he was able to account for the delay. Though his knowledge of railroad operating was limited, common sense told him that the freight would not be likely to leave, now, ahead of the ten o'clock passenger. That meant another half-hour of suspense to be paid for in such coin as one might be able to offer. The fugitive paid in keen agonies of apprehension. Surely, long before this the watchman would have returned to the bank, and the hue and cry being raised, the pursuit must now be afoot. In that case, the dullest policeman on the force would know enough to make straight for the railroad yard.

Smith knelt at the crack of the car door and listened, while the minutes dragged slowly in procession. Once, through the crack, he had a glimpse of the smoky flare of a kerosene torch in the hands of a passing car-inspector; and once again, one of the trainmen walked back over the tops of the cars, making a creaky thundering overhead as he tramped from end to end of the "empty." But as yet there was no hue and cry, or, if there were, it had not reached the railroad yard.

Keenly alive to every passing sound, Smith finally heard the passenger-train coming in from the east; heard the hoarse stridor of the engine's pop-valve at the station stop, and the distance-diminished rumblings of the baggage and express trucks over the wooden station platform. The stop was a short one, and in a few minutes the passenger-train came down through the yard, its pace measured by the sharp staccato blasts of the exhaust. It was the signal of release, and as the quickening staccato trailed away into silence, Smith braced himself for the slack-taking jerk of the starting freight.

The jerk did not come. Minute by minute the interval lengthened, and at last the listener in the "empty" heard voices and saw through the crack of the door a faint nimbus of lantern light approaching from the rear of the train. The voices came nearer. By the dodging movements of the light rays, Smith knew instantly what was coming. His pursuers were out, and they were overhauling the waiting freight-train, searching it for a stowaway.

He hardly dared breathe when the lantern-bearers reached his car. There were a number of them, just how many he could not determine. But McCloskey, the Lawrenceville chief of police, was one of the number. Also, there was an Irish yardman who was carrying one of the lanterns and swinging it under the cars to show that the truss-rods and brake-beams were empty.

"'Tis not the likes of him that do be brake-beamin' their way out of town, Chief," the Irishman was saying. "'Tis more likely he's tuk an autymobile and the middle of the big road."

"There's no automobile missing, and his own car is still in the garage," Smith heard the police chief say. And then: "Hold your lantern up here, Timmy, till we see if this car door is fastened shut."

It was a measure of the distance that the bank clerk and small-city social leader had already travelled on the road toward a complete metamorphosis that the only answer to this threat of discovery was a tightening of the muscles, a certain steeling of thews and sinews for the wild-beast spring if the door should be opened. One thought dominated all others: if they took him they should not take him alive.

Happily or unhappily, as one may wish to view it, the danger passed. "The door's fastened, all right," said one of the searchers, and the menace went on, leaving Smith breathing hard and chuckling grimly to himself over the cunning forethought which had prompted him to grope for the bit of wire bale-tie.

Past this there was another interval of waiting—a brief one, this time. Then the long freight began to move out over the switches. When he could no longer see the sheen of the city electrics in the strip of sky visible through his door crack, Smith gathered up the leavings of hay on the car floor and stretched himself out flat on his back. And it was another measure of the complete triumph of the elemental underman over the bank clerk that he immediately fell asleep and did not awaken until a jangling of draw-bars and a ray of sunlight sifting through the crack of the door told him that the train had arrived at some destination, and that it was morning.

Sitting up to rub his eyes and look at his watch, the fugitive made a hasty calculation. If the train had been in motion all night, this early morning stopping-place should be Indianapolis. Getting upon his feet, he applied an investigative eye to the crack. The train, or at least his portion of it, was side-tracked in a big yard with many others. Working the pick-lock wire again, he unhasped the door and opened it. There was no one in sight in this particular alley of the crowded yard, and he dropped to the ground and slid the door back into place.

Making a note of the initials and number, so that he might find the car again, he crawled under three or four standing trains and made his way to a track-side lunch-counter. The thick ham sandwich and the cup of muddy coffee eaten and drunk with the appetite of a starved vagrant set up another mile-stone in the distances traversed. Was it, indeed, only on the morning of yesterday that he had sent his toast back because, forsooth, the maid at Mrs. Gilman's select boarding-house for single gentlemen had scorched it a trifle? It seemed as incredible as a fairytale.

Beyond the quenching of his hunger and the stuffing of his pockets with two more of the sad sandwiches, he went back to his box car, knowing that, in the nature of things, his flight was as yet only fairly begun. His train, or some train in which his car was a unit, was just pulling out, and he was barely in time to slide the door and scramble in. Once inside, he made haste to close the opening before the train should emerge from the shelter of its mate on the next track. But before he could brace himself for the shove, a hand came down from the car roof, a brakeman's coupling-stick was thrust into the riding-rail of the door, and the closing operation was effectively blocked.

Smith stood back and waited for a head to follow the hand. It came presently; the bare, tousled head of a young brakeman who had taken off his cap and was lying on his stomach on the car roof to look under the eaves into the interior. Smith made a quick spring and caught the hanging head in the crook of his elbow. "You're gone," he remarked to the inverted face crushed in the vise of forearm and biceps. "If you turn loose, you'll break your back as you come over, and if you don't turn loose, I can pull your head off."

"Leggo of me!" gasped the poor prisoner, drumming with his toes on the roof. "Wha—whadda you want with my head? You can't do nothin' with it when you get it!"

"I have got it," said Smith, showing his teeth. "By and by, when we get safely out of town, I'm going to jump up and bite you."

The brakeman tried to cry out that he was slipping; that the fall would kill him. Smith felt him coming and shifted his hold just in time to make the fall an assisted somersault, landing the man clumsily, but safely, inside of the car. The trigging stick had been lost in the scuffle, and Smith's first care was to slide the door.

"Say; what kind of a 'bo are you, anyway?" gasped the railroad man, flattening himself against the side of the car and struggling to regain his suddenly lost prestige; the time-honored authority of the trainman over the ride-stealer. "Don't you know you might 'a' killed me, pullin' me off'm the roof that way?"

"I can do it yet, if you feel that you've missed anything that was rightfully coming to you," Smith laughed. Then: "Do you happen to have a pipe and a bit of tobacco in your clothes?"

"My gosh!" said the brakeman, "I like your nerve!" Nevertheless, he rummaged in his pocket and handed over a corn-cob pipe and a sack of tobacco. "Maybe you'll want a match, too."

"No, thanks; I have one."

Smith filled the pipe, lighted it, and returned the tobacco. The nickel mixture was not quite like the Turkish blend in the humidor jar on the Kincaid Terrace mantel, but it sufficed. At the pipe-puffing the brakeman looked him over curiously.

"Say; you're no Weary Willie," he commented gruffly; "you're wearin' too good clothes. What's your lay?"

More and more Smith could feel the shacklings of the reputable yesterdays slipping from him. Civilization has taken its time ambling down the centuries, but the short cuts to the primitive are neither hard to find nor long to traverse.

"My 'lay' just now is to get a free ride on this railroad," he said. "How far is this 'empty' going?"

"To St. Louis," was the reply, extorted by the very matter-of-fact calmness of the question. "But you're not goin' to St. Louis in it—not by a jugful. You're goin' to hop off at the first stop we make."

"Am I? Wait until I have finished my smoke. Then we'll open the door and scrap for it; the best man to stay in the car, and the other to take a chance turning handsprings along the right of way. Does that appeal to you?"

"No, by jacks! You bet your life it don't!"

"All right; what's the other answer?"

If the brakeman knew any other answer he did not suggest it. A few miles farther along, the train slowed for a stop. The brakeman felt his twisted neck tenderly and said: "If you'll tell me that you ain't runnin' away from some sheriff 'r other...."

"Do I look it?"

"I'm dogged if I know what you do look like—champeen middle-weight, maybe. Lemme open that door."

Smith took a final whiff and returned the pipe. "Suppose I say that I'm broke and haven't had a chance to pawn my watch," he suggested. "How does that strike you?"

The trainman slid the door open a foot or so as the train ground and jangled to a stand at the grade crossing with another railroad.

"I'll think about it," he growled. "You pulled me off'm the roof; but you kep' me from breakin' my back, and you've smoked my pipe. My run ends at Terre Haute."

"Thanks," said Smith; and at that the tousle-headed young fellow dropped off and disappeared in the direction of the caboose.

Smith closed the door and hooked it with his wire, and the train jogged on over the crossing. Hour after hour wore away and nothing happened. By the measured click of the rail joints under the wheels it was evident that the freight was a slow one, and there were many halts and side-trackings. At noon Smith ate one of the pocketed sandwiches. The ham was oversalted, and before long he began to be consumed with thirst. He stood it until it became a keen torture, and then he found the bit of wire again and tried to pick the hasp-lock, meaning to take advantage of the next stop for a thirst-quenching dash.

For some reason the wire refused to work, and he could not make it free the hasp. After many futile attempts he whittled another peep-hole, angling it so that it pointed toward the puzzling door hook. Then he saw what had been done. Some one—the somersaulting brakeman, no doubt—had basely inserted a wooden peg in the staple in place of the hook and the empty box car was now a prison-van.

Confronting the water famine, Smith drew again upon the elemental resources and braced himself to endure. When night came the slow train was still jogging along westward somewhere in Illinois, and the box-car prisoner was so thirsty that he did not dare to eat the meat in the remaining sandwich; could eat the bread only in tiny morsels, chewed long and patiently. Still he would not make the outcry that the tricky brakeman had doubtless counted upon; the noise that would bring help at any one of the numerous stops—and purchase relief at the price of an arrest for ride-stealing.

Grimly resolute, Smith made up his mind to hang on until morning. Every added mile was a mile gained in the flight from the gallows or the penitentiary, and the night's run would put him just that much farther beyond the zone of acute danger. Such determination fights and wins its own battle, and though he dreamed of lakes and rivers and cool-running brooks and plashing fountains the greater part of the night, he slept through it and awoke to find his car side-tracked in a St. Louis yard.

One glance through the whittled peep-hole showed him that the imprisoning peg was still in its staple, so now there was no alternative but the noise. A brawny switchman was passing, and he came and unhasped the door in response to Smith's shower of kicks upon it.

"Come down out o' that, ye scut! 'Tis the stone pile f'r the likes of yez in this State, and it's Michael Toomey that'll be runnin' ye in," remarked the brawny person, when the door had been opened.

"Wait," said Smith hoarsely. He had caught sight of a bucket of water with a dipper in it standing by the door of the switch shanty, and he jumped down and ran for it. With the terrible thirst assuaged, he wheeled and went back to the big switchman. "Now I'm ready to be run in," he said. "But first, you know, you've got to prove that you're the better man," and with that he whipped off his coat and squared himself for the battle.

It was joined at once, the big man being Irish and nothing loath. Also, it was short and sweet. Barring a healthy and as yet unsatisfied appetite, Smith was in the pink of condition, and the little trainer in the Lawrenceville Athletic Club had imparted the needful skill. In three swift rounds the big switchman was thrashed into a proper state of submission and hospitality, and again, being Irish, he bore no grudge.

"You're a pugnayshus young traithor, and I'm fair sick for to be doin' ye a fayvor," spluttered the big man, after the third knock-out. "What is ut ye'll be wantin'?"

Smith promptly named three things; breakfast directions, a morning paper, and a railroad man's advice as to the best means of getting forward on his journey. His new ally put him in the way of compassing all three, and when the westward faring was resumed—this time in the hollow interior of a huge steel smoke-stack loaded in sections on a pair of flat cars—he went eagerly through the newspaper. The thing he was looking for was there, under flaring headlines; a day late, to be sure, but that was doubtless owing to Lawrenceville's rather poor wire service.

ATTEMPTED MURDER OF BANK PRESIDENT

Society-Leader Cashier Embezzles $100,000 and Makes Murderous Assault on President

Lawrenceville, May 15.—J. Montague Smith, cashier of the Lawrenceville Bank and Trust Company, and a leader in the Lawrenceville younger set, is to-day a fugitive from justice with a price on his head. At a late hour last night the watchman of the bank found President Dunham lying unconscious in front of his desk. Help was summoned, and Mr. Dunham, who was supposed to be suffering from some sudden attack of illness, was taken to his hotel. Later, it transpired that the president had been the victim of a murderous assault. Discovering upon his return to the city yesterday evening that the cashier had been using the bank's funds in an attempt to cover a stock speculation of his own, Dunham sent for Smith and charged him with the crime. Smith made an unprovoked and desperate assault upon his superior officer, beating him into insensibility and leaving him for dead. Since it is known that he did not board any of the night trains east or west, Smith is supposed to be in hiding somewhere in the vicinity of the city. A warrant is out, and a reward of $1,000 for his arrest and detention has been offered by the bank. It is not thought possible that he can escape. It was currently reported not long since that Smith was engaged to a prominent young society woman of Lawrenceville, but this has proved to be untrue.

Smith read the garbled news story with mingled thankfulness and rage; thankfulness because it told him that he was not a murderer, and rage, no less at Dunham's malignant ingenuity than at his own folly in setting the seal of finality upon the false accusation by running away. But the thing was done, and it could not be undone. Having put himself on the wrong side of the law, there was nothing for it now but a complete disappearance; exile, a change of identity, and an absolute severance with his past.

While he was folding the St. Louis newspaper and putting it into his pocket, he was wondering, half cynically, what Verda Richlander was thinking of him. Was it she, herself, who had told the newspaper people that there was nothing in the story of the engagement? That she would side with his accusers and the apparent, or at least uncontradicted, facts he could hardly doubt. There was no very strong reason why she should not, he told himself, rather bitterly. He had not tried to bind her to him in any shackling of sentiment. Quite the contrary, they had both agreed to accept the modern view that sentiment should be regarded as a mildly irruptive malady which runs, or should run, its course, like measles or chicken-pox, in early adolescence. That being the case, Miss Verda's leaf—like all other leaves in the book of his past— might be firmly pasted down and forgotten. As an outlaw with a price on his head he had other and vastly more important things to think about.

Twenty-four hours beyond this final decision he reached Kansas City, where there was a delay and some little diplomacy to be brought into play before he could convince a freight crew on the Union Pacific that he had to be carried, free of cost, to Denver. In the Colorado capital there was another halt and more trouble; but on the second day he found another empty box car and was once more moving westward, this time toward a definite destination.

During the Denver stop-over he had formulated his plan, such as it was. In a newspaper which he had picked up, he had lighted upon an advertisement calling for laborers to go over into the Timanyoni country to work on an irrigation project. By applying at the proper place he might have procured free transportation to the work, but there were two reasons why he did not apply. One was prudently cautionary and was based on the fear that he might be recognized. The other was less easily defined, but no less mandatory in the new scheme of things. The vagabonding had gotten into his blood, and he was minded to go on as he had begun, beating his way to the job like other members of the vagrant brotherhood.

IV
The High Hills

Train Number Seventeen, the Nevada through freight, was two hours late issuing from the western portal of Timanyoni Canyon. Through the early mountain-climbing hours of the night and the later flight across the Red Desert, the dusty, travel-grimed young fellow in the empty box car midway of the train had slept soundly, with the hard car floor for a bed and his folded coat for a pillow. But on the emergence of the train from the echoing canyon depths the sudden cessation of the crash and roar of the shut-in mountain passage awoke him and he got up to open the door and look out.

It was still no later than a lazy man's breakfast time, and the May morning was perfect, with a cobalt sky above and a fine tingling quality in the air to set the blood dancing in the veins. Over the top of the eastern range the sun was looking, level-rayed, into a parked valley bounded on all sides by high spurs and distant snow peaks. In its nearer reaches the valley was dotted with round hills, some of them bare, others dark green to their summits with forestings of mountain pine and fir. Now that it was out of the canyon, the train was skirting the foot of the southern boundary spur, the railroad track holding its level by heading the gulches and rounding the alternating promontories.

From the outer loopings of the curves, the young tramp at the car door had momentary glimpses of the Timanyoni, a mountain torrent in its canyon, and the swiftest of upland rivers even here where it had the valley in which to expand. A Copah switchman had told him that the railroad division town of Brewster lay at the end of the night's run, in a river valley beyond the eastern Timanyonis, and that the situation of the irrigation project which was advertising for laborers in the Denver newspapers was a few miles up the river from Brewster.

For reasons of his own, he was not anxious to make a daylight entry into the town itself. Sooner or later, of course, the scrutiny of curious eyes must be met, but there was no need of running to meet the risk. Not that the risk was very great. While he was killing time in the Copah yard the day before, waiting for a chance to board the night freight, he had picked up a bit of broken looking-glass and put it in his pocket. The picture it gave back when he took it out and looked into it was that of a husky young tramp with a stubble beard a week old, and on face and neck and hands the accumulated grime of two thousand miles of freight-train riding. Also, the week's wear and tear had been, if anything, harder on the clothes than on the man. His hat had been lost in one of the railroad-yard train-boardings and he had replaced it in Denver with a workman's cap. It was a part of the transformation, wrought and being wrought in him, that he was able to pocket the bit of looking-glass with a slow grin of satisfaction. When one is about to apply for a job as a laboring man it is well to look the part.

As the train swept along on its way down the grades the valley became more open and the prospect broadened. At one of the promontory roundings the box-car passenger had a glimpse of a shack-built construction camp on the river's margin some distance on ahead. A concrete dam was rising in sections out of the river, and dominating the dam and the shacks two steel towers, with a carrying cable stretched between them, formed the piers of the aerial spout conveyer for the placing of the material in the forms.

A mile or more short of the construction camp the railroad made another of the many gulch loopings; and on its next emergence the train had passed the site of the dam, leaving it fully a mile in the rear. Here the young man at the car door saw the ditch company's unloading side-track with a spur branching away from the main line and crossing the river on a temporary trestle. There were material yards on both sides of the stream, and in one of the opposing hills a busy quarry.

The train made no stop at the construction siding, but a half-mile farther along the brakes began to grind and the speed was slackened. Sliding the car door another foot or two, the young tramp with the week-old stubble beard on his face leaned out to look ahead. His opportunity was at hand. A block semaphore was turned against the freight and the train was slowing in obedience to the signal. Waiting until the brakes shrilled again, the tramp put his shoulder to the sliding door, sat for a moment in the wider opening, and then swung off.

After the train had gone on he drew himself up, took a deep chest-filling breath of the crisp morning air, and looked about him. The sun was an hour high over the eastern mountains, and the new world spread itself in broad detail. His alighting was upon one of the promontory embankments. To the westward, where the curving railroad track was lost in the farther windings of the river, lay the little intermountain city of Brewster, a few of its higher buildings showing clear-cut in the distance. Paralleling the railroad, on a lower level and nearer the river, a dusty wagon road pointed in one direction toward the town, and in the other toward the construction camp.

The young man who had crossed four States and the better part of a fifth as a fugitive and vagrant turned his back upon the distant town as a place to be avoided. Scrambling down the railroad embankment, he made his way to the wagon road, crossed it, and kept on until he came to the fringe of aspens on the river's edge, where he broke all the trampish traditions by stripping off the travel-worn clothes and plunging in to take a soapless bath. The water, being melted snow from the range, was icy-cold and it stabbed like knives. Nevertheless, it was wet, and some part of the travel dust, at least, was soluble in it. He came out glowing, but a thorn from his well-groomed past came up and pricked him when he had to put the soiled clothes on again. There was no present help for that, however; and five minutes later he had regained the road and was on his way to the ditch camp.

When he had gone a little distance he found that the wagon road dodged the railroad track as it could, crossing and recrossing the right of way twice before the construction camp came into view. The last of the crossings was at the temporary material yard for which the side-track had been installed, and from this point on, the wagon road held to the river bank. The ditch people were doubtless getting all their material over the railroad so there would be little hauling by wagon. But there were automobile tracks in the dust, and shortly after he had passed the material yard the tramp heard a car coming up behind him. It was a six-cylinder roadster, and its motor was missing badly.

He gave the automobile passing room when it came along, glancing up to note that its single occupant was a big, bearded man, wearing his gray tweeds as one to whom clothes were merely a convenience. He was chewing a black cigar, and the unoccupied side of his mouth was busy at the passing moment heaping objurgations upon the limping motor. A hundred yards farther along the motor gave a spasmodic gasp and stopped. When the young tramp came up, the big man had climbed out and had the hood open. What he was saying to the stalled motor was picturesque enough to make the young man stop and grin appreciatively.

"Gone bad on you?" he inquired.

Colonel Dexter Baldwin, the Timanyoni's largest landowner,

and a breeder of fine horses who tolerated motor-cars only because they could be driven hard and were insensate and fit subjects for abusive language, took his head out of the hood.

"The third time this morning," he snapped. "I'd rather drive a team of wind-broken mustangs, any day in the year!"

"I used to drive a car a while back," said the tramp. "Let me look her over."

The colonel stood aside, wiping his hands on a piece of waste, while the young man sought for the trouble. It was found presently in a loosened magneto wire; found and cleverly corrected. The tramp went around in front and spun the motor, and when it had been throttled down, Colonel Baldwin had his hand in his pocket.

"That's something like," he said. "The garage man said it was carbon. You take hold as if you knew how. What's your fee?"

The tramp shook his head and smiled good-naturedly.

"Nothing; for a bit of neighborly help like that."

The colonel put his coat on, and in the act took a better measure of the stalwart young fellow who looked like a hobo and talked and behaved like a gentleman. Colonel Dexter was a fairly shrewd judge of men, and he knew that the tramping brotherhood divides itself pretty evenly on a distinct line of cleavage, with the born vagrant on one side and the man out of work on the other.

"You are hiking out to the dam?" he asked brusquely.

"I am headed that way, yes," was the equally crisp rejoinder.

"Hunting a job?"

"Just that."

"What sort of a job?"

"Anything that may happen to be in sight."

"That usually means a pick and shovel or a wheelbarrow on a construction job. We're needing quarrymen and concrete handlers, and we could use a few more rough carpenters on the forms. But there isn't much office work."

The tramp looked up quickly.

"What makes you think I'm hunting for an office job?" he queried.

"Your hands," said the colonel shortly.

The young man looked at his hands thoughtfully. They were dirty again from the tinkering with the motor, but the inspection went deeper than the grime.

"I'm not afraid of the pick and shovel, or the wheelbarrow, and on some accounts I guess they'd be good for me. But on the other hand, perhaps it is a pity to spoil a middling good office man to make an indifferent day-laborer—to say nothing of knocking some honest fellow out of the only job he knows how to do."

Colonel Baldwin swung in behind the steering-wheel of the roadster and held a fresh match to the black cigar. Though he was from Missouri, he had lived long enough in the high hills to know better than to judge any man altogether by outward appearances.

"Climb in," he said, indicating the vacant seat at his side. "I'm the president of the ditch company. Perhaps Williams may be able to use you; but your chances for office work would be ten to one in the town."

"I don't care to live in the town," said the man out of work, mounting to the proffered seat; and past that the big roadster leaped away up the road and the roar of the rejuvenated motor made further speech impossible.

It was a full fortnight or more after this motor-tinkering incident on the hill road to the dam, when Williams, chief engineer of the ditch project, met President Baldwin in the Brewster offices of the ditch company and spent a busy hour with the colonel going over the contractors' estimates for the month in prospect. In an interval of the business talk, Baldwin remembered the good-looking young tramp who had wanted a job.

"Oh, yes; I knew there was something else that I wanted to ask you," he said. "How about the young fellow that I unloaded on you a couple of weeks ago? Did he make good?"

"Who—Smith?"

"Yes; if that's his name."

The engineer's left eyelid had a quizzical droop when he said dryly: "It's the name he goes by in camp; 'John Smith.' I haven't asked him his other name."

The ranchman president matched the drooping eyelid of unbelief with a sober smile. "I thought he looked as if he might be out here for his health—like a good many other fellows who have no particular use for a doctor. How is he making it?"

The engineer, a hard-bitten man with the prognathous lower jaw characterizing the tribe of those who accomplish things, thrust his hands into his pockets and walked to the window to look down into the Brewster street. When he turned to face Baldwin again, it was to say: "That young fellow is a wonder, Colonel. I put him into the quarry at first, as you suggested, and in three days he had revolutionized things to the tune of a twenty-per-cent saving in production costs. Then I gave him a hack at the concrete-mixers, and he's making good again in the cost reduction. That seems to be his specialty."

The president nodded and was sufficiently interested to follow up what had been merely a casual inquiry.

"What are you calling him now?—a betterment engineer? You know your first guess was that he was somebody's bookkeeper out of a job."

Williams wagged his head.

"He's a three-cornered puzzle to me, yet. He isn't an engineer, but when you drag a bunch of cost money up the trail, he goes after it like a dog after a rabbit. I'm not anxious to lose him, but I really believe you could make better use of him here in the town office than I can on the job."

Baldwin was shaking his head dubiously.

"I'm afraid he'd have to loosen up on his record a little before we could bring him in here. Badly as we're needing a money man, we can hardly afford to put a 'John Smith' into the saddle—at least not without knowing what his other name used to be."

"No; of course not. I guess, after all, he's only a 'lame duck,' like a good many of the rest of them. Day before yesterday, Burdell, the deputy sheriff, was out at the camp looking the gangs over for the fellow who broke into Lannigan's place last Saturday night. When he came into the office Smith was busy with an estimate, and Burdell went up and touched him on the shoulder, just to let him know that it was time to wake up. Suffering cats! It took three of us to keep him from breaking Burdell in two and throwing him out of the window!"

"That looks rather bad," was the president's comment. Colonel Dexter Baldwin had been the first regularly elected sheriff of Timanyoni County in the early days and he knew the symptoms. "Was Burdell wearing his star where it could be seen?"

The engineer nodded.

"What explanation did Smith make?"

"Oh, he apologized like a gentleman, and said he was subject to little nervous attacks like that when anybody touched him unexpectedly. He took Burdell over to Pete Simm's shack saloon and bought him a drink. Perkins, the timekeeper, says he's going to get a megaphone so he can give due notice in advance when he wants to call Smith's attention."

The colonel pulled out a drawer in the desk, found his box of diplomatic cigars and passed it to the engineer, saying: "Light up a sure-enough good one, and tell me what you think Smith has been doing back yonder in the other country."

Williams took the cigar but he shied at the conundrum.

"Ask me something easy," he said. "I've stacked up a few

guesses. He's from the Middle West—as the Bible says, his 'speech bewrayeth' him—and he's had a good job of some kind; the kind that required him to keep abreast of things. If there's anything in looks, you'd say he wasn't a thief or an embezzler, and yet it's pretty apparent that he's been used to handling money in chunks and making it work for its living. I've put it up that there's a woman in it. Perhaps the other fellow got in his way, or came up behind him and touched him unexpectedly, or something of that sort. Anyway, I'm not going to believe he's a crooked crook until I have to."

Colonel Baldwin helped himself to one of his own cigars, and the talk went back to business. In the irrigation project, Williams was a stockholder as well as the chief of construction, and Baldwin had more than once found him a safe adviser. There was need for counsel. The Timanyoni Ditch Company was in a rather hazardous condition financially, and the president and Williams rarely met without coming sooner or later to a threshing out of the situation.

The difficulties were those which are apt to confront a small and local enterprise when it is so unfortunate as to get in the way of larger undertakings. Colonel Baldwin, and a group of his neighbors on the north side of the river, were reformed cattlemen and horse breeders. Instead of drifting farther west in advance of the incoming tide of population following the coming of the railroad, they had availed themselves of their homestead rights and had taken up much of the grass-land in the favorable valleys, irrigating it at first with water taken out of the river in private or neighborhood ditches.

Later on came the sheep-feeding period, and after that the utilization of larger crop-raising areas. The small ditches proving inadequate for these, Colonel Baldwin had formed a stock company among his neighbors in the grass-lands and his friends in Brewster for the building of a substantial dam in the eastern hills. The project had seemed simple enough in the beginning. The stock was sold for cash and each stockholder would be a participating user of the water. Williams, who had been a United States reclamation man before he came to the Timanyoni, had made careful estimates, and the stock subscription provided money enough to cover the cost of the dam and the main ditch.

After some little bargaining, the dam site and the overflow land for the reservoir lake had been secured, and the work was begun. Out of a clear sky, however, came trouble and harassment. Alien holders of mining claims in the reservoir area turned up and demanded damages. Some few homesteaders who had promised to sign quitclaims changed their minds and sued for relief, and after the work was well under way it appeared that there was a cloud on the title of the dam site itself. All of these clashings were carried into court, and the rancher promoters found themselves confronting invisible enemies and obstacle-raisers at every turn.

The legal fight, as they soon found out, cost much money in every phase of it; and now, when the dam was scarcely more than half completed, a practically empty treasury was staring them in the face. This was the situation which called for its regular threshing out in every conference between Colonel Baldwin and his chief of construction. There was no disguising the fact that a crisis was approaching, a financial crisis which no one among the amateur promoters was big enough to cope with.

"We've got to go in deeper, Colonel; there is nothing else to do," was the engineer's summing up of the matter at the close of the conference. "The snow is melting pretty rapidly on the range now, and when we get the June rise we'll stand to lose everything we have if we can't keep every wheel turning to get ready for the high water."

Baldwin was holding his cigar between his fingers and scowling at it as if it had mortally offended him.

"Assessments on the stock, you mean?" he said. "I'm afraid our crowd won't stand for that. A good part of it is ready to lie down in the harness right now."

"How about a bond issue?" asked the engineer.

"Lord of heavens! What do we, or any of us, know about bond issues? Why, we knew barely enough about the business at the start to chip in together and buy us a charter and go to work on a plan a little bit bigger than the neighborhood ditch idea. You couldn't float bonds in Timanyoni Park, and we're none of us foxy enough to go East and float 'em."

"I guess that's right, too," admitted Williams. "Besides, with the stock gone off the way it has, it would take a mighty fine-haired financial sharp to sell bonds."

"What's that?" demanded the president. "Who's been selling any stock?"

"Buck Gardner, for one; and that man Bolling, up at the head of Little Creek, for another. Maxwell, the railroad superintendent, told me about it, and he says that the price offered, and accepted, was thirty-nine."

"Dad burn a cuss with a yellow streak in him!" rasped the Missouri colonel. "We had a fair and square agreement among ourselves that if anybody got scared he was to give the rest of us a chance to buy him out. Who bought from these welshers?"

"Maxwell didn't know that. He said it was done through

Kinzie's bank. From what I've heard on the outside, I'm inclined to suspect that Crawford Stanton was the buyer."

"Stanton, the real-estate man?"

"The same."

Again the president stared thoughtfully at the glowing end of his cigar.

"There's another of the confounded mysteries," he growled. "Who is Crawford Stanton, and what is he here for? I know what he advertises, but everybody in Brewster knows that he hasn't made a living dollar in real estate since he came here last winter. Williams, do you know, I'm beginning to suspect that there is a mighty big nigger in our little wood-pile?"

"You mean that all these stubborn hold-ups have been bought and paid for? You'll remember that is what Billy Starbuck tried to tell us when the first of the missing mining-claim owners began to shout at us."

"Starbuck has a long head, and what he doesn't know about mining claims in this part of the country wouldn't fill a very big book. I remember he said there had never been any prospecting done in the upper Timanyoni gulches, and now you'd think half the people in the United States had been nosing around up there with a pick and shovel at one time or another. But it was a thing that Starbuck told me no longer ago than yesterday that set me to thinking," Baldwin went on. "As you know, the old Escalante Spanish Grant corners over in the western part of this park. When the old grants were made, they were ruled off on the map without reference to mountain ranges or other natural barriers."

Williams nodded.

"Well, as I say, one corner of the Escalante reaches over the Hophras and out into the park, covering about eight or ten square miles of the territory just beyond us on our side of the river. Starbuck told me yesterday that a big Eastern colonization company had got a bill through Congress alienating that tract."

The chief of construction bounded out of his chair and began to walk the floor. "By George!" he said; and again: "By George! That's what we're up against, Colonel! Where will those fellows get the water for their land? There is no site for a dam lower down than ours, and, anyway, that land lies too high to be watered by anything but a high-line ditch!"

"Nice little brace game, isn't it?" growled Baldwin. "If we hadn't been a lot of hayseed amateurs, we might have found out long ago that some one was running in a cold deck on us. What's your notion? Are we done up, world without end?"

Williams's laugh was grim.

"What we need, Colonel, is to go out on the street and yell for a doctor," he said. "It's beginning to look as if we had acquired a pretty bad case of malignant strangle-itis."

Baldwin ran his fingers through his hair and admitted that he had lost his sense of humor.

"It's hell, Williams," he said soberly. "You know how recklessly I've waded into this thing—how recklessly we've all gone into it for that matter. I'll come down like a man and admit that it has climbed up the ladder to a place where I can't reach it. This Eastern crowd is trying to freeze us out, to get our dam and reservoir and ditch rights for their Escalante scheme. When they do, they'll turn around and sell us water—at fifty dollars an inch, or something like that!"

"What breaks my heart is that we haven't been able to surround the sure-enough fact while there was still time to do something," lamented the ex-reclamation man. "The Lord knows it's been plain enough, with Stanton right here on the ground, and probably every one of the interferences traceable directly to him. He has begun to close in on us; his purchase of the Gardner and Bolling stockholdings is the beginning of the end. You know as well as I do, Colonel, what a contagious disease 'the yellows' is. Others will get it, and the first thing we know, Stanton will own a majority of the stock and be voting us all out of a job. You'll have to come around to my suggestion, after all, and advertise for a doctor." It was said of the chief of construction that he would have joked on his death-bed, and, as a follower for the joke, he added: "Why don't you call Smith in and give him the job?"

"Smith be damned," growled the colonel, who, as we have seen, had become completely color-blind on the sense-of-humor side.

"I wouldn't put it beyond him to develop into the young Napoleon of finance that we seem to be needing just now," Williams went on, carrying the jest to its legitimate conclusion.

Baldwin, like other self-made promoters in their day of trouble, was in the condition of the drowning man who catches at straws.

"You don't really mean that, Williams, do you?" he asked.

"No, I didn't mean it when I said it," was the engineer's admission; "I was only trying to get a rise out of you. But really, Colonel, on second thought I don't know but it is worth considering. As I say, Smith seems to know the money game from start to finish. What is better still, he is a fighter from the word go—what you might call a joyous fighter. Suppose you drive out to-morrow or next day and pry into him a little."

The rancher president had relapsed once more into the slough of discouragement.

"You are merely grabbing for handholds, Bartley—as I was a minute ago. We are in a bad row of stumps when we can sit here and talk seriously about roping down a young hobo and putting him into the financial harness. Let's go around to Frascati's and eat before you go back to camp. It's bread-time, anyway."

The chief of construction said no more about his joking suggestion at the moment, but when they were walking around the square to the Brewster Delmonico's he went back to the dropped subject in all seriousness, saying: "Just the same, I wish you could know Smith and size him up as I have. I can't help believing, some way, that he's all to the good."

V
The Specialist

Though the matter of calling in an expert doctor of finance to diagnose the alarming symptoms in Timanyoni Ditch had been left indeterminate in the talk between Colonel Baldwin and himself, Williams did not let it go entirely by default. On the day following the Brewster office conference the engineer sent for Smith, who was checking the output of the crushers at the quarry, and a little later the "betterment" man presented himself at the door of the corrugated-iron shack which served as a field office for the chief.

Williams looked the cost-cutter over as he stood in the doorway. Smith was thriving and expanding handsomely in the new environment. He had let his beard grow and it was now long enough to be trimmed to a point. The travel-broken clothes had been exchanged for working khaki, with lace boots and leggings, and the workman's cap had given place to the campaign felt of the engineers. Though he had been less than a month on the job, he was already beginning to tan and toughen under the healthy outdoor work—to roughen, as well, his late fellow members of the Lawrenceville Cotillon Club might have said, since he had fought three pitched battles with as many of the camp bullies, and had in each of them approved himself a man of his hands who could not only take punishment, but could hammer an opponent swiftly and neatly into any desired state of subjection.

"Come in here and sit down; I want to talk to you," was the way Williams began it; and after Smith had found a chair and had lighted a gift cigar from the headquarters desk-box, the chief went on: "Say, Smith, you're too good a man for anything I've got for you here. Haven't you realized that?"

Smith pulled a memorandum-book from his hip pocket and ran his eye over the private record he had been keeping.

"I've shown you how to effect a few little savings which total up something like fifteen per cent of your cost of production and operation," he said. "Don't you think I'm earning my wages?"

"That's all right; I've been keeping tab, too, and I know what you're doing. But you are not beginning to earn what you ought to, either for yourself or the company," put in the chief shrewdly. And then: "Loosen up, Smith, and tell me something about yourself. Who are you, and where do you come from, and what sort of a job have you been holding down?"

Smith's reply was as surprising as it was seemingly irrelevant.

"If you're not too busy, Mr. Williams, I guess you'd better make out my time-check," he said quietly.

Williams took a reflective half-minute for consideration, turning the sudden request over deliberately in his mind, as his habit was.

"I suppose, by that you mean that you'll quit before you will consent to open up on your record?" he assumed.

"You've guessed it," said the man who had sealed the book of his past.

Again Williams took a little time. It was discouraging to have his own and the colonel's prefigurings as to Smith's probable state and standing so promptly verified.

"I suppose you know the plain inference you're leaving, when you say a thing like that?"

Smith made the sign of assent. "It leaves you entirely at liberty to finish out the story to suit yourself," he admitted, adding: "The back numbers—my back numbers—are my own, Mr. Williams. I've kept a file of them, as everybody does, but I don't have to produce it on request."

"Of course, there's nothing compulsory about your producing it. But unless you are what they call in this country a 'crooked' crook, you are standing in your own light. You have such a staving good head for figures and finances that it seems a pity for you to be wasting it here on an undergraduate's job in cost-cutting. Any young fellow just out of a technical school could do what you're doing in the way of paring down expenses."

The cost-cutter's smile was mildly incredulous.

"Nobody seemed to be doing it before I came," he offered.

"No," Williams allowed, "that's the fact. To tell the plain truth, we've had bigger things to wrestle with; and we have them yet, for that matter—enough of them to go all around the job twice and tie in a bow-knot."

"Finances?" queried Smith, feeling some of the back-number instincts stirring within him.

The chief engineer nodded; then he looked up with a twinkle in his closely set gray eyes. "If you'll tell me why you tried to kill Burdell the other day, maybe I'll open up the record—our record—for you."

This time the cost-cutter's smile was good-naturedly derisive, and it ignored the reference to Burdell.

"You don't have to open up your record—for me; it's the talk of the camp. You people are undercapitalized—to boil it down into one word. Isn't that about the way it sizes up?"

"That is the way it has turned out; though we had capital enough to begin with. We've been bled to death by damage suits."

Smith shook his head. "Why haven't you hired a first-class attorney, Mr. Williams?"

"We've had the best we could find, but the other fellows have beaten us to it, every time. But the legal end of it hasn't been the whole thing or the biggest part of it. What we are needing most is a man who knows a little something about corporation fights and high finance." And at this the engineer forgot the Smith disabilities, real or inferential, and went on to explain in detail the peculiar helplessness of the Timanyoni Company as the antagonist of the as yet unnamed land and irrigation trust.

Smith heard him through, nodding understandingly when the tale was told.

"It's the old story of the big fish swallowing the little one; so old that there is no longer any saving touch of novelty in it," he commented. "I've been wondering if there wasn't something of that kind in your background. And you say you haven't any Belmonts or Morgans or Rockefellers in your company?"

"We have a bunch of rather badly scared-up ranch owners and local people, with Colonel Baldwin in command, and that's all. The colonel is a fighting man, all right, and he can shoot as straight as anybody, when you have shown him what to shoot at. But he is outclassed, like all the rest of us, when it comes to a game of financial freeze-out. And that is what we are up against, I'm afraid."

"There isn't the slightest doubt in the world about that," said the one who had been called in as an expert. "What I can't understand is why some of you didn't size the situation up long ago—before it got into its present desperate shape. You are at the beginning of the end, now. They've caught you with an empty treasury, and these stock sales you speak of prove that they have already begun to swallow you by littles. Timanyoni Common—I suppose you haven't any Preferred—at thirty-nine is an excellent gamble for any group of men who can see their way clear to buying the control. With an eager market for the water—and they can sell the water to you people, even if they don't put their own Escalante project through—the stock can be pushed to par and beyond, as it will be after you folks are all safely frozen out. More than that, they can charge you enough, for the water you've got to have, to finance the Escalante scheme and pay all the bills; and their investment, at the present market, will be only thirty-nine cents in the dollar. It's a neat little play."

Williams was by this time far past remembering that his adviser was a man with a possible alias and presumably a fugitive from justice.

"Can't something be done, Smith? You've had experience in these things; your talk shows it. Have we got to stand still and be shot to pieces?"

"The necessity remains to be demonstrated. But you will be shot to pieces, to a dead moral certainty, if you don't put somebody on deck with the necessary brains, and do it quickly," said Smith with frank bluntness.

"Hold on," protested the engineer. "Every man to his trade. When I said that we had nobody but the neighbors and our friends in the company, I didn't mean to give the impression that they were either dolts or chuckleheads. As a matter of fact, we have a pretty level-headed bunch of men in Timanyoni Ditch—though I'll admit that some of them are nervous enough, just now, to want to get out on almost any terms. What I meant to say was that they don't happen to be up in all the crooks and turnings of the high-finance buccaneers."

"I didn't mean to reflect upon Colonel Baldwin and his friends," rejoined the ex-cashier good-naturedly. "It is nothing especially discrediting to them that they are not up in all the tricks of a trade which is not theirs. The financing of a scheme like this has come to be a business by itself, Mr. Williams, and it is hardly to be expected that a group of inexperienced men could do it successfully."

"I know that, blessed well. That is what I said from the beginning, and I think Colonel Baldwin leaned that way, too. But it seemed like a very simple undertaking. A number of stockmen and crop growers wanted a dam and a ditch, and they had the money to pay for them. That seemed to be all there was to it in the beginning."

Smith was leaning back in his chair and smoking reflectively.

"Did you call me in here to get an expert opinion?" he asked, half humorously.

"Something of that kind—yes; just on the bare chance that you could, and would, give us one," Williams admitted.

"Well, I'm hardly an expert," was the modest reply; "but if I were in your place I should hire the best financial scrapper that money could pay for. I can't attempt to tell you what such a man would do, but he would at least rattle around in the box and try to give you a fighting chance, which is more than you seem to have now."

The construction chief turned abruptly upon his cost-cutter.

"Keeping in mind what you said a few minutes ago about 'back numbers,' would it be climbing over the fence too far for me to ask if your experience has been such as would warrant you in tackling a job of this kind?"

"That is a fair question, and I can answer it straight," said the man under fire. "I've had the experience."

"I thought so; and that brings on more talk. I'm not authorized to make you any proposal. But Colonel Baldwin and I were talking the matter over yesterday and your name was mentioned. I told the colonel that it was very evident that you were accustomed to handling bigger financial matters than these labor-and-material cost-cuttings you've been figuring on out here. If the colonel should ask you to, would you consider as a possibility the taking of the doctor's job on this sick project of ours?"

"No," was the brief rejoinder.

"Why not?"

Smith looked away out of the one square window in the shack at the busy scene on the dam stagings.

"Let us say that I don't care to mix and mingle with my kind, Mr. Williams, and let it go at that," he said.

"You are not interested in that side of it?"

"Interested, but not to the point of enlisting."

"You don't think of anything that might make you change your mind?"

"There is nothing that you could offer which would be a sufficient inducement."

"Why isn't there?"

"Because I'm not exactly a born simpleton, Mr. Williams. There are a number of reasons which are purely personal to me, and at least one which cuts ice on your side of the pond. Your financial 'doctor,' as you call him, would have to be trusted absolutely in the handling of the company's money and its negotiable securities. You would have a perfect right to demand any and every assurance of his fitness and trustworthiness. You could, and should, put him under a fairly heavy bond. I'll not go into it any deeper than to say that I can't give a bond."

Williams took his defeat, if it could be called a defeat, without further protest.

"I thought it might not be amiss to talk it over with you," he said. "I don't know that the colonel will make any move, but if he does, he will deal with you direct. You say it is impossible, and perhaps it is. But it won't do any harm for you to think it over, and if I were you, I shouldn't burn all the bridges behind me. There ought to be considerable money in it for the right man, if he succeeds, and nothing much to lose if he should fail."

Smith went back to his work in the quarry with a troubled mind. The little heart-to-heart talk with Williams had been sharply depressive. It had shown him, as nothing else could, how limited for all the remainder of his life his chances must be. That he would be pursued, that descriptions and photographs of the ex-cashier of the Lawrenceville Bank and Trust Company were already circulating from hand to hand among the paid man-catchers, he did not doubt for a moment. While he could remain as a workman unit in an isolated construction camp, there was some little hope that he might be overlooked. But to become the public character of Williams's suggestion in a peopled city was to run to meet his fate.

In a way the tentative offer was a keen temptation. One of the lustiest growths pushing its way up through the new soil of the metamorphosis was a strong and mounting conviction that J. Montague Smith, of the Lawrenceville avatar, had been only half a man; was, at his best, only a pale shadow of the plain John Smith to whom accident and a momentary impulse of passion had given birth. With a clear field he would have asked for nothing better than a chance to take the leadership in the fight which Williams had outlined, and the new and elemental stirrings were telling him that he could win the fight. But with a price on his head it was not to be thought of.

That night, when he rolled himself in his blankets in the bunk tent, he had renewed his prudent determination and it was crystallizing itself in words.

"No, not for money or gratitude or any other argument they can bring to bear," he said to himself, and thereupon fell asleep with the mistaken notion that he had definitely pushed the temptation aside for good and all.

VI
The Twig

It is said that the flow of a mighty river may owe its most radical change in direction to the chance thrusting of a twig into the current at some critical instant in the rise or fall of the flood. To the reincarnated Smith, charting his course upon the conviction that his best chance of immunity lay in isolation and a careful avoidance of the peopled towns, came the diverting twig in this wise.

On the second morning following the unofficial talk with Bartley Williams in the iron-sheeted headquarters office at the dam, a delayed consignment of cement, steel, and commissary supplies was due at the side-track a mile below the camp. Perkins, the timekeeper, took the telephone call from Brewster giving notice of the shipment, and started the camp teams to meet the train, sending a few men along to help with the unloading. Later, he called Smith in from the quarry and gave him the invoices covering the shipment.

"I guess you'd better go down to the siding and check this stuff in, so that we'll know what we're getting," was his suggestion to the general utility man; and Smith put the invoices into his pocket and took the road, a half-hour or more behind the teams.

When the crookings of the tote-road let him get his first sight of the side-track, he saw that the train was already in and the mixed shipment of camp supplies had been transferred to the wagons. A few minutes sufficed for the checking, and since there was nothing more to be done, he sent the unloading gang back to camp with the teams, meaning to walk back, himself, after he should have seen the car of steel and the two cars of cement kicked in at the upper end of the side-track.

While he was waiting for the train to pull up and make the shift he was commenting idly upon the clumsy lay-out of the temporary unloading yard, and wondering if Williams were responsible for it. The siding was on the outside of a curve and within a hundred yards of the river bank. There was scanty space for the unloading of material, and a good bit of what there was was taken up by the curving spur which led off from the siding to cross the river on a trestle, and by the wagon road itself, which came down a long hill on the south side of the railroad and made an abrupt turn to cross the main track and the siding fairly in the midst of things.

As the long train pulled up to clear the road crossing, Smith stepped back and stood between the two tracks. A moment later the cut was made, and the forward section of the train went on to set the three loaded cars out at the upper switch, leaving the rear half standing on the main line. From his position between the tracks there was a clear view past the caboose at the end of the halted section and beyond, to the road crossing and the steep grade down which the dusty wagon road made a rough gash in the shoulder of the mountain spur which had crowded it from the river-bank side of the railroad right of way. At the bottom of the steep grade, where the road swerved to cross the two tracks, there was a little sag; and between the sag and the crossing a sharp bit of up-grade made to gain the level of the railroad embankment.

One of the men of the unloading gang, a leather-faced grade shoveller who had helped to build the Nevada Short Line, had lagged behind the departing wagons to fill and light his pipe.

"Wouldn't that jar you up right good and hard f'r a way to run a railroad," he said to Smith, indicating the wholly deserted standing section of the freight with the burnt match-end. "Them fellies 've all gone off up ahead, a-leavin' this yere hind end without a sign of a man'r a flag to take keer of it. S'pose another train 'd come boolgin' 'round that curve. Wouldn't it rise merry hell with things 'long about this-away?"

Smith was listening only with the outward ear to what the pipelighter was saying. Somewhere in the westward distances a thunderous murmur was droning upon the windless air of the June morning, betokening, as it seemed, the very catastrophe the ex-grade-laborer was prefiguring. Smith stripped his coat for a flag and started to run toward the crossing, but before he had caught his stride a dust cloud swept up over the shoulder of the wagon-road hill and the portentous thunderings were accounted for. A big gray automobile, with the cut-out open, was topping the side-hill grade, and Smith recognized it at once. It was Colonel Dexter Baldwin's roadster, and it held a single occupant—namely, the young woman who was driving it.

Smith stopped running and transferred his anxiety from the train and railroad affairs to the young woman. Being himself a skilful driver of cars—and a man—he had a purely masculine distrust of the woman, any woman, behind a steering-wheel. To be sure, there was no danger, as yet. Turning to look up the track, he saw that the three loaded cars had been set out, that the forward section of the train had been pulled up over the switch, and that it was now backing to make the coupling with the standing half. He hoped that the trainmen had seen the automobile, and that they would not attempt to make the coupling until after the gray car had crossed behind the caboose. But in the same breath he guessed, and guessed rightly, that they were too far around the curve to be able to see the wagon-road approach.

Still there was time enough, and room enough. The caboose on the rear end of the standing section was fully a hundred feet clear of the road crossing; and if the entire train should start backward at the coupling collision, the speed at which the oncoming roadster was running should take it across and out of danger. Nevertheless, there was no margin for the unexpected. Smith saw the young woman check the speed for the abrupt turn at the bottom of the hill, saw the car take the turn in a skidding slide, heard the renewed roar of the motor as the throttle was opened for a run at the embankment grade. Then the unexpected dropped its bomb. There was a jangling crash and the cars on the main track were set in motion toward the crossing. The trainmen had tried to make their coupling, the drawheads had failed to engage, and the rear half of the train was surging down upon the point of hazard.

Smith's shout, or the sight of the oncoming train, one of the two, or both, put the finishing touch on the young woman's nerve. There was still time in which to clear the train, but at the critical instant the young woman apparently changed her mind and tried to stop the big car short of the crossing. The effort was unsuccessful. When the stop was made, the front wheels of the roadster were precisely in the middle of the main track, and the motor was killed.

By this time Smith had thrown his coat away and was racing the backing train, with the exgrade-laborer a poor second a dozen yards to the rear. Having ridden in the roadster, Smith knew that it had no self-starter. "Jump!" he yelled. "Get out of the car!" and then his heart came into his mouth when he saw that she was struggling to free herself and couldn't; that she was entangled in some way behind the low-hung tiller-wheel.

Smith was running fairly abreast of the caboose when he made this discovery, and the hundred feet of clearance had shrunk to fifty. In imagination he could already see the gray car overturned and crushed under the wheels of the train. In a flying spurt he gained a few yards on the advancing menace and hurled himself against the front of the stopped roadster. He did not attempt to crank the motor. There was time only for a mighty heave and shove to send the car backing down the slope of the crossing approach; for this and for the quick spring aside to save himself; and the thing was done.

VII
A Notice to Quit

Once started and given its push, the gray roadster drifted backward from the railroad crossing and kept on until it came to rest in the sag at the turn in the road. Running to overtake it, Smith found that the young woman was still trying, ineffectually, to free herself. In releasing the clutch her dress had been caught and Smith was glad enough to let the extricating of the caught skirt and the cranking of the engine serve for a breath-catching recovery.

When he stepped back to "tune" the spark the young woman had subsided into the mechanician's seat and was retying her veil with fingers that were not any too steady. She was small but well-knit; her hair was a golden brown and there was a good deal of it; her eyes were set well apart, and in the bright morning sunlight they were a slaty gray—of the exact shade of the motor veil she was rearranging. Smith had a sudden conviction that he had seen the wide-set eyes before; also the straight little nose and the half boyish mouth and chin, though where he had seen them the conviction could give no present hint.

"I sup-pup-pose I ought to say something appropriate," she was beginning, half breathlessly, while Smith stood at the fender and grinned in character-not with the ex-leader of the Lawrenceville younger set, but with the newer and more elemental man of all work on a desert dam-building job. "Wha-what is the proper thing to say when you have just been sus-snatched out of the way of a railroad train?"

As J. Montague, the rescuer would have had a neatly turned rejoinder at his tongue's end; but the well-mannered phrases were altogether too conventional to suggest themselves to a strapping young barbarian in ill-fitting khaki and leggings and a slouch felt. Being unable to recall them, he laughed and pushed the J. Montague past still farther into the background.

"You don't have to say anything. It's been a long time since I've had a chance to make such a bully grand-stand play as this." And then: "You're Colonel Baldwin's daughter, aren't you?"

She nodded, saying:

"How did you know?"

"I know the car. And you have your father's eyes."

She did not seem to take it amiss that he was making her eyes a basis for comparisons. One William Starbuck, a former cattleman and her father's time-tried friend, paid Miss Corona the compliment of saying that she never allowed herself to get "bogged down in the haughtinesses." She was her father's only son, as well as his only daughter, and she divided her time pretty evenly in trying to live up to both sets of requirements.

"You have introduced me; wo-won't you introduce yourself?" she said, when a second crash of the shifting freight-train spent itself and gave her an opening.

"I'm Smith," he told her; adding: "It's my real name."

Her laugh was an instant easing of tensions.

"Oh, yes; you're Mr. Williams's assistant. I've heard Colonel-da—my father, speak of you."

"No," he denied in blunt honesty, "I'm not Williams's assistant; at least, the pay-roll doesn't say so. Up at the camp they call me 'The Hobo,' and that's what I was a week or so ago when your father picked me up and gave me a lift to the dam in this car."

The young woman had apparently regained whatever small fraction of self-possession the narrow escape had shocked aside.

"Are they never going to take that miserable train out of the way?" she exclaimed. "I've got to see Mr. Williams, and there isn't a minute to spare. That is why I was breaking all the speed limits."

"They are about ready to pull out now," he returned, with a glance over his shoulder at the train. "I'm a sort of general utility man up at the camp: can you use me in any way?"

"I'm afraid you won't do," she replied, with a little laughing grimace that made him wonder where and when in the past he had seen some young woman do the same thing under exactly similar conditions. "It's a matter of business—awfully urgent business. Colonel-da—I mean my father, has gone up to Red Butte, and a little while ago they telephoned over to the ranch from the Brewster office to say that there was going to be some more trouble at the dam."

"They?" he queried.

"Mr. Martin, the head bookkeeper. He said he'd been trying to get Mr. Williams, but the wires to the camp were out of order."

"They're not," said Smith shortly, remembering that Perkins had been talking from the camp to the Brewster railroad agent within the half-hour. "But never mind that: go on."

Again she let him see the piquant little grimace.

"You say that just as if you were Mr. Williams's assistant," she threw back at him. "But I haven't time to quarrel with you this morning, Mr. Real-name Smith. If you'll take your foot off the fender I'll go on up to the dam and find Mr. Williams."

"You couldn't quarrel with me if you should try," was the good-natured rejoinder, and Smith tried in vain to imagine himself taking his present attitude with any of the young women he had known in his cotillon days—with Verda Richlander, for example. Then he added: "You won't find Williams at the camp. He started out early this morning to ride the lower ditch lines beyond Little Creek, and he said he wouldn't be back until some time to-morrow. Now will you tell me what you're needing—and give me a possible chance to get my pay raised?"

"Oh!" she exclaimed, with a little gasp of disappointment, presumably for the Williams absence. "I've simply got to find Mr. Williams—or somebody! Do you happen to know anything about the lawsuit troubles?"

"I know all about them; Williams has told me."

"Then I'll tell you what Mr. Martin telephoned. He said that three men were going to pretend to relocate a mining claim in the hills back of the dam, somewhere near the upper end of the reservoir lake-that-is-to-be. They're doing it so that they can get out an injunction, or whatever you call it, and then we'll have to buy them off, as the others have been bought off."

Smith was by this time entirely familiar with the maps and profiles and other records of the ditch company's lands and holdings.

"All the land within the limits of the flood level has been bought and paid for—some of it more than once, hasn't it?" he asked.

"Oh, yes; but that doesn't make any difference. These men will claim that their location was made long ago, and that they are just now getting ready to work it. It's often done in the case of mining claims."

"When is all this going to happen?" he inquired.

"It is already happening," she broke out impatiently. "Mr. Martin said the three men left town a little after daybreak and crossed on the Brewster bridge to go up on the other side of the Timanyoni. They had a two-horse team and a camping outfit. They are probably at work long before this time."

The young woman had taken her place again behind the big tiller-wheel, and Smith calmly motioned her out of it.

"Take the other seat and let me get in here," he said; and when she had changed over, he swung in behind the wheel and put a foot on the clutch pedal.

"What are you going to do?" she asked.

"I'm going to take you on up to the camp, and then, if you'll lend me this car, I'll go and do what you hoped to persuade Williams to do—run these mining-claim jokers into the tall timber."

"But you can't!" she protested; "you can't do it alone! And, besides, they are on the other side of the river, and you can't get anywhere with the car. You'll have to go all the way back to Brewster to get across the river!"

It was just here that he stole another glance at the very-much-alive little face behind the motor veil; at the firm, round chin and the resolute, slaty-gray eyes.

"I suppose I ought to take you to the camp," he said. "But you may go along with me, if you want to—and are not afraid."

She laughed in his face.

"I was born here in the Timanyoni, and you haven't been here three weeks: do you think I'd be afraid to go anywhere that you'll go?"

"We'll see about that," he chuckled, matching the laugh; and with that he let the clutch take hold and sent the car rolling gently up to the level of the railroad embankment and across the rails of the main track.

On the right of way of the paralleling side-track he steered off the crossing and pulled the roadster around until it was headed fairly for the upper switch. Then he climbed down and recovered his coat which had been flung aside in the race with the train. Resuming his place behind the tiller-wheel, he put the motor in the reverse and began to back the car on the siding, steering so that the wheels on one side hugged the inside of one rail.

"What in the world are you trying to do?" questioned the young woman who had said she was not afraid.

"Wait," he temporized; "just wait a minute and get ready to hang on like grim death. We're going across on that trestle."

He fully expected her to shriek and grab for the steering-wheel. That, he told himself, was what the normal young woman would do. But Miss Corona disappointed him.

"You'll put us both into the river, and smash Colonel-daddy's car, but I guess the Baldwin family can stand it if you can," she remarked quite calmly.

Smith kept on backing until the car had passed the switch from which the spur branched off to cross to the material yard on the opposite side of the river. A skilful bit of juggling put the roadster over on the ties of the spur-track. Then he turned to his fellow risk.

"Sit low, and hang on with both hands," he directed. "Now!" and he opened the throttle.

The trestle was not much above two hundred feet long, and, happily, the cross-ties were closely spaced. Steered to a hair, the big car went bumping across, and in his innermost recesses Smith was saying to his immediate ancestor, the well-behaved bank clerk: "You swab! you never saw the day when you could do a thing like this ... you thought you had me tied up in a bunch of ribbon, didn't you?"

If Miss Baldwin were frightened, she did not show it; and when the crossing was safely made, Smith caught a little side glance that told him he was making good. He jerked the roadster out of the entanglement of the railroad track and said: "You may sit up now and tell me which way to go. I don't know anything about the roads over here."

She pointed out the way across the hills, and a four-mile dash followed that set the blood dancing in Smith's veins. He had never before driven a car as fast as he wanted to; partly because he had never owned one powerful enough, and partly because the home-land speed laws—and his own past métier—would not sanction it. Up hill and down the big roadster raced, devouring the interspaces, and at the topping of the last of the ridges the young woman opened the small tool-box in the dividing arm between the seats and showed her reckless driver a large and serviceable army automatic snugly holstered under the lid.

"Daddy always keeps it there for his night drives on the horse ranges," she explained. But Smith was shaking his head.

"We're not going to need anything of that sort," he assured her, and the racing search for three men and a two-horse team was continued.

Beyond the final hill, in a small, low-lying swale which was well hidden from any point of view in the vicinity of the distant dam, they came upon the interlopers. There were three men and two horses and a covered wagon, as Martin's telephone message had catalogued them. The horses were still in the traces, and just beyond the wagon a long, narrow parallelogram, of the length and breadth of a legal mining claim, had been marked out by freshly driven stakes. In one end of the parallelogram two of the men were digging perfunctorily, while the third was tacking the legal notice on a bit of board nailed to one of the stakes.

Smith sent the gray car rocketing down into the swale, brought it to a stand with a thrust of the brakes, and jumped out. Once more the primitive Stone Age man in him, which had slept so long and so quietly under the Lawrenceville conventionalities, was joyously pitching the barriers aside.

"It's moving day for you fellows," he announced cheerfully, picking the biggest of the three as the proper subject for the order giving. "You're on the Timanyoni Ditch Company's land, and you know it. Pile into that wagon and fade away!"

The big man's answer was a laugh, pointed, doubtless, by the fact that the order giver was palpably unarmed. But on second thought he began to supplement the laugh with an oath. Smith's right arm shot out, and when the blow landed there were only two left to close in on him. In such sudden hostilities the advantages are all with the beginner. Having superior reach and a good bit more skill than either of the two tacklers, Smith held his own until he could get in a few more of the smashing right-handers, but in planting them he took punishment enough to make him Berserk-mad and so practically invincible. There was a fierce mingling of arms, legs, and bodies, sufficiently terrifying, one would suppose, to a young woman sitting calmly in an automobile a hundred yards away; but she neither cried out nor attempted to go to the rescue with the weapon which it seemed as if Smith might be needing.

The struggle was short in just proportion to its vigor, and at the end of it two of the trespassers were knocked out, and Smith was dragging the third over to the wagon, into which he presently heaved the man as if he had been a sack of meal. Miss Baldwin, sitting in the car, saw her ally dive into the covered wagon and come out with a pair of Winchesters. Pausing only long enough to smash the guns, one after the other, over the wagon-wheel, he started back after the two other men. They were not waiting to be carried to the wagon; they were up and running in a wide semicircle to reach their hope of retreat unslain, if that might be. It was all very brutal and barbarous, no doubt, but the colonel's daughter was Western born and bred, and she clapped her hands and laughed in sheer enthusiasm when she saw Smith make a show of chasing the circling runners.

He did not return to her until after he had pulled up the freshly driven stakes and thrown them away, and by that time the wagon, with the horses lashed to a keen gallop, was disappearing over the crest of the northern ridge.

"That's one way to get rid of them, isn't it?" said the emancipated bank man, jocosely, upon taking his place in the car to cramp it for the turn. "Was that something like the notion you had in mind?"

"Mercy, no!" she rejoined. And then: "Are you sure you are not hurt?"

"Not worth mentioning," he evaded. "Those duffers couldn't hurt anybody, so long as they couldn't get to their guns."

"But you have saved the company at your own expense. They will be sure to have you arrested."

"We won't cross that bridge until we come to it," he returned. "And, besides, there were no witnesses. You didn't see anything."

"Of course, I didn't; not the least little thing in the world!" she agreed, laughing with him.

"I thought not. There were too many of us for any single eye-witness to get more than the general effect." Then, in easy assertion of his victor rights: "If we were back in the country from which I have lately escaped it would be proper for me to ask your permission to drive you safely home. Since we are not, I shall assume the permission and do it anyway."

"Oh, is that necessary?" she asked, meaning, as he took it, nothing more than comradely deprecation at putting him to the trouble of it.

"Not absolutely necessary, perhaps, but decently prudent. You might drop me opposite the dam, but you'd have to pass those fellows somewhere on the way and they might try to make it unpleasant for you."

She made no further comment, and he sent the car spinning along over the hills to the westward. A mile short of the trestle river crossing they overtook and passed the wagon. Because he had the colonel's daughter with him, Smith put on a burst of speed and so gave the claim-jumpers no chance to provoke another battle. With the possible unpleasantnesses thus left in the rear, Smith knew well enough that there was really no reason for his going any farther than the spur-track trestle. None the less, he held to his announced determination, driving briskly down the north-side river road and on toward the grass-land ranches.

In the maze of cross-roads opposite the little city on the south bank of the river, Smith was out of his reckoning, and was obliged to ask his companion to direct him.

"I thought you weren't ever going to say anything any more," she sighed, in mock despair. "Take this road to the right."

"I can't talk and drive a speed-wagon at the same time," he told her, twisting the gray car into the road she had indicated, and he made the assertion good by covering the four remaining miles in the same preoccupied fashion.

There was a reason, of a sort, for his silence; two of them, to be exact. For one, he was troubled by that haunting sense of familiarity which was still trying to tell him that this was not his first meeting with Colonel Baldwin's daughter; and the other was much bigger, and more depressing. Though he was continually assuring himself that he had buried the former bank clerk and all of his belongings in a deep grave, some of the bank-clerk convictions still refused to remain decently in the coffin. One of these—and it had been daggering him sharply for the past half-hour—was the realization that in breaking with his past, he had broken also with the world of women—good women—at least to the extent of ever asking one of them to marry him.

Truly, though shadows are insubstantial things for the greater part, there is one exception. The shadow of a crime may involve both the innocent and the guilty quite as effectually as the thing itself, and Smith saw himself shut out automatically from the married beatitudes.... He pushed the thought aside, coming back to the other one—the puzzle of familiarity—when Miss Baldwin pointed to a transplanted Missouri farm mansion, with a columned portico, standing in a grove of cottonwoods on the left-hand side of the road, telling him it was Hillcrest.

There was a massive stone portal fronting the road, and when he got down to open the gates the young woman took the wheel and drove through; whereupon, he decided that it was time for him to break away, and said so.

"But how will you get back to the camp?" she asked.

"I have my two legs yet, and the walking isn't bad."

"No; but you might meet those men again."

"That is the least of my troubles."

Miss Corona Baldwin, like the Missouri colonel, her father, came upon moments now and then when she had the ultimate courage of her impulses.

"I should have said you hadn't a trouble in the world," she asserted, meeting his gaze level-eyed.

The polite paraphrases of the coffined period were slipping to the end of his tongue, but he set his teeth upon them and said, instead: "That's all you know about it. What if I should tell you that you've been driving this morning with an escaped convict?"

"I shouldn't believe it," she said calmly.

"Well, you haven't—not quite," he returned, adding the qualifying phrase in sheer honesty.

She had untied her veil and was asking him hospitably if he wouldn't come in and meet her mother. Something in the way she said it, some little twist of the lips or look of the eyes, touched the spring of complete recognition and the familiarity puzzle vanished instantly.

"You forget that I am a workingman," he smiled. "My gang in the quarry will think I've found a bottle somewhere." And then: "Did you ever lose a glove, Miss Baldwin—a white kid with a little hole in one finger?"

"Dozens of them," she admitted; "and most of them had holes, I'm afraid. But what has that got to do with your coming in and meeting mamma and letting her thank you for saving my life?"

"Nothing at all, of course," he hastened to say; and with that he bade her good-by rather abruptly and turned his back upon the transplanted Missouri mansion, muttering to himself as he closed the portal gates behind him: "'Baldwin,' of course! What an ass I was not to remember the name! And now I've got the other half of it, too; it's 'Corona.'"

VIII
Timanyoni Ditch

Smith had his vote of thanks from Colonel Dexter Baldwin in person late in the afternoon of the day following the summary eviction of the sham mine locators in the upper reservoir; presidential thanks for his prompt defense of the company's interests, and a warm outhanding of fatherly gratitude for the rescue at the unloading side-track. The vote was passed in Williams's sheet-iron office at the dam, the colonel having driven out to the camp for the express purpose; and the chief of construction himself was not present.

"You've loaded us up with a tolerably heavy obligation, Smith—Corry's mother and me," was the way the colonel summed up in the personal field. "If you hadn't been on deck and strictly on the job at that railroad crossing yesterday morning——"

"Don't mention it, Colonel," Smith broke in, protesting honestly as plain "John" where a "J. Montague" might have made self-gratulatory capital. "There is only one thing in this world more onerous than owing an obligation, and that is the feeling that you've got to live up to one. I did nothing more than any man would have done for any woman. You know it, and I know it. Let's leave it that way and forget it."

The tall Missourian's laugh was entirely approbative.

"I like that," he said. "It's a good, man-fashion way of looking at it. Corry wanted me to tell her what I was going to say to you, and I said I'd be hanged if I knew. I owe you one for making it easy. You know how I feel about it—how any father would feel; and that's enough."

"Plenty," was the brief rejoinder.

"But there's another chapter to it that neither of us can cross out; you'll have to come out to the ranch and let Corry's mother have a hack at you," Baldwin went on. "I couldn't figure you out of that if I should try. And now about those claim-jumpers: I suppose you didn't know any of them by name?"

"No."

"Corry says you gave them the time of their lives. By George, I wish I'd been there to see!" and the colonel slapped his leg and laughed. "Did they look like the real thing—sure-enough prospectors?"

"They looked like a bunch of hired assassins," said Smith, with a grin. "It's some more of the interference, isn't it?"

The colonel's square jaw settled into the fighting angle.

"How much do you know about this business mix-up of ours, Smith?" he asked.

"All that Williams could tell me in a little heart-to-heart talk we had the other day."

"You agreed with him that there was a tolerably big nigger in the wood-pile, didn't you?"

"I had already gathered that much from the camp gossip."

"Well, it's so. We're just about as helpless as a bunch of cattle in a sink-hole," was the ranchman president's confirmation of the camp guesses. "As long as it was a straightaway stunt of buying land and building a dam and digging a few ditches, we were in the fight. We knew what we wanted, and we had the money to go out and buy it. But now it looks as if we were aiming to get it where the chicken got the cleaver. If our hunch about the Escalante irrigation trust is right, we are not only going to lose our money and our work; we've run slap up against a proposition that will shut us out of the water altogether and force us to buy it of these Eastern sharks—at their own price. When it comes to that, we may as well make 'em a present of the entire Little Creek district. They can take it whenever they have a mind to."

Smith was thinking of the young woman with the resolute slaty-gray eyes when he said: "That is, of course, if you lie down and let them put the steam-roller over you. But you're not going to do that, are you?"

Baldwin shook his head as one who will not permit himself to minimize a hazard.

"Keep that notion of the cattle in a sink-hole in front of you, Smith, and you'll get a pretty fair idea of the chances. What in the name of the great horn spoon can we do—more than we have done?"

"There are a number of things that might be done," said Smith, falling back reflectively upon the presumably dead and buried bank-cashier part of him. "In the first place, these trust people can't take your dam and your ditch right of way until after they have bought up a voting control of your stock. It is very pointedly up to you and your fellow stockholders to say whether or not you are going to let them scare or force you into selling, isn't it?"

"I reckon maybe it is. But two of our men have already sold out, and more will follow. These Eastern sharks 've got the bulge on us; they have the money, and we're just about as good as dead broke."

"Of course," said the younger man. "That was part of the game; to swamp you with costly lawsuits, use up your capital, and break your credit. It's done every day in business, and in a thousand different ways, some of them pure robberies, but most of them legally defensible. You folks have made the mistake of letting it go too far on too small a capitalization. You're left without a fighting fund. Still, while there is life there is always hope. And if you can manage to stay in the game and play it out, there is big money in it for all of you; enough to make it well worth while for you to put up the fight of your lives."

"Big money?—you mean in saving our investment?"

"Oh, no; not at all; in cinching the other fellows," Smith put in genially. "As Williams explained it to me, there is the biggest kind of a killing in it for you people, if you can hold on and win out."

Colonel Dexter Baldwin lifted his soft hat and ran his fingers through his grizzled hair.

"Say, Smith; you mustn't forget that I'm from Missouri," he said half quizzically.

"But I shouldn't think you'd need to be 'shown' in this particular instance," was the smiling rejoinder. "Why are these Eastern capitalists spending their good money on a scheme to freeze out your little handful of ranch owners, Colonel? Surely you've asked yourself that question long before this, haven't you?"

"Why, yes; it's because they want to get something for nothing, isn't it?"

"In a general sense, of course, that is the basis of all crooked business schemes. But the chance to sell you people water from your own dam isn't the only thing or the main thing in this case; that part of it is merely incidental. Didn't Williams tell me that they are obliged to have this dam site, or, at least, one as high up the river as this, in order to get the water over to their newly alienated grant in the western half of the park?"

"I don't know what Bartley told you, but that is the fact."

"No way of dodging that, is there? They couldn't possibly build a dam of their own, lower down, and make it work, could they? I'm asking because what I don't know about irrigation engineering would fill a Carnegie library in a good-sized little city."

"You've got it straight," said the colonel. "A good part of the Escalante Grant lies higher than our Little Creek ranches. From any point farther down the river than this, they'd have to pump the water to get it up to the Escalante mesas."

"Very good. Then they're simply obliged to have your dam, or—Don't you see the alternative now, Colonel?"

"Heavens to Betsy!" exclaimed the breeder of fine horses, bringing his fist down upon Williams's desk with a crash that made the ink-bottles dance. And then: "The Lord have mercy! What a lot of fence-posts we are—the whole kit and b'ilin' of us! If they get the dam, they sell water to us; if they don't get it, we sell it to them!"

"That's it, exactly," Smith put in quietly. "And I should say that your stake in the game is worth the stiffest fight you can make to save it. Don't you agree with me?"

"Great Jehu! I should say so!" ejaculated the amateur trust fighter. Then he broke down the barriers masterfully. "That settles it, Smith. You can't wiggle out of it now, no way or shape. You've got to come over into Macedonia and help us. Williams tells me you refused him, but you can't refuse me."

If Smith hesitated, it was only partly on his own account. He was thinking again of the young woman with the honest eyes when he said: "Do you know why I turned Williams down when he spoke to me the other day?"

Colonel Dexter Baldwin had his faults, like other men, but they were not those of indirection.

"I reckon I do know, son," he said, with large tolerance. "You're a 'lame duck' of some sort; you've made that pretty plain in your talks with Williams, haven't you? But that's our lookout. Bartley is ready to swear that you are not a crooked crook, whatever else it is that you're dodging for, and if we want to shut our eyes to the way you won't loosen up about yourself.... Besides, there's yesterday; and what you did down at the railroad crossing and out yonder in the hills——"

"We agreed to forget the yesterday incidents," the lame duck reminded him quickly. And then: "I ought to say 'No,' Colonel Baldwin; say it straight out, and stick to it. If I don't say it—if I ask for a little time—it is because I want to weigh up a few things—the things I can't talk about to you or to Williams. If, in the end, I should be fool enough to say 'Yes,' it will be merely because, the way things have turned out with me, I'd a little rather fight than eat. But even in that case it is only fair to you to say that, right in the middle of the scrap, I may fall to pieces on you."

Baldwin was too shrewd to try to push his advantage when there was, or seemed to be, a chance that the desired end was as good as half attained. And it was a purely manful prompting that made him get up and thrust out his hand to the young fellow who was trying to be as frank as he dared to be.

"Put it there, John," he said heartily. "Nobody in the Timanyoni is going to pry into you an inch farther than you care to let 'em; and if you get into trouble by helping us, you can count on at least one backer who will stand by you until the cows come home. Now then, hunt up your coat, and we'll drive over to Hillcrest for a bite to eat. I know you won't be easy in your mind until you've had it out with Corry's mother—about that little railroad trick—and you may as well do it now and have it over with. No; excuses don't go, this time. I had my orders from the Missus before I left town, and I know better than to go home without you. Never mind the commissary khaki. It won't be the first time that the working-clothes have figured at the Hillcrest table—not by a long shot."

And because he did not know how to frame a refusal that would refuse, Smith got his coat and went.

IX
Relapsings

Given his choice between the two, Smith would cheerfully have faced another hand-to-hand battle with the claim-jumpers in preference to even so mild a dip into the former things as the dinner at Hillcrest foreshadowed. The reluctance was not forced; it was real. The primitive man in him did not wish to be entertained. On the fast auto drive down to Brewster, across the bridge, and out to the Baldwin ranch Smith's humor was frankly sardonic. Dinners, social or grateful, were such childish things; so little worth the time and attention of a real man with work to do!

It mattered nothing that he had lived twenty-five years and more without suspecting this childishness of things social. That door was closed and another had been opened; beyond the new opening the prospect was as yet rather chaotic and rugged, to be sure, but the color scheme, if somewhat raw, was red-blood vivid, and the horizons were illimitable. Smith sat up in the mechanician's seat and straightened the loose tie under the soft collar of his working-shirt, smiling grimly as his thought leaped back to the dress clothes he had left lying on the bed in his Lawrenceville quarters. He cherished a small hope that Mrs. Baldwin might be shocked at the soft shirt and the khaki. It would serve her right for taking a man from his job.

The colonel did not try to make him talk, and the fifteen-mile flight down the river and across into the hills was shortly accomplished. At the stone-pillared portal he got out to open the gates. Down the road a little distance a horseman was coming at a smart gallop—at least, the rider figured as a man for the gate-opener until he saw that it was Corona Baldwin, booted and spurred and riding a man's saddle.

Smith let the gray car go on its way up the drive without him and held the gates open for the horse and its rider.

"So you weakened, did you? I'm disappointed in you," was Miss Baldwin's greeting. "You've made me lose my bet with Colonel-daddy. I said you wouldn't come."

"I had no business to come," he answered morosely. "But your father wouldn't let me off."

"Of course, he wouldn't; daddy never lets anybody off, unless they owe him money. Where are your evening clothes?"

Smith let the lever of moroseness slip back to the grinning

notch. "They are about two thousand miles away, and probably in some second-hand shop by this time. What makes you think I ever wore a dress suit?" He had closed the gates and was walking beside her horse up the driveway.

"Oh, I just guessed it," she returned lightly, "and if you'll hold your breath, I'll guess again."

"Don't," he laughed. "You are going to say that at some time in my life I knew better than to accept anybody's dinner invitation undecorated. Maybe there was such a time, but if so, I am trying to forget it."

Her laugh was good-naturedly derisive.

"You'll forget it just so long as you are able to content yourself in a construction camp. I know the symptoms. There are times when I feel as if I'd simply blow up if I couldn't put on the oldest things I've got and go and gallop for miles on Shy, and other times when I want to put on all the pretty things I have and look soulful and talk nonsense."

"But you've been doing that—the galloping, I mean—all your life, haven't you?"

"Not quite. There were three wasted years in a finishing school back East. It is when I get to thinking too pointedly about them that I have to go out to the stable and saddle Shy."

They had reached the steps of the pillared portico, and a negro stable-boy, one of the colonel's importations from Missouri, was waiting to take Miss Baldwin's horse. Smith knew how to help a woman down from a side-saddle; but the two-stirruped rig stumped him. The young woman saw his momentary embarrassment and laughed again as she swung out of her saddle to stand beside him on the step.

"The women don't ride that way in your part of the country?" she queried.

"Not yet."

"I'm sorry for them," she scoffed. And then: "Come on in and meet mamma; you look as if you were dreading it, and, as Colonel-daddy says, it's always best to have the dreaded things over with."

Smith did not find his meeting with the daughter's mother much of a trial. She was neither shocked at his clothes nor disposed to be hysterically grateful over the railroad-crossing incident. A large, calm-eyed, sensible matron, some ten or a dozen years younger than the colonel, Smith put her, and with an air of refinement which was reflected in every interior detail of her house.

Smith had not expected to find the modern conveniences in a Timanyoni ranch-house, but they were there. The room to which the

Indian house-boy led him had a brass bedstead and a private bath, and the rugs, if not true Tabriz, were a handsome imitation. Below stairs it was much the same. The dining-room was a beamed baronial hall, with a rough-stone fireplace big enough to take a cord-wood length, and on the hearth andirons which might have come down from the Elizabethan period. It was mid-June and the fireplace was empty, but its winter promise was so hospitable that Smith caught himself hoping that he might stay out of jail long enough to be able to see it in action.

The dinner was strictly a family meal, with the great mahogany table shortened to make it convenient for four. There were cut glass and silver and snowy napery, and Smith was glad that the colonel did most of the talking. Out of the past a thousand tentacles were reaching up to drag him back into the net of the conventional. With the encompassments to help, it was so desperately easy to imagine himself once more the "débutantes' darling," as Westfall had often called him in friendly derision. When the table-talk became general, he found himself joining in, and always upon the lighter side.

By the time the dessert came on, the transformation was complete. It was J. Montague, the cotillon leader, who sat back in his chair and told amiable little after-dinner stones, ignoring the colonel's heartinesses, and approving himself in the eyes of his hostess as a dinner guest of the true urban quality. Now and then he surprised a look in the younger woman's eyes which was not wholly sympathetic, he thought; but the temptation to show her that he was not at all the kind of man she had been taking him for was too strong to be resisted. Since she had seen fit to charge him with a dress-clothes past he would show her that he could live up to it.

Contrary to Smith's expectations, the colonel did not usurp him immediately after dinner. A gorgeous sunset was flaming over the western Timanyonis and there was time for a quiet stroll and a smoke under the silver-leafed cottonwoods with his hostess for a companion. In the little talk and walk, Smith found himself drawn more and more to the calm-eyed, well-bred matron who had given a piquant Corona to an otherwise commonplace world. He found her exceedingly well-informed; she had read the books that he had read, she had heard the operas that he had always wanted to hear, and if any other bond were needed, he found it in the fact that she was a native of his own State.

Under such leadings the relapse became an obsession. He abandoned himself shamelessly to the J. Montague attitude, and the events crowding so thickly between the tramp-like flight from

Lawrenceville and the present were as if they had not been. Mrs. Baldwin saw nothing of the rude fighter of battles her daughter had drawn for her, and wondered a little. She knew Corona's leanings, and was not without an amused impression that Corona would not find this later Smithsonian phase altogether to her liking.

A little later the daughter, who had been to the horse corral with her father, came to join them, and the mother, smiling inwardly, saw her impression confirmed. Smith was talking frivolously of thés dansants and dinner-parties and club meets; whereat the mother smiled and Miss Corona's lip curled scornfully.

Smith got what he had earned, good measure, pressed down, shaken together and running over, a few minutes after Mrs. Baldwin had gone in, leaving him to finish his cigar under the pillared portico with Corona to keep him company. He never knew just what started it, unless it was his careful placing of a chair for the young woman and his deferential—and perfectly natural—pause, standing, until she was seated.

"Do, for pity's sake, sit down!" she broke out, half petulantly. And when he had obeyed: "Well, you've spoiled it all, good and hard. Yesterday I thought you were a real man, but now you are doing your best to tell me that you were only shamming."

Smith was still so far besotted as to be unable to imagine wherein he had offended.

"Really?" he said. "I'm sorry to have disappointed you. All I need now to make me perfectly happy is to be told what I have done."

"It isn't what you've done; it's what you are," she retorted.

"Well, what am I?" he asked patiently.

Her laugh was mocking. "You are politely good-natured, for one thing; but that wasn't what I meant. You have committed the unpardonable sin by turning out to be just one of the ninety-nine, after all. If you knew women the least little bit in the world, you would know that we are always looking for the hundredth man."

Under his smile, Smith was searching the Lawrenceville experience records minutely in the effort to find something that would even remotely match this. The effort was a complete failure. But he was beginning to understand what this astonishingly frank young woman meant. She had seen the depth of his relapse, and was calmly deriding him for it. A saving sense of humor came to remind him of his own sardonic musings on the silent drive from the camp with the colonel; how he had railed inwardly at the social trivialities.

"You may pile it on as thickly as you please," he said, the

good-natured smile twisting itself into the construction-camp grin. Then he added: "I may not be the hundredth man, but you, at least, are the hundredth woman."

"Why? Because I say the first thing that asks to be said?"

"That, and some other things," he rejoined guardedly. Then, with malice aforethought: "Is it one of the requirements that your centennial man should behave himself like a boor at a dinner-table, and talk shop and eat with his knife?"

"You know that isn't what I meant. Manners don't make the man. It's what you talked about—the trumpery little social things that you found your keenest pleasure in talking about. I don't know what has ever taken you out to a construction camp and persuaded you to wear khaki. Perhaps it was only what Colonel-daddy calls a 'throw-back.' I don't believe you ever did a day's hard work in your life before you came to the Timanyoni."

Smith looked at his hands. They were large and shapely, but the only callouses they could show were accusingly recent.

"If you mean manual labor, you are right," he admitted thoughtfully. "Just the same, I think you are a little hard on me."

It was growing dark by this time, and the stars were coming out. Some one had turned the lights on in the room the windows of which opened upon the portico, and the young woman's chair was so placed that he could still see her face. She was smiling rather more amicably when she said:

"You mustn't take it too hard. It isn't you, personally, you know; it's the type. I've met it before. I didn't meet any other kind during my three years in the boarding-school; nice, pleasant young gentlemen, as immaculately dressed as their pocketbooks would allow, up in all the latest little courtesies and tea-table shop-talk. They were all men, I suppose, but I'm afraid a good many of them had never found it out—will never find it out. I've been calling it environment; I don't like to admit that the race is going down-hill."

By this time the sardonic humor was once more in full possession and he was enjoying her keenly.

"Go on," he said. "This is my night off."

"I've said enough; too much, perhaps. But a little while ago at the dinner-table, and again out there in the grove where you were walking with mamma, you reminded me so forcibly of a man whom I met just for a part of one evening about a year ago."

"Tell me about him," he urged.

"I was coming back from school and I stopped over in a small town in the Middle West to visit some old friends of mamma's. There were young people in the family, and one evening they gave a lawn-party for me. I met dozens of the pleasant young gentlemen, more than I had ever seen together at any one time before; clerks and book-keepers, and rich farmers' sons who had been to college."

"But the man of whom I am reminding you?"

"He was one of them. He drove over from some neighboring town in his natty little automobile and gave me fully an hour of his valuable time. He made me perfectly furious!"

"Poor you!" laughed Smith; but he was thankful that the camp sunburn and his four weeks' beard were safeguarding his identity. "I hope you didn't tell him so. He was probably doing his level best to give you a good time in the only definition of the term that the girls of his own set had ever given him. But why the fury in his case in particular?"

"Just because, I suppose. He was rather good-looking, you know; and down underneath all the airy little things he persisted in talking about it seemed as if I could now and then get tiny glimpses of something that might be a real man, a strong man. I remember he told me he was a bank cashier and that he danced. He was quite hopeless, of course. Without being what you would call conceited, you could see that the crust was so thick that nothing short of an earthquake would ever break it."

"But the earthquakes do come, once in a blue moon," he said, still smiling at her. "Let's get it straight. You are not trying to tell me that you object to decent clothes and good manners per se, are you?"

"Not at all; I like them both. But the hundredth man won't let either his clothes or his manners wear him; he'll wear them."

"Still, you think the type of man you have been describing is entirely hopeless; that was the word you used, I believe."

The colonel was coming out, and he had stopped in the doorway to light a long-stemmed pipe. The young woman got up and fluffed her hair with the ends of her fingers—a little gesture which Smith remembered, recalling it from the night of the far-away lawn-party.

"Daddy wants you, and I'll have to vanish," she said; "but I'll answer your question before I go. Types are always hopeless; it's only the hundredth man who isn't. It's a great pity you couldn't go on whipping claim-jumpers all the rest of your life, Mr. Smith. Don't you think so? Good night. We'll meet again at breakfast. Daddy isn't going to let you get away short of a night's lodging, I know."

Two cigars for Smith and four pipes for the colonel further along, the tall Missourian rose out of the split-bottomed chair which he had drawn up to face the guest's and rapped the ashes from the bowl of the corn-cob into the palm of his hand.

"I think you've got it all now, Smith, every last crook and turn of it, and I reckon you're tired enough to run away to bed. You see just where we stand, and how little we've got to go on. If I've about talked an arm off of you, it's for your own good. I don't know how you've made up your mind, or if you've made it up at all; but it was only fair to show you how little chance we've got on anything short of a miracle. I wouldn't want to see you butt your head against a stone wall, and that's about what it looks like to me."

Smith took a turn up and down the stone-flagged floor of the portico with his hands behind him. Truly, the case of Timanyoni Ditch was desperate; even more desperate than he had supposed. Figuring as the level-headed bank cashier of the former days, he told himself soberly that no man in his senses would touch it with a ten-foot pole. Then the laughing gibes of the hundredth woman—gibes which had cut far deeper than she had imagined—came back to send the blood surging through his veins. It would be worth something to be able to work the miracle the colonel had spoken of; and afterward....

Colonel Dexter Baldwin was still tapping his palm absently with the pipe when Smith came back and said abruptly:

"I have decided, Colonel. I'll start in with you to-morrow morning, and we'll pull this mired scheme of yours out of the mud, or break a leg trying to. But you mustn't forget what I told you out at the camp. Right in the middle of things I may go rotten on you and drop out."

X
The Sick Project

Brewster, owing its beginnings to the completion of the Nevada Short Line, and the fact that the railroad builders designated it as a division headquarters, had grown into city-charter size and importance with the opening of the gold-mines in the Gloria district, and the transformation of the surrounding park grass-lands into cultivated ranches. To the growth and prosperity of the intermountain city a summer hotel on the shore of Lake Topaz—reached only by stage from Brewster—had added its influence; and since the hotel brought people with well-lined pocketbooks, there was a field for the enthusiastic real-estate promoters whose offices filled all the odd corners in the Hophra House block.

In one of these offices, on the morning following Smith's first dinner at Hillcrest, a rather caustic colloquy was in progress between the man whose name appeared in gilt lettering on the front windows and one of his unofficial assistants. Crawford Stanton, he of the window name, was a man of many personalities. To summer visitors with money to invest, he was the genial promoter, and if there were suggestions of iron hardness in the sharp jaw and in the smoothly shaven face and flinty eyes, there was also a pleasant reminder of Eastern business methods and alertness in the promoter's manner. But Lanterby, tilting uneasily in the "confidential" chair at the desk-end, knew another and more biting side of Mr. Stanton, as a hired man will.

"Good Gad! do you sit there and tell me that the three of them let that hobo of Williams's push them off the map?" Stanton was demanding raucously. "I thought you had at least sense enough to last you overnight. I told you to pick out a bunch with sand—fellows that could hang on and put up a fight if they had to. And you say all this happened the day before yesterday: how does it come that you are just now reporting it?"

The hard-faced henchman in the tilting chair made such explanations as he could.

"Boogerfield and his two partners 've been hidin' out somewhere; I allow they was plumb ashamed to come in and tell how they'd let one man run 'em off. You'd think that curly-whiskered helper o' Williams's was a holy terror, to hear Boogerfield talk. They'd left their artillery in the chuck-wagon, and they say he come at 'em barehanded—with the colonel's girl settin' in the ortamobile a-lookin' on. Boogerfield wants to know who's goin' to pay him for them two Winchesters that His Whiskers bu'sted over the wagon-wheel."

Mr. Crawford Stanton was carelessly unconcerned about the claim-jumpers' loss, either in gear or skin.

"Damn the Winchesters!" he said morosely. "What do you know about this fellow Smith? Who is he, and where did he come from?"

Lanterby told all that was known of Smith, and had no difficulty in compressing it into a single sentence. Stanton leaned back in his chair and the lids of the flinty eyes narrowed thoughtfully.

"There's a lot more to it than that," he said incisively at the end of the reflective pause. Then he added a curt order: "Make it your job to find out."

Lanterby moved uneasily in his insecure seat, but before he could speak, his employer went on again, changing the topic abruptly, but still keeping within the faultfinding boundaries.

"What sort of a screw has gone loose in your deal with the railroad men? I thought you told me you had it fixed with the yard crews so that Williams's material would have a chance to season a while in the Brewster yards before it was delivered. They got two cars of cement and one of steel the day before yesterday, and the delivery was made within three hours after the stuff came in from the East."

Again Lanterby tried to explain.

"Dougherty, the yardmaster, took the bank roll I slipped him, all right enough, and promised to help out. But he's scared of Maxwell. He told me this mornin' that Colonel Baldwin has been kickin' like blazes to Maxwell about the delays."

"Maxwell is a thick-headed ass!" exploded the faultfinder. "I've done everything on earth except to tell him outright in so many words that his entire railroad outfit, from President Brewster down, is lined up on the other side of the fight. But go on with your dickering. Jerk Dougherty into line and tell him that nothing is going to happen to him if he doesn't welsh on us. Hint to him that we can pull a longer string than Dick Maxwell can, if it comes to a show-down. Now go out and find Shaw. I want him, and I want him right now."

The hard-faced man who looked as if he might be a broken-down gambler unjointed his leg-hold upon the tilted chair and went out; and a few minutes later another of Stanton's pay-roll men drifted in. He was a young fellow with sleepy eyes and cigarette stains on his fingers, and he would have passed readily for a railroad clerk out of a job, which was what he really was.

"Well?" snapped Stanton when the incomer had taken the chair lately vacated by Lanterby.

"I shadowed the colonel, as you told me to," said the young man. "He went up to Red Butte to see if he couldn't rope in some of the old-timers on his ditch project. He was trying to sell some treasury stock. His one-horse company is about out of money. Mickle, a clerk in Kinzie's bank, tells me that the ditch company's balance is drawn down to a few thousand dollars, with no more coming in."

"Did the colonel succeed in making a raise in Red Butte?"

"Nary," said the spy nonchalantly. "Drake, the banker up

there, was his one best bet; but I got a man I know to give Drake a pointer, and he curled up like a hedgehog when you poke it with a sharp stick."

"That's better. The colonel came back yesterday, didn't he?"

"Yesterday afternoon. His wife and daughter met him at the railroad-station with the automobile, and told him something or other that made him hire old man Shuey to drive the women out home while he took the roadster and went up to the dam."

"You went along?" queried Stanton.

"As soon as I could find somebody to drive me; yes. That wasn't right away, though; and when I got there I had to leave my buzz-wagon back in the hills a piece and walk into camp. When I inquired around I found that the colonel was shut up in Williams's office with a fellow named Smith. They were finishing up whatever they'd been talking about when I got a place to listen in; but I heard enough to make me suspect that something new had broken loose. Just as they were getting ready to quit, the colonel was saying: 'That settles it, Smith; you've got to come over into'—I didn't catch the name of the place—'and help us. Williams tells me you refused him, but you can't refuse me.' There was more of it, but they had opened the door and I had to skin out. A little later they drove off together in the colonel's car, coming on through town to go out to the ranch, I suppose, because Smith didn't show up any more at the camp."

Again the gentleman with the sharp jaw took time for narrow-eyed reflection.

"You'll have to switch over from the colonel to this fellow Smith for the present, Shaw," he decided, at length. "Lanterby is supposed to be on that part of the job, but he's altogether too coarse-handed. I want to know who Smith is, and where he hails from, and how he comes to be butting in. Lanterby said at first, and says yet, that he is just a common hobo tumbling in from the outside. It's pretty evident that Lanterby has another guess coming. You look him up and do it quick."

The young man glanced up with a faint warming of avarice in his sleepy eyes. "It'll most likely run into money—for expenses," he suggested.

"For graft, you mean," snapped Stanton. Then he had it out with this second subordinate in crisp English. "I'm onto you with both feet, Shaw; every crook and turn of you. More than that, I know why you were fired out of Maxwell's office; you've got sticky fingers. That's all right with me up to a certain point, but beyond that point you get off. Understand?"

Shaw made no answer in direct terms, but if his employer had been watching the heavy-lidded eyes he might have seen in them the shadow of a thing much more dangerous than plain dishonesty: a passing shadow of the fear that makes for treachery when the sharp need for self-protection arises.

"I'll try to find out about the hobo," he said, with fair enough lip-loyalty, and after he had rolled a fresh cigarette he went away to begin the mining operations which might promise to unearth Smith's record.

It was ten o'clock when Shaw left the real-estate office in the Hophra House block. Half an hour earlier Smith had come to town with the colonel in the roadster, and the two had shut themselves up in the colonel's private room in the Timanyoni Ditch Company's town office in the Barker Building, which was two squares down the street from the Hophra House. Summoned promptly, Martin, the bookkeeper, had brought in his statements and balance-sheets, and the new officer, who was as yet without a title, had struck out his plan of campaign.

"'Amortization' is the word, Colonel," was Smith's prompt verdict after he had gone over Martin's summaries. "The best way to get at it now is to wipe the slate clean and begin over again."

The ranchman president was chuckling soberly.

"Once more you'll have to show me, John," he said. "We folks out here in the hills are not up in all the Wall Street crinkles."

"You don't know the word? It means to scrap the old machinery to make room for the new," Smith explained. "In modern business it is the process of extinguishing a corporation: closing it up and burying it in another and bigger one, usually. That is what we must do with Timanyoni Ditch."

"I'm getting you, a little at a time," said the colonel, taking his first lesson in high finance as a duck takes to the water. Then he added: "It won't take much of a lick to kill off the old company, in the shape it's got into now. How will you work it?"

Smith had the plan at his fingers' ends. With the daring of all the perils had come a fresh access of fighting fitness that made him feel as if he could cope with anything.

"We must close up the company's affairs and then reorganize promptly and, with just as little noise as may be, form another company—which we will call Timanyoni High Line—and let it take over the old outfit, stock, liabilities, and assets entire. You say your present capital stock is one hundred thousand dollars; is it all paid in?"

"Every dollar of it except a little for a few shares of treasury stock that we've been holding for emergencies. As I told you last night, I went up to Red Butte and tried to sell that treasury stock to Drake, the banker; but he wouldn't bite."

"Which was mighty lucky for us," Smith put in. "It would have queered us beautifully if he had, and the story had got out that the president of Timanyoni Ditch had sold a block of treasury stock at thirty-nine."

"Well, he didn't take it," said the colonel. "He was so blame' chilly that I like to froze to death before I could get out of the bank."

"All right; then we'll go on. This new company that I am speaking of will be capitalized at, say, an even half million. To the present holders of Timanyoni Ditch we'll give the new stock for the old, share for share, with a bonus of twenty-five shares of the new stock for every twenty-five shares of the old surrendered and exchanged. This will be practically giving the present shareholders two for one. Will that satisfy them?"

This time Colonel Dexter Baldwin's smile was grim.

"You're just juggling now, John, and you know it. Out here on the woolly edge of things a dollar is just a plain iron dollar, and you can't make it two merely by calling it so."

"Never you mind about that," cut in the new financier. "The first rule of investment is that a dollar is worth just what it will earn in dividends; no more, and equally no less. You know, and I know, that if we can pull this thing through there is a barrel of money in it for all concerned. But we'll skip that part of it and stick to the details. At two to one for the amortization of the old company we shall still have something like three hundred thousand dollars treasury stock upon which to realize for the new capital needed, and that will be amply sufficient to complete the dam and the ditches and to provide a fighting fund. Now then, tell me this: how near can we come to placing that treasury stock right here in Timanyoni Park? In other words, can the money be had here at any price?"

"You mean that you don't want to go East to raise it?"

"I mean that we haven't time. More than that, it's up to us to keep this thing in the family, so to speak; and the moment we go into other markets, we are getting over into the enemy's country. I'm not saying that the money couldn't be raised in New York; but if we should go there, the trust would have an underhold on us, right from the start."

"I see," said the colonel, who was indeed seeing many things that his simple-hearted philosophy had never dreamed of; and then he answered the direct question. "There is plenty of money right here in the Timanyonis; not all of it in Brewster, perhaps, but in the country among the Gloria and Little Butte mine owners, smelter men, and the better class of ranchmen. Take Dick Maxwell, the railroad superintendent—he's a miner on the side, you know—he could put ten or twenty thousand more into it without turning a hair; and so could some of the others."

Smith nodded. He was getting his second wind now, and the race promised to be a keen joy.

"But they would have to be 'shown,' you think?" he suggested. "All right; we'll proceed to show them. Now we can come down to present necessities. We've got to keep the work going—and speed it up to the limit: we ought to double Williams's force at once—put on a night shift to work by electric light. I took the liberty of telephoning Williams from Hillcrest this morning while you were reading your newspaper. I told him to wire advertisements for more labor to the newspapers in Denver, offering wages high enough to make the thing look attractive."

The colonel blinked twice and swallowed hard.

"Say, John," he said, leaning across the table-desk; "you've sure got your nerve with you. Do you know what our present bank balance happens to be?"

"No; I was just coming to that," said the reorganizer, smiling easily. "How much is it?"

"It is under five thousand dollars, and a good part of that is owing to the cement people!"

"Never mind; don't get nervous," was the reassuring rejoinder. "We are going to make it bigger in a few minutes, I hope. Who is your banker here?"

"Dave Kinzie, of the Brewster City National."

"Tell me a little something about Mr. Kinzie before we go down to see him; just brief him for me as a man, I mean."

The colonel was shaking his head slowly.

"He's what you might call a twenty-ton optimist, Dave is; solid, a little slow and sure, but the biggest boomer in the West, if you can get him started—believes in the resources of the country and all that. But you can't borrow money from him without security, if that's what you're aiming to do."

"Can't we?" smiled the young man who knew banks and bankers. "Let's go and see. You never know until you try, Colonel; and even then you're not always dead certain. Take me around and introduce me to this Mr. David Kinzie—and, hold on; it may be as well to give me a handle of some sort before we begin to talk money with other people. What are you going to call me in this new scheme of things?"

The big Missourian's laugh was a hearty guffaw.

"Gosh all Friday! the way it's starting out you're the whole works, Smith! Just name your own name, and we'll cinch it for you."

"I suppose you've already got a secretary and treasurer?"

"We had up to a few days ago, before Buck Gardner sold out his stock to Crawford Stanton."

"Haven't you had a board meeting since?"

"Yes; but only to accept Gardner's resignation. We didn't elect anybody else—nobody wanted the place; every last man of 'em shied."

"Naturally; not seeing any immediate prospects of having anything to treasure," laughed Smith. "But that will do. You may introduce me to Kinzie as your acting financial secretary, if you like. Now one more question: what is Kinzie's attitude toward Timanyoni Ditch?"

"At first it was all kinds of friendly; he is a stockholder in a small way, and he's heart and soul for anything that promises to build up the country, as I told you. But after a while he began to cool down a little, and now—well, I don't know; I hate to think it of Dave, but I'm afraid he's leaning the other way, toward these Eastern fellows. Little things he has let fall, and this last deal in which he tried to cover Stanton's tracks in the stock-buying from Gardner and Bolling; they all point that way."

"That is natural, too," said Smith, whose point of view was always unobscured in any battle of business. "The big company would be a better customer for the bank than your little one could ever hope to be. I guess that's all for the present. If you're ready, we'll go down and face the music. Take me to the Brewster City National and introduce me to Mr. Kinzie; then you can stand by and watch the wheels go round."

"By Janders!" said the colonel with an open smile; "I believe you'd just as soon tackle a banker as to eat your dinner; and I'd about as soon take a horsewhipping. Come on; I'll steer you up against Dave, but I'm telling you right now that the steering is about all you can count on from me."

It was while they were crossing the street together and turning down toward the Alameda Avenue corner where the Brewster City National Bank windows looked over into the windows of the Hophra House block opposite, that Mr. Crawford Stanton had his third morning caller, a thick-set barrel-bodied man with little pig-like eyes, closely cropped hair, a bristling mustache, and a wooden leg of the home-made sort—a peg with a hollowed bowl for the bent knee and a slat-like extension to go up the outside of the leg to be stapled to a leathern belt. Across one of the swarthy cheeks there was a broad scar that looked, at first sight, like a dash of blue paint. It was a knife slash got in the battle with Mexican Ruiz in which the thickset man had lost his leg. After the Mexican had brought him down with a bullet, he had added his mark as he had said he would; laying the big man's cheek open and rubbing the powder from a chewed cartridge into the wound. Afterward, the men of the camps called the cripple "Pegleg" or "Blue Pete" indifferently, though not to his face. For though the fat face was always relaxed in a good-natured smile, the crippled saloon-keeper was of those who kill with the knife; and since he could not pursue, he was fain to cajole the prey within reach.

Stanton looked up from his desk when the pad-and-click of the cripple's step came in from the street.

"Hello, Simms," he said, in curt greeting. "Want to see me?"

"Uh-huh; for a minute or so. Busy?"

"Never too busy to talk business. Sit down."

Simms threw the brim of his soft hat up with a backhanded stroke and shook his head. "It ain't worth while; and I gotta get back to camp. I blew in to tell y'u there's a fella out there that needs th' sand-bag."

"Who is it?"

"Fella name' Smith. He's showin' 'em how to cut too many corners—pace-settin', he calls it. First thing they know, they'll get the concrete up to where the high water won't bu'st it out."

Stanton's laugh was impatient.

"Don't make any mistake of that sort, Simms," he said. "We don't want the dam destroyed; we'd work just as hard as they would to prevent that. All we want is to have other people think it's likely to go out—think it hard enough to keep them from putting up any more money. Let that go. Is there any more fresh talk—among the men?" Stanton prided himself a little upon the underground wire-pulling which had resulted in putting Simms on the ground as the keeper of the construction-camp canteen. It was a fairly original way of keeping a listening ear open for the camp gossip.

"Little," said the cripple briefly. "This here blink-blank fella Smith's been tellin' Williams that I ort to be run off th' reservation; says th' booze puts the brake on for speed."

"So it does," agreed Stanton musingly. "But I guess you can stay a while longer. What do the men say about Smith?"

"Whole heap o' things. The best guess is that he's a jail-break' from somewheres back in the States. He ain't no common 'bo; that's a dead cinch. Gatrow, the quarry foreman, puts it up that he done something he had to run for."

"Get him drunk and find out," suggested Stanton shortly.

"Not him," said the round-faced villain, with the ingratiating smile wrinkling at the corners of the fat-embedded eyes. "He's the take-a-drink-or-let-it-alone kind."

"Well, keep your eye on him and your ears open. I have a notion that he's been sent here—by some outfit that means to buck us. If he hasn't any backing——"

The interruption was the hurried incoming of the young man with sleepy eyes and the cigarette stains on his fingers, and for once in a way he was stirred out of his customary attitude of cynical indifference.

"Smith and Colonel Baldwin are over yonder in Kinzie's private office," he reported hastily. "Before they shut the door I heard Baldwin introducing Smith as the new acting financial secretary of the Timanyoni Ditch Company!"

XI
When Greek Meets Greek

Smith allowed himself ten brief seconds for a swift eye-measuring of the square-shouldered, stockily built man with a gray face and stubbly mustache sitting in the chair of authority at the Brewster City National before he chose his line of attack.

"We are not going to cut very deeply into your time this morning, Mr. Kinzie," he began when the eye-appraisal had given him his cue. "You know the history of Timanyoni Ditch up to the present, and you have no doubt had your own misgivings about the wisdom of its financing on such a small scale, and as a purely local enterprise. Others have had the same misgivings, and—well, to cut out the details, there is to be a complete reorganization of the company on a new basis, and we are here to offer to take your personal allotment of the stock off your hands at par for cash. Colonel Baldwin has stipulated that his friends in the original deal must be protected, and——"

"Here, here—hold on," interrupted the bank president; "you're hitting it up a little bit too fast for me, Mr. Smith. Before we get down to any talk of buying and selling, suppose you tell me something about yourself and your new company. Who are you? and whereabouts do you hold forth when you are at home?"

Smith laughed easily. "If we were trying to borrow money of you, we might have to go into preliminaries and particulars, Mr. Kinzie. As it is, I'm sure you are not going to press for the answers to these very natural questions of yours. Further than that, we shall have to ask you to hold anything that may be said here in strict confidence—as between a banker and his customer. We are not alone in the fight for the water-rights on the other side of the river, as you know, and until we are safely fortified we shall have to be prudently cautious. But that is another matter. What we want to know now is this: will you let us protect you by taking your Timanyoni Ditch stock at par? That's the principal question at issue just now."

Kinzie met the issue fairly. "I don't know you yet, Mr. Smith; but I do know Colonel Baldwin, here, and I guess I'll take a chance on things as they stand. I'll keep my stock."

The new secretary's smile was rather patronizing than grateful.

"As you please, Mr. Kinzie, of course," he said smoothly. "But I'm going to tell you frankly that you'll keep it at your own risk. I am not sure what plan will be adopted, but I assume it will be amortization and a retirement of the stock of the original company. All that we need to enable us to bring this about is the voting control of the old stock, and we already have that, as you know."

The banker pursed his lips until the stubbly gray mustache stood out stiffly. Then he cut straight to the heart of the matter.

"You mean that there will be a majority pool of the old stock, and that the pool will ignore those stockholders who don't come in?"

"Something like that," said Smith pleasantly. And then: "We're going to be generously liberal, Mr. Kinzie; we are giving Colonel Baldwin's friends a fair chance to come in out of the wet. Of course, if they refuse to come in—if they prefer to stay out——"

Kinzie was smiling sourly.

"You'll have to take care of your own banker, won't you, Mr. Smith?" he asked. "Why don't you loosen up and tell me a little more? What have you fellows got up your sleeve, anyway?"

At this, the new financial manager slacked off on the hawser of secrecy a little—just a little.

"Mr. Kinzie, we've got the biggest thing, and the surest, that ever came to Timanyoni Park; not in futures, mind you, but in facts already as good as accomplished. If it were necessary—as it isn't—I could go to New York to-day and put a million dollars behind our reorganization plan in twenty-four hours. You'd say so, yourself, if I were at liberty to explain. But again we're dodging and wasting your time and ours. Think the matter over—about your stock—and let me know before noon. It's rather cruel to hurry you so, but time is precious with us and——"

"You sit right down there, young man, and put a little of this precious time of yours against mine," said Kinzie, pointing authoritatively at the chair which Smith had just vacated. "You mustn't go off at half-cock, that way. You'll need a bank here to do business with, won't you?"

Smith did not sit down. Instead, he smiled genially and fired his final shot.

"No, Mr. Kinzie; we shan't need a local bank—not as a matter of absolute necessity. In fact, on some accounts, I don't know but that it would be better for us not to have one."

"Sit down," insisted the bank president; and this time he would take no denial. Then he turned abruptly upon Baldwin, who had been playing his part of the silent listener letter-perfect.

"Baldwin, we are old friends, and I'd trust you to the limit—on any proposition that doesn't ask for more than straight-from-the-shoulder honesty. How much is this young friend of ours talking through his hat?"

"Not any, whatever, Dave. He's got the goods." Baldwin was wise enough to limit himself carefully as to quantity in his reply.

"It's straight, is it? No gold-brick business?"

"So straight that if we can't pay twenty per cent on what money we put in, I'll throw up my three thousand acres over yonder on Little Creek and go back to cow-punching."

Again the banker made a comical bristle brush of his cropped mustache.

"I want your business, Dexter; I've got to have it. But I'm going to be plain with you. You two are asking me to believe that you've gone outside and dug up a new bunch of backers. That may be all right, but Timanyoni Ditch has struck a pretty big bone that maybe your new backers know about—and maybe they don't. You've had a lot of bad luck, so far; getting your land titles cleared, and all that; and you're going to have more. I've——"

It was Smith's turn again and he cut in smartly.

"That is precisely what I was driving at. Our banker can't run with the hare and hunt with the hounds. You'll excuse me if I say that you haven't been altogether fair with Timanyoni Ditch, or with

Colonel Baldwin, Mr. Kinzie. A friendly banker doesn't help sell out his customer. You know that, as well as I do. Still, you did it."

Kinzie threw up his hands and tried to defend himself. "It was a straight business transaction, Mr. Smith. As long as we're in the banking business, we buy and sell for anybody who comes along."

"No, we don't, Mr. Kinzie; we protect our customers first. In the present instance you thought your customer was a dead one, anyway, so it wouldn't make much difference if you should throw another shovelful of dirt or so onto the coffin. Wasn't that the way of it?"

The president was fairly pushed to the ropes and he showed it.

"Answer me one question, both of you," he snapped. "Are you big enough to fight for your own hand against Stanton's crowd?"

"You'll see; and the sight is going to cost you something," said Smith, and the blandest oil could have been no smoother than his tone.

"Is that right, Dexter?"

"That's the way it looks to me, Dave," said the ranchman capitalist, who, whatever might be his limitations in the field of high finance, was not lacking the nerve to fight unquestioning in any partner's quarrel.

The president of the Brewster City National turned back to Smith.

"What do you want, Mr. Smith?" he asked, not too cordially.

"Nothing that you'd give us, I guess; a little business loyalty, for one thing——"

"And a checking balance for immediate necessities for another?" suggested the banker.

With all his trained astuteness—trained in Kinzie's own school, at that—Smith could not be sure that the gray-faced old Westerner was not setting a final trap for him, after all. But he took the risk, saying, with a decent show of indifference: "Of course, it would be more convenient here than in Denver or Chicago. But there is no hurry about that part of it."

The president took a slip of paper from a pigeonhole and wrote rapidly upon it. Once more his optimism was locking horns with prudent caution. It was the optimism, however, that was driving the pen. Baldwin's word was worth something, and it might be disastrous to let these two get away without anchoring them solidly to the Brewster City National.

"Sign this, you two," he said. "I don't know even the name of your new outfit yet, but I'll take a chance on one piece of two-name paper, anyhow."

Smith took up the slip and glanced at it. It was an accommodation note for twenty thousand dollars. With the money fairly in his hands, he paused to drive the nail of independence squarely home before he would sign.

"We don't want this at all, Mr. Kinzie, unless the bank's good-will comes with it," he said with becoming gravity.

"I'll stand with you," was the brusque rejoinder. "But it's only fair to you both to say that you've got the biggest kind of a combination to buck you—a national utilities corporation with the strongest sort of political backing."

"I doubt if you can tell us anything that we don't already know," said Smith coolly, as he put his name on the note; and when Baldwin had signed: "Let this go to the credit of Timanyoni Ditch, if you please, Mr. Kinzie, and we'll transfer it later. It's quite possible that we shan't need it, but we are willing to help out a little on your discount profits, anyway. Further along, when things shape themselves up a bit more definitely, you shall know all there is to know, and we'll give you just as good a chance to make money as you'll give us."

When they were safely out of the bank and half a square away from it, Dexter Baldwin pushed his hat back and mopped his forehead. "They say a man can't sweat at this altitude," he remarked. "I'm here to tell you, Smith, that I've lost ten pounds in the last ten minutes. Where in the name of the jumping Jehoshaphat did you get your nerve, boy? You stand to lose an even hundred-and-fifty-dollar bill on this deal; don't you know that?"

"How so?" asked the plunger.

"I'd have bet you that much against the old campaign hat you're wearing that you couldn't 'touch' Dave Kinzie for twenty dollars—let alone twenty thousand—in a month of Sundays! You made him believe we'd got outside backing from somewhere."

"I didn't say anything like that, did I?"

"No; but you opened the door and he walked in."

"That's all right: I'm not responsible for Mr. Kinzie's imagination. We were obliged to have a little advertising capital; we couldn't turn a wheel without it. Now that we have it, we'll get busy. We've got to furnish a new suite of offices, install a bigger office force, incorporate Timanyoni High Line, and open its stock subscription books, all practically while the band plays. Time is the one thing we can't waste. Put me in touch with a good business lawyer and I'll start the legal machinery. Then you can get into your car and go around and interview your crowd, man by man. I want to know exactly where we stand with the old stockholders before we make any move in public. Can you do that?"

Baldwin lifted his hat and shoved his fingers through his hair.

"I reckon I can; there are only sixty or seventy of 'em. And Bob Stillings is your lawyer. Come around the corner and I'll introduce you."

XII
The Rocket and the Stick

For a full fortnight after the preliminary visit to the Brewster City National Bank, Smith was easily the busiest man in Timanyoni County. Establishing himself in the Hophra House, and discarding the working khaki only because he was shrewd enough to dress the new part becomingly, he flung himself into what Colonel Baldwin called the "miracle-working" campaign with a zest that knew no flagging moment.

Within the fourteen-day period new town offices were occupied on the second floor of the Brewster City National Building; Stillings, most efficient of corporation counsels, had secured the new charter; and the stock-books of Timanyoni High Line had been opened, with the Brewster City National named as the company's depository and official fiduciary agent.

At the dam the building activities had been generously doubled. An electric-light plant had been installed, and Williams was working day and night shifts both in the quarries and on the forms. Past this, the new financial manager, himself broadening rapidly as his field broadened, was branching out in other directions. After a brief conference with a few of his principal stockholders he had instructed Stillings to include the words "Power and Light" in the cataloguing of the new company's possible and probable charter activities, and by the end of the fortnight the foundations of a power-house were going in below the dam, and negotiations were already on foot with the Brewster city council looking toward the sale of electric current to the city for lighting and other purposes.

Notwithstanding all the demands made upon him as the chief energizer in the working field, Smith had made the planting of his financial anchor securely to windward his first care. Furnished with a selected list by Colonel Baldwin, he had made a thorough canvas of possible investors, and by the time the new stock was printed and ready for delivery through Kinzie's bank, an iron-clad pool of the majority of the original Timanyoni Ditch stock had been organized, and Smith had sold to Maxwell, Starbuck, and other local capitalists a sufficient amount of the new treasury stock to give him a fighting chance; this, with a promise of more if it should be needed.

The stock-selling campaign was a triumph, and though he did not recognize it as such, it marked the longest step yet taken in the march of the metamorphosis. As the cashier in Dunham's bank Smith had been merely a high-grade clerk. There had been no occasion for the development of the precious quality of initiative, and he had hardly known the meaning of the word. But now there seemed to be no limit to the new powers of accomplishment. Men met him upon his own ground, and a lilting sense of triumph gave him renewed daring when he found that he could actually inspire them with some portion of his own confidence and enthusiasm.

But in all this there had been no miracle, one would say; nothing but enterprise and shrewd business acumen and lightning-like speed in bringing things to pass. If there were a miracle, it lay in this: that not to Maxwell or to any of the new investors had Smith revealed the full dimensions of the prize for which Timanyoni High Line was entering the race. Colonel Baldwin and one William Starbuck, Maxwell's brother-in-law, by courtesy, and his partner in the Little Alice mine, alone knew the wheel within the wheel; how the great Eastern utility corporation represented by Stanton had spent a million or more in the acquisition of the Escalante Grant, which would be practically worthless as agricultural land without the water which could be obtained only by means of the Timanyoni dam and canal system.

With all these strenuous stirrings in the business field, it may say itself that Smith found little time for social indulgences during the crowded fortnight. Day after day the colonel begged him to take a night off at the ranch, and it was even more difficult to refuse the proffered hospitality at the week-end. But Smith did refuse it.

With the new life and the larger ambition had come a sturdy resolve to hold himself aloof from entanglements of every sort. That Corona Baldwin was going to prove an entanglement he was wise enough to foresee from the moment in which he had identified her with the vitalizing young woman whose glove he had carried off. In fact, she was already associated in his thoughts with every step in the business battle. Was he not taking a very temerarious risk of discovery and arrest merely for the sake of proving to her that her "hopeless case" of the lawn-party could confute her mocking little theories about men and types without half trying?

It was not until after Miss Corona—driving to town with her father, as she frequently did—had thrice visited the new offices that Smith began to congratulate himself, rather bitterly, to be sure, upon his wisdom in staying away from Hillcrest. For one thing, he was learning that Corona Baldwin was an exceedingly charming young woman of many moods and tenses, and that in some of the moods, and in practically all of the tenses, she was able to make him see rose-colored. When she was not with him, he had no difficulty in assuring himself that the rose-colored point of view was entirely out of the question for a man in daily peril of meeting the sheriff. But when she was present, calm sanity had a way of losing its grip, and the rose-colored possibilities reasserted themselves with intoxicating accompaniments.

Miss Corona's fourth visit to the handsome suite of offices over the Brewster City National chanced to fall upon a Saturday. Her father, president of the new company, as he had been of the old, had a private office of his own, but Miss Corona soon drifted out to the railed-off end of the larger room, where the financial secretary had his desk.

"Colonel-daddy tells me that you are coming out to Hillcrest for the week-end," was the way in which she interrupted the financial secretary's brow-knittings over a new material contract. "I have just wagered him a nice fat little round iron dollar of my allowance that you won't. How about it?"

Smith looked up with his best-natured grin.

"You win," he said shortly.

"Thank you," she laughed. "In a minute or so I'll go back to the president's office and collect." Then: "One dinner, lodging, and breakfast of us was about all you could stand, wasn't it? I thought maybe it would be that way."

"What made you think so?"

"You should never ask a woman why; it's a frightfully unsafe thing to do."

"I know," he mocked. "There have been whole books written about the lack of logic on your side of the sex fence."

She had seated herself in the chair reserved for inquiring investors. There was a little interval of glove-smoothing silence, and then, like a flash out of a clear sky, she smiled across the desk-end at him and said:

"Will you forgive me if I ask you a perfectly ridiculous question?"

"Certainly. Other people ask them every day."

"Is—is your name really and truly John Smith?"

"Why should you doubt it?"

It was just here that Smith was given to see another one of Miss Corona's many moods—or tenses—and it was a new one to him. She was visibly embarrassed.

"I—I don't want to tell you," she stammered.

"All right; you needn't."

"If you're going to take it that easy, I will tell you," she retorted. "Mr. Williams thought your name was an alias; and I'm not sure that he doesn't still think so."

"The Smiths never have to have aliases. It's like John Doe or Richard Roe, you know."

"Haven't you any middle name?"

"I have a middle initial. It is 'M.'" He was looking her fairly in the eyes as he said it, and the light in the new offices was excellent. Thanks to her horseback riding, Miss Corona's small oval face had a touch of healthy outdoor tan; but under the tan there came, for just a flitting instant, a flush of deeper color, and at the back of the gray eyes there was something that Smith had never seen there before.

"It's—it's just an initial?" she queried.

"Yes; it's just an initial, and I don't use it ordinarily. I'm not ashamed of the plain 'John.'"

"I don't know why you should be," she commented, half absently, he thought. And then: "How many 'John M. Smiths' do you suppose there are in the United States?"

"Oh, I don't know; a million or so, I guess."

"I should think you would be rather glad of that," she told him. But when he tried to make her say why he should be glad, she talked pointedly of other things and presently went back to her father's office.

It was not until after she had gone out with her father, and he had made her wager good by steadfastly refusing to spend the week-end at the ranch, that Smith began to put two and two together, erroneously, as it happened, though he could not know this. Mrs. Baldwin's home town in his native State was the little place that her daughter had visited and where the daughter had had a lawn-party given in her honor. Was it not more than probable that the colonel's wife was still keeping up some sort of a correspondence with her home people and that through this, or some mention in a local paper, Corona had got hold of the devastating story of one J. Montague Smith?

There were fine little headings of perspiration standing on the fugitive's forehead when the small sum in addition had progressed thus far. But if he had only known it, there was no need, as yet, for the sweat of apprehension. Like some other young women, Miss Baldwin suffered from spasmodic attacks of the diary-keeping malady; she had been keeping one at the time of her return from school, and the lawn-party in the little town in the Middle West had its due entry.

In a moment of idle curiosity on the Saturday forenoon, she had looked into the year-old diary to find the forgotten name of the man of whom Smith was still persistently reminding her. It was there in all its glory: "J. Montague Smith." Could it be possible?—but, no; John Smith, her father's John Smith, had come to the construction camp as a hobo, and that was not possible, not even thinkable, of the man she had met. None the less, it was a second attack of the idle curiosity that had moved her to go to town with her father on the Saturday afternoon of questionings.

After the other members of the office force had taken their departure, Smith still sat at his desk striving to bring himself back with some degree of clear-headedness to the pressing demands of his job. Just as he was about to give it up and go across to the Hophra House for his dinner, William Starbuck drifted in to open the railing gate and to come and plant himself in the chair of privilege at Smith's desk-end.

"Well, son; you've got the animals stirred up good and plenty, at last," he said, when he had found the "makings" and was deftly rolling a cigarette—his one overlapping habit reaching back to his range-riding youth. "Dick Maxwell got a wire to-day from his kiddie's grandpaw—and my own respected daddy-in-law—Mr. Hiram Fairbairn; you know him—the lumber king."

"I'm listening," said Smith.

"Dick's wire was an order; instructions from headquarters to keep hands off of your new company and to work strictly in cahoots—'harmony' was the word he used—with Crawford Stanton. How does that fit you?"

The financial secretary's smile was the self-congratulatory face-wrinkling of the quarry foreman who has seen his tackle hitch hold to land the big stone safely at the top of the pit.

"What is Maxwell going to do about it?" he asked.

"Dick is all wool and a yard wide; and what he signs his name to is what he is going to stand by. You won't lose him, but the wire shows us just about where we're aiming to put our leg into the gopher-hole and break it, doesn't it?"

"I'm not borrowing any trouble. Mr. Fairbairn and his

colleagues are just a few minutes too late, Starbuck. We've got our footing—inside of the corral."

The ex-cow-puncher, who was now well up on the middle rounds of fortune's ladder, shook his head doubtfully.

"Don't you make any brash breaks, John. Mr. Hiram Fairbairn and his crowd can swing twenty millions to your one little old dollar and a half, and they're not going to leave any of the pebbles unturned when it comes to saving their investment in the Escalante. I don't care specially for my own ante—Stella and I will manage to get a bite to eat, anyway. But for your own sake and Colonel Dexter's, you don't want to let the grass grow under your feet; not any whatsoever. You go ahead and get that dam finished, pronto, if you have to put a thousand men on it and work 'em Sundays as well as nights. That's all; I just thought I'd drop in and tell you."

Smith went to his rooms in the hotel a few minutes later to change for dinner. Having been restocking his wardrobe to better fit his new state and standing as the financial head of Timanyoni High Line, he found the linen drawer in his dressing-case overflowing. Opening another, he began to arrange the overflow methodically. The empty drawer was lined with a newspaper, and he took the paper out to fold it afresh. In the act he saw that it was a copy of the Chicago Tribune some weeks old. As he was replacing it in the drawer bottom, a single head-line on the upturned page sprang at him like a thing living and venomous. He bent lower and read the underrunning paragraph with a dull rage mounting to his eyes and serving for the moment to make the gray of the printed lines turn red.

Lawrenceville, May 19.—The grand jury has found a true bill against Montague Smith, the absconding cashier of the Lawrenceville Bank and Trust, charged with embezzling the bank's funds. The crime would have been merely a breach of trust and not actionable but for the fact that Smith, by owning stock in the bankrupt Westfall industries lately taken over by the Richlander Company, had so made himself amenable to the law. Smith disappeared on the night of the 14th and is still at large. He is also wanted on another criminal count. It will be remembered that he brutally assaulted President Dunham on the night of his disappearance. The reward of $1,000 for his apprehension and arrest has been increased to $2,000 by the bank directors.

XIII
The Narrow World

At the fresh newspaper reminder that his sudden bound upward from the laboring ranks to the executive headship of the irrigation project had merely made him a more conspicuous target for the man-hunters, Smith scanted himself of sleep and redoubled his efforts to put the new company on a sound and permanent footing. In the nature of things he felt that his own shrift must necessarily be short. Though his own immediate public was comparatively small, the more or less dramatic coup in Timanyoni High Line had advertised him thoroughly. He was rapidly coming to be the best-known man in Brewster, and he cherished no illusions about lost identities, or the ability to lose them, in a land where time and space have been wired and railroaded pretty well out of existence.

Moreover, Dunham's bank was a member of a protective association, and Smith knew how wide a net could be spread and drawn when any absconding employee was really wanted. The doubling of the reward gave notice that Dunham was vindictively in earnest, and in that event it would be only a question of time until some one of the hired man-hunters would hit upon the successful clew.

It was needful that he should work while the day was his in which to work; and he did work. There was still much to be done. Williams was having a threat of labor troubles at the dam, and Stillings had unearthed another possible flaw in the land titles dating back to the promotion of a certain railroad which had never gotten far beyond the paper stage and the acquiring of some of its rights of way.

Smith flung himself masterfully at the new difficulties as they arose, and earned his meed of praise from the men for whom he overcame them. But under the surface current of the hurrying business tide a bitter undertow was beginning to set in. In every characterizing change it is inevitable that there should be some loss in the scrapping of the old to make way for the new. Smith saw himself in two aspects. In one he stood as a man among men, with a promise of winning honors and wealth; with the still more ecstatic promise of being able, perhaps, to win the love of the vivifying young woman who had once touched the spring of sentiment in him—and was touching it again. In the other he was a fugitive and an outlaw, waiting only for some spreader of the net to come and tap him on the shoulder.

He took his first decided backward step on the night when he went into a hardware store and bought a pistol. The free, fair-fighting spirit which had sent him barehanded against the three claim-jumpers was gone and in its place there was a fell determination, undefined as yet, but keying itself to the barbaric pitch. With the weapon in his pocket he could look back over the transforming interspaces with a steadier eye. Truly, he had come far since that night in the Lawrenceville Bank when a single fierce gust of passion had plucked him away from all the familiar landmarks.

And as for Corona Baldwin, there were days in which he set his jaw and told himself that nothing, even if it were the shedding of blood, should stand in the way of winning her. It was his right as a man; he had done nothing to make himself the outlaw that the Lawrenceville indictment declared him to be; therefore he would fight for his chance—slay for it, if need be. But there were other days when the saner thought prevailed and he saw the pit of selfishness into which the new barbarisms were plunging him. The Baldwins were his friends, and they were accepting him in the full light of the inference that he was a man under a cloud. Could he take a further advantage of their generosity by involving them still more intimately in his own particular entanglement? He assured himself that he couldn't and wouldn't; that though he might, indeed, commit a murder when the pinch came, he was still man enough to stay away from Hillcrest.

He was holding this latter view grimly on an evening when he had worked himself haggard over the draft of the city ordinance which was to authorize the contract with the High Line Company for lights and power. It had been a day of nagging distractions. A rumor had been set afoot—by Stanton, as Smith made no doubt—hinting that the new dam would be unsafe when it should be completed; that its breaking, with the reservoir behind it, would carry death and destruction to the lowlands and even to the city. Timid stockholders, seeing colossal damage suits in the bare possibility, had taken the alarm, and Smith had spent the greater part of the day in trying to calm their fears. For this cause, and some others, he was on the ragged edge when Baldwin dropped in on his way home from the dam and protested.

"Look here, John; you're overdoing this thing world without end! It's six o'clock, man!—quitting-time. Another week of this grinding and you'll be hunting a nice, quiet cot in the railroad hospital, and then where'll we be? You break it off short, right now, and go home with me and get your dinner and a good night's rest. No, by Jupiter, I'm not going to let you off, this trip. Get your coat and hat and come along, or I'll rope you down and hog-tie you."

For once in a way, Smith found that there was no fight left in him, and he yielded, telling himself that another acceptance of the Baldwin hospitality, more or less, could make no difference. But no sooner was the colonel's gray roadster headed for the bridge across the Timanyoni than the exhilarating reaction set in. In a twinkling the business cares, and the deeper worries as well, fled away, and in their place heart-hunger was loosed. If Corona would give him this one evening, rest him, revive him, share with him some small portion of her marvellous vitality....

He did not overrate the stimulative effect of her presence; of the mere fact of propinquity. When the roadster drew up at the portico of the transplanted Missouri plantation mansion she was waiting on the steps. It was dinner-time, and she had on an evening gown of some shimmering, leafy stuff that made her look more like a wood-nymph than he had ever supposed any mere mortal woman could look. When she stood on tiptoes for her father's kiss, Smith knew the name of his malady, however much he may have blinked it before; knew its name, and knew that it would have to be reckoned with, whatever fresh involvements might be lying in wait for him behind the curtain of the days to come.

After dinner, a meal at which he ate little and was well content to satisfy the hunger of his soul by the road of the eye, Smith went out to the portico to smoke. The most gorgeous of mountain sunsets was painting itself upon the sky over the western Timanyonis, but he had no eyes for natural grandeurs, and no ears for any sound save one—the footstep he was listening for. It came at length, and he tried to look as tired as he had been when the colonel made him close his desk and leave the office; tried and apparently succeeded.

"You poor, broken-down Samson, carrying all the brazen gates of the money-Philistines on your shoulders! You had to come to us at last, didn't you? Let me be your Delilah and fix that chair so that it will be really comfortable." She said it only half mockingly, and he forgave the sarcasm when she arranged some of the hammock pillows in the easiest of the porch chairs and made him bury himself luxuriously in them.

Still holding the idea, brought over from that afternoon of the name questioning, that she had in some way discovered his true identity, Smith was watching narrowly for danger-signals when he thanked her and said:

"You say it just as it is. I had to come. But you could never be anybody's Delilah, could you? She was a betrayer, if you recollect."

He made the suggestion purposely, but it was wholly ignored, and there was no guile in the slate-gray eyes.

"You mean that you didn't want to come?"

"No; not that. I have wanted to come every time your father has asked me. But there are reasons—good reasons—why I shouldn't be here."

If she knew any of the reasons she made no sign. She was sitting in the hammock and touching one slippered toe to the flagstones for the swinging push. From Smith's point of view she had for a background the gorgeous sunset, but he could not see the more distant glories.

"We owe you much, and we are going to owe you more," she said. "You mustn't think that we don't appreciate you at your full value. Colonel-daddy thinks you are the most wonderful somebody that ever lived, and so do a lot of the others."

"And you?" he couldn't resist saying.

"I'm just plain ashamed—for the way I treated you when you were here before. I've been eating humble-pie ever since."

Smith breathed freer. Nobody but a most consummate actress could have simulated her frank sincerity. He had jumped too quickly to the small sum-in-addition conclusion. She did not know the story of the absconding bank cashier.

"I don't know why you should feel that way," he said, eager, now, to run where he had before been afraid to walk.

"I do. And I believe you wanted to shame me. I believe you gave up your place at the dam and took hold with daddy more to show me what an inconsequent little idiot I was than for any other reason. Didn't you, really?"

He laughed in quiet ecstasy at this newest and most adorable of the moods.

"Honest confession is good for the soul: I did," he boasted. "Now beat that for frankness, if you can."

"I can't," she admitted, laughing back at him. "But now you've accomplished your purpose, I hope you are not going to give up. That would be a little hard on Colonel-daddy."

"Oh, no; I'm not going to give up—until I have to."

"Does that mean more than it says?"

"Yes, I'm afraid it does."

She was silent for the length of time that it took the flaming crimson in the western sky to fade to salmon.

"I know I haven't earned the right to ask you any of the whys," she said at the end of the little pause.

"Women like you—only there are not any more of them, I think—don't have to earn things. The last time you were in the office you said enough to let me know that you and your father and Williams—all of you, in fact—suspect that I am out here under a cloud of some sort. It is true."

"And that is why you say you won't give up until you have to?"

"That is the reason; yes."

There was another little interval of silence and then she said: "I suppose you couldn't tell me—or anybody—could you?"

"I can tell you enough so that you will understand why I may not be permitted to go on and finish what I have begun in Timanyoni High Line. When I left home I thought I was a murderer."

He would not look at her to see how she was taking it, but he could not help hearing her little gasp.

"Oh!" she breathed; and then: "You say you 'thought.' Wasn't it so?"

"It happened not to be. The man didn't die. I suppose I might say that I didn't try to kill him; but that would hardly be true. At the moment, I didn't care. Have you ever felt that way?—you know what I mean, just utterly blind and reckless as to consequences?"

"I have a horrible temper, if that covers it."

"It's something like that," he conceded; "only, up to the moment when it happened I hadn't known that I had any temper. Perhaps I might say that the provocation was big enough, though the law won't say so."

The pink flush had faded out of the high western horizon and the stars were coming out one at a time. The colonel had come up from the ranch bunk-house where the men slept, and was smoking his long-stemmed corn-cob pipe on the lawn under the spreading cottonwoods. Peace was the key-note of the perfect summer night, and even for the man under the shadow of the law there was a quiet breathing space.

"I don't believe you could ever kill a man in cold blood," said the young woman in the hammock. "I'm sure you know that, yourself, and it ought to be a comfort to you."

"It might have been once, but it isn't any more."

"Why not?"

"I suppose it is because I left a good many things behind me when I ran away—besides the man I thought was dead. In that other life I never knew what it meant to fight for the things I wanted;

perhaps it was because I never wanted anything very badly, or possibly it was because the things I did want came too easily."

"They are not coming so easily now?"

"No; but I'm going to have them at any cost. You will know what I mean when I say that nothing, not even human life, seems so sacred to me as it used to."

"Have you ever talked with daddy about all these things?"

"No. You don't know men very well; they don't talk about such things to one another. The average man tells some woman, if he can be lucky enough to find one who will listen."

"You haven't told me all of it," she said, after another hesitant pause. "You have carefully left the woman out of it. Was she pretty?"

Smith buried his laugh so deep that not a flicker of it came to the surface.

"Is that the open inference always?—that a man tries to kill another because there is a woman in it?"

"I merely asked you if she was pretty."

"There was a woman," he answered doggedly; "though she had nothing to do with the trouble. I was going to call on her the night I—the night the thing happened. I hope she isn't still waiting for me to ring the door-bell."

"You haven't told her where you are?"

"No; but she's not losing any sleep about that. She isn't that kind. Indeed, I'm not sure that she wouldn't turn the letter over to the sheriff, if I should write her. Let's clear this up before we go any further. It was generally understood, in the home town, you know, that we were to be married some time, though nothing definite had ever been said by either of us. There wasn't any sentiment, you understand; I was idiotic enough at the time to believe that there wasn't any such thing as sentiment. It has cost me about as much to give her up as it has cost her to give me up—and that is a little less than nothing."

Again the silence came between. The colonel was knocking his pipe bowl against a tree trunk and an interruption was threatening. When the low voice came again from the hammock it was troubled.

"You are disappointing me, now. You are taking it very lightly, and apparently you neither know nor care very much how the woman may be taking it. Perhaps there wasn't any sentiment on your part."

Smith was laughing quietly. "If you could only know Verda Richlander," he said. "Imagine the most beautiful thing you can think of, and then take the heart out of it, and—but, hold on, I can do better than that," and he drew out his watch and handed it to her with the back case opened.

She took the watch and stopped the hammock swing to let the light from the nearest window fall upon the photograph.

"She is very beautiful; magnificently beautiful," she said, returning the watch. And an instant later: "I don't see how you could say what you did about the sentiment. If I were a man——"

The colonel had mounted the steps and was coming toward them. The young woman slipped from the hammock and stood up.

"Don't go," said Smith, feeling as if he were losing an opportunity and leaving much unsaid that ought to be said. But the answer was a quiet "good night" and she was gone.

Smith went back to town with the colonel the next morning physically rested, to be sure, but in a frame of mind bordering again upon the sardonic. In the cold light of the following day, after-dinner confidences, even with the best-beloved, have a way of showing up all their puerilities and inadequacies. Two things, and two alone, stood out clearly: one was that he was most unmistakably in love with Corona Baldwin, and the other was that he had shown her the weakest side of himself by appealing like a callow boy to her sympathies.

Hence there was another high resolve not to go to Hillcrest again until he could go as a free man; a resolve which, it is perhaps needless to say, was broken thereafter as often as the colonel asked him to go. Why, in the last resort, Smith should have finally chosen another confidant in the person of William Starbuck, the reformed cow-puncher, he scarcely knew. But it was to Starbuck that he appealed for advice when the sentimental situation had grown fairly desperate.

"I've told you enough so that you can understand the vise-nip of it, Billy," he said to Starbuck one night when he had dragged the mine owner up to the bath-room suite in the Hophra House, and had told him just a little, enough to merely hint at his condition. "You see how it stacks up. I'm in a fair way to come out of this the biggest scoundrel alive—the piker who takes advantage of the innocence of a good girl. I'm not the man she thinks I am. I am standing over a volcano pit every minute of the day. If it blows up, I'm gone, obliterated, wiped out."

"Is it aiming to blow up?" asked Starbuck sagely.

"I don't know any more about that than you do. It is the kind that usually does blow up sooner or later. I've prepared for it as well as I can. What Colonel Baldwin and the rest of you needed was a financial manager, and Timanyoni High Line has its fighting chance—which was more than Timanyoni Ditch had when I took hold. If I should drop out now, you and Maxwell and the colonel and Kinzie could go on and make the fight; but that doesn't help out in this other matter."

Starbuck smoked in silence for a long minute or two before he said: "Is there another woman in it, John?"

"Yes; but not in the way you mean. It never came to anything more than a decently frank friendship, though the whole town had it put up that it was all settled and we were going to be married."

"Huh! I wonder if that's what she'd say? You say it never came to anything more than a friendship: maybe that's all right from your side of the fence. But how about the girl?"

The harassed one's smile was grimly reminiscent.

"If you knew her you wouldn't ask, Billy. She is the modern, up-to-date young woman in all that the term implies. When she marries she will give little and ask little, outside of the ordinary amenities and conventionalities."

"That's what you say; and maybe it's what you think. But when you have to figure a woman into it, you never can tell, John. Are you keeping in touch with this other girl?"

Smith shook his head.

"No; I shall probably never see her or hear from her again. Not that it matters a penny's worth to either of us. And your guess was wrong if you thought that things past are having any effect on things present. Corona Baldwin stands in a class by herself."

"She's a mighty fine little girl, John," said Starbuck slowly. "Any one of a dozen fellows I could name would give all their old shoes to swap chances with you."

"That isn't exactly the kind of advice I'm needing," was the sober rejoinder.

"No; but it was the kind you were wanting, when you tolled me off up here," laughed the ex-cow-puncher. "I know the symptoms. Had 'em myself for about two years so bad that I could wake up in the middle of the night and taste 'em. Go in and win. Maybe the great big stumbling-block you're worrying about wouldn't mean anything at all to an open-minded young woman like Corona; most likely it wouldn't."

"If she could know the whole truth—and believe it," said Smith musingly.

"You tell her the truth, and she'll take care of the believing part of it, all right. You needn't lose any sleep about that."

Smith drew a long breath and removed his pipe to say: "I

haven't the nerve, Billy, and that's the plain fact. I have already told her a little of it. She knows that I——"

Starbuck broke in with a laugh. "Yes; it's a shouting pity about your nerve! You've been putting up such a blooming scary fight in this irrigation business that we all know you haven't any nerve. If I had your job in that, I'd be going around here toting two guns and wondering if I couldn't make room in the holster for another."

Smith shook his head.

"I was safe enough so long as Stanton thought I was the resident manager and promoter for a new bunch of big money in the background. But he has had me shadowed and tracked until now I guess he is pretty well convinced that I actually had the audacity to play a lone hand; and a bluffing hand, at that. That makes a difference, of course. Two days after I had climbed into the saddle here, he sent a couple of his strikers after me. I don't know just what their orders were, but they seemed to want a fight—and they got it. It was in Blue Pete's doggery, up at the camp."

"Guns?" queried Starbuck.

"Theirs; not mine, because I didn't have any. I managed to get the shooting-irons away from them before we had mixed very far."

"You're just about the biggest, long-eared, stiff-backed, stubborn wild ass of the wallows that was ever let loose in a half-reformed gun-country!" grumbled the ex-cow-man. "You're fixing to get yourself all killed up, Smith. Haven't you sense enough to see that these rustlers will rub you out in two twitches of a dead lamb's tail if they've made up their minds that you are the High Line main guy and the only one?"

"Of course," said the wild ass easily. "If they could lay me up for a month or two——"

"Lay up, nothing!" retorted Starbuck. "Lay you down, about six feet underground, is what I mean!"

"Pshaw!" exclaimed the one whose fears ran in a far different channel from any that could be dug by mere corporation violence. "This is America, in the twentieth century. We don't kill our business competitors nowadays."

"Don't we?" snorted Starbuck. "That will be all right, too. We'll suppose, just for the sake of argument, that my respected and respectable daddy-in-law, or whatever other silk-hatted old money-bags happens to be paying Crawford Stanton's salary and commission, wouldn't send out an order to have you killed off. Maybe Stanton, himself, wouldn't stand for it if you'd put it that barefaced. But daddy-in-law, and Stanton, and all the others, hire blacklegs and sharpers and gunmen and thugs. And every once in a while somebody takes a wink for a nod—and bang! goes a gun."

"Well, what's the answer?" said Smith.

"Tote an arsenal, yourself, and be ready to shoot first and ask questions afterward. That's the only way you can live peaceably with such men as Jake Boogerfield and Lanterby and Pete Simms."

Smith got out of his chair and took a turn up and down the length of the room. When he came back to stand before Starbuck, he said: "I did that, Billy. I've been carrying a gun for a week and more; not for these ditch pirates, but for somebody else. The other night, when I was out at Hillcrest, Corona happened to see it. I'm not going to tell you what she said, but when I came back to town the next morning, I chucked the gun into a desk drawer. And I hope I'm going to be man enough not to wear it again."

Starbuck dropped the subject abruptly and looked at his watch.

"You liked to have done it, pulling me off up here," he remarked. "I'm due to be at the train to meet Mrs. Billy, and I've got just about three minutes. So long."

Smith changed his street clothes leisurely after Starbuck had gone, and made ready to go down to the café dinner, turning over in his mind, meanwhile, the problem whose solution he had tried to extract from his late visitor. The workable answer was still as far off and as unattainable as ever when he went down-stairs and stopped at the desk to toss his room-key to the clerk.

The hotel register was lying open on the counter, and from force of habit he ran his eye down the list of late arrivals. At the end of the list, in sprawling characters upon which the ink was yet fresh, he read his sentence, and for the first time in his life knew the meaning of panic fear. The newest entry was:

"Josiah Richlander and daughter, Chicago."

Smith was not misled by the place-name. There was only one "Josiah Richlander" in the world for him, and he knew that the Lawrenceville magnate, in registering from Chicago, was only following the example of those who, for good reasons or no reason, use the name of their latest stopping-place for a registry address.

XIV
A Reprieve

For the length of time it took him to read Josiah Richlander's signature on the Hophra House register and to grasp the full meaning of the Lawrenceville magnate's presence in Brewster, Smith's blood ran cold and there was a momentary attack of shocked consternation, comparable to nothing that any past experience had to offer. It had been a foregone conclusion from the very outset that, sooner or later, some one who knew him would drift in from the world beyond the mountains; but in all his imaginings he had never dreamed of the Richlander possibility. Verda, as he knew, had been twice to Europe—and, like many of her kind, had never been west of the Mississippi in her native land. Why, then, had she——

But there was no time to waste in curious speculations as to the whys and wherefores. Present safety was the prime consideration. With Josiah Richlander and his daughter in Brewster, and guests under the same roof with him, discovery, identification, disgrace were knocking at the door. Smith had a return of the panicky chill when he realized how utterly impossible it would be for a man with his business activities to hide, even temporarily, not in the hotel, to be sure, but anywhere in a town of the Brewster dimensions. And the peril held no saving element of uncertainty. He could harbor no doubt as to what Josiah Richlander would do if discovery came. For so long a time as should be consumed in telegraphing between Brewster and Lawrenceville, Smith thought he might venture to call himself a free man. But that was the limit.

It was the dregs of the J. Montague subconsciousness yet remaining in him that counselled flight, basing the prompting upon a bit of panic-engendered reasoning. Miss Verda and her father could hardly be anything more than transient visitors in Brewster. Possibly he might be able to keep out of their way for the needful day or so. To resolve in such an urgency was to act. One minute later he had hailed a passing auto-cab at the hotel entrance, and the four miles between the city and Colonel Baldwin's ranch had been tossed to the rear before he remembered that he had expressly declined a dinner invitation for that same evening at Hillcrest, the declination basing itself upon business and having been made by word of mouth to Mrs. Baldwin in person when she had called at the office with her daughter just before the luncheon hour.

Happily, the small social offense went unremarked, or at least unrebuked. Smith found his welcome at the ranch that of a man who has the privilege of dropping in unannounced. The colonel was jocosely hospitable, as he always was; Mrs. Baldwin was graciously lenient—was good enough, indeed, to thank the eleventh-hour guest for reconsidering at the last moment; and Corona——

Notwithstanding all that had come to pass; notwithstanding, also, that his footing in the Baldwin household had come to be that of a family friend, Smith could never be quite sure of the bewitchingly winsome young woman who called her father "Colonel-daddy." Her pose, if it were a pose, was the attitude of the entirely unspoiled child of nature and the wide horizons. When he was with her she made him think of all the words expressive of transparency and absolute and utter unconcealment. Yet there were moments when he fancied he could get passing glimpses of a subtler personality at the back of the wide-open, frankly questioning eyes; a wise little soul lying in wait behind its defenses; prudent, all-knowing, deceived neither by its own prepossessions or prejudices, nor by any of the masqueradings of other souls.

Smith, especially in this later incarnation which had so radically changed him, believed as little in the psychic as any hardheaded young business iconoclast of an agnostic century could. But on this particular evening when he was smoking his after-dinner pipe on the flagstoned porch with Corona for his companion, there were phenomena apparently unexplainable on any purely material hypothesis.

"I am sure I have much less than half of the curiosity that women are said to have, but, really, I do want to know what dreadful thing has happened to you since we met you in the High Line offices this morning—mamma and I," was the way in which one of the phenomena was made to occur; and Smith started so nervously that he dropped his pipe.

"You can be the most unexpected person, when you try," he laughed, but the laugh scarcely rang true. "What makes you think that anything has happened?"

"I don't think—I know," the small seeress went on with calm assurance. "You've been telling us in all sorts of dumb ways that you've had an upsetting shock of some kind; and I don't believe it's another lawsuit. Am I right, so far?"

"I believe you are a witch, and it's a mighty good thing you didn't live in the Salem period," he rejoined. "They would have hanged you to a dead moral certainty."

"Then there was something?" she queried; adding, jubilantly: "I knew it!"

"Go on," said the one to whom it had happened; "go on and tell me the rest of it."

"Oh, that isn't fair; even a professional clairvoyant has to be told the color of her eyes and hair."

"Wha-what!" the ejaculation was fairly jarred out of him and for the moment he fancied he could feel a cool breeze blowing up the back of his neck.

The clairvoyant who did not claim to be a professional was laughing softly.

"You told me once that a woman was adorable in the exact degree in which she could afford to be visibly transparent; yes, you said 'afford,' and I've been holding it against you. Now I'm going to pay you back. You are the transparent one, this time. You have as good as admitted that the 'happening' thing isn't a man; 'wha-what' always means that, you know; so it must be a woman. Is it the Miss Richlander you were telling me about?"

There are times when any mere man may be shocked into telling the simple truth, and Smith had come face to face with one of them. "It is," he said.

"She is in Brewster?"

"Yes."

"When did she come?"

"This evening."

"And you ran away? That was horribly unkind, don't you think—after she had come so far?"

"Hold on," he broke in. "Don't let's go so fast. I didn't ask her to come. And, besides, she didn't come to see me."

"Did she tell you that?"

"I have taken precious good care that she shouldn't have the chance. I saw her name—and her father's—on the hotel register; and just about that time I remembered that I could probably get a bite to eat out here."

"You are queer! All men are a little queer, I think—always excepting Colonel-daddy. Don't you want to see her?"

"Indeed, I don't!"

"Not even for old times' sake?"

"No; not even for old times' sake. I've given you the wrong impression completely, if you think there is any obligation on my part. It never got beyond the watch-case picture stage, as I have told you. It might have drifted on to the other things in the course of time, simply because neither of us might have known any better than to let it drift. But that's all a back number, now."

"Just the same, her coming shocked you."

"It certainly did," he confessed soberly; and then: "Have you forgotten what I told you about the circumstances under which I left home?"

"Oh!" she murmured, and as once before there was a little gasp to go with the word. Then: "She wouldn't—she wouldn't——"

"No," he answered; "she wouldn't; but her father would."

"So her father wanted her to marry the other man, did he? What was he like—the other man? I don't believe you've ever told me anything about him."

Smith's laugh was an easing of strains.

"Now your 'control' is playing tricks on you. There were a dozen other men, more or less."

"And her picture was in the watch-case of each?"

"You've pumped me dry," he returned, the sardonic humor reasserting itself. "I haven't her watch-case list; I never had it. But I guess it's within bounds to suppose that she got the little pictures from the photographer by the half-dozen, at least. Young women in my part of the world don't think much of the watch-case habit; I mean they don't regard it seriously."

A motor-car was coming up the driveway and Smith was not altogether sorry when he saw Stillings, the lawyer, climb out of it to mount the steps. It was high time that an interruption of some sort was breaking in, and when the colonel appeared and brought Stillings with him to the lounging end of the porch, a business conference began which gave Miss Corona an excuse to disappear, and which accounted easily for the remainder of the evening.

Borrowing a horse from the Hillcrest corral the following morning, Smith returned to Brewster by way of the dam, making the long détour count for as much as possible in the matter of sheer time-killing. It was a little before noon when he reached town by the roundabout route, and after putting the horse up at the livery-stable in which Colonel Baldwin was a half owner, he went to the hotel to reconnoitre. The room-clerk who gave him his key gave him also the information he craved.

"Mr. Richlander? Oh, yes; he left early this morning by the stage. He is interested in some gold properties up in the range beyond Topaz. Fine old gentleman. Do you know him, Mr. Smith?"

"The name seemed familiar when I saw it on the register last evening," was Smith's evasion; "but it is not such a very uncommon name. He didn't say when he was coming back?"

"No."

Smith took a fresh hold upon life and liberty. While the world is perilously narrow in some respects, it is comfortably broad in others, and a danger once safely averted is a danger lessened. Snatching a hasty luncheon in the grill-room, the fighting manager of Timanyoni High Line hurried across to the private suite in the Kinzie Building offices into which he had lately moved and once more plunged into the business battle.

Notwithstanding a new trouble which Stillings had wished to talk over with his president and the financial manager the night before—the claim set up by the dead-and-gone paper railroad to a right of way across the Timanyoni at the dam—the battle was progressing favorably. Williams was accomplishing the incredible in the matter of speed, and the dam was now nearly ready to withstand the high-water stresses when they should come. The power-house was rising rapidly, and the machinery was on the way from the East. Altogether things were looking more hopeful than they had at any period since the hasty reorganization. Smith attacked the multifarious details of his many-sided job with returning energy. If he could make shift to hold on for a few days or weeks longer....

He set his teeth upon a desperate determination to hold on at any cost; at all costs. If Josiah Richlander should come back to Brewster—but Smith would not allow himself to think of this. At the worst, the period of peril could not be long. Smith knew his man, and was well assured that it would take something more alluring than a gold-mine to keep the Lawrenceville millionaire away from his business at home for any considerable length of time. With the comforting conclusion for a stimulus, the afternoon of hard work passed quickly and there was only a single small incident to break the busy monotonies. While Smith was dictating the final batch of letters to the second stenographer a young man with sleepy eyes and yellow creosote stains on his fingers came in to ask for a job. Smith put him off until the correspondence was finished and then gave him a hearing.

"What kind of work are you looking for?" was the brisk query.

"Shorthand work, if I can get it," said the man out of a job.

"How rapid are you?"

"I have been a court reporter."

Smith was needing another stenographer and he looked the applicant over appraisingly. The appraisal was not entirely satisfactory. There was a certain shifty furtiveness in the half-opened eyes, and the rather weak chin hinted at a possible lack of the discreetness which is the prime requisite in a confidential clerk.

"Any business experience?"

"Yes; I've done some railroad work."

"Here in Brewster?"

Shaw lied smoothly. "No; in Omaha."

"Any recommendations?"

The young man produced a handful of "To Whom it May Concern" letters. They were all on business letter-heads, and were apparently genuine, though none of them were local. Smith ran them over hastily and he had no means of knowing that they had been carefully prepared by Crawford Stanton at no little cost in ingenuity and painstaking. How careful the preparation had been was revealed in the applicant's ready suggestion.

"You can write or wire to any of these gentlemen," he said; "only, if there is a job open, I'd be glad to go to work on trial."

The business training of the present makes for quick decisions. Smith snapped a rubber band around the letters and shot them into a pigeonhole of his desk.

"We'll give you a chance to show what you can do," he told the man out of work. "If you measure up to the requirements, the job will be permanent. You may come in to-morrow morning and report to Mr. Miller, the chief clerk."

The young man nodded his thanks and went out, leaving just as the first stenographer was bringing in his allotment of letters for the signatures. Having other things to think of, Smith forgot the sleepy-eyed young fellow instantly. But it is safe to assume that he would not have dismissed the incident so readily if he had known that Shaw had been waiting in the anteroom during the better part of the dictating interval, and that on the departing applicant's cuffs were microscopic short-hand notes of a number of the more important letters.

XV
"Sweet Fortune's Minion"

It was late dinner-time when Smith closed the big roll-top desk in the new private suite in the Kinzie Building offices and went across the street to the hotel. A little farther along, as he was coming down from his rooms to go to dinner, he saw Starbuck in the lobby talking to Williams; but since they did not see him, he passed on without stopping.

The great dining-room of the Hophra House was on the ground floor; a stucco-pillared immensity with scenic mural decorations after Bierstadt and a ceiling over which fat cupids and the classical nude in goddesses rioted in the soft radiance of the shaded electrics. The room was well filled, but the head waiter found Smith a small table in the shelter of one of the pillars and brought him an evening paper.

Smith gave his dinner order and began to glance through the paper. The subdued chatter and clamor of the big room dinned pleasantly in his ears, and the disturbing thought of peril imminent was losing its keenest cutting edge when suddenly the solid earth yawned and the heavens fell. Half absently he realized that the head waiter was seating some one at the place opposite his own; then the faint odor of violets, instantly reminiscent, came to his nostrils. He knew instinctively, and before he could put the newspaper aside, what had happened. Hence the shock, when he found himself face to face with Verda Richlander, was not so completely paralyzing as it might have been. She was looking across at him with a lazy smile in the glorious brown eyes, and the surprise was quite evidently no surprise for her.

"I told the waiter to bring me over here," she explained; and then, quite pleasantly: "It is an exceedingly little world, isn't it, Montague?"

He nodded gloomily.

"Much too little for a man to hide in," he agreed; adding: "But I think I have known that, all along; known, at least, that it would be only a question of time."

The waiter had come to take Miss Richlander's dinner order, and the talk paused. After the man had gone she began again.

"Why did you run away?" she asked.

Smith shrugged his shoulders helplessly.

"What else was there for me to do. Besides, I believed, at the time, that I had killed Dunham. I could have sworn he was dead when I left him."

She was toying idly with the salad-fork. "Sometimes I am almost sorry that he wasn't," she offered.

"Which is merely another way of saying that you were unforgiving enough to wish to see me hanged?" he suggested, with a sour smile.

"It wasn't altogether r that; no." There was a pause a nd then she went on: "I suppose you know what has been happening since you ran away—what has been done in Lawrenceville, I mean?"

"I know that I have been indicted by the grand jury and that there is a reward out for me. It's two thousand dollars, isn't it?"

She let the exact figure of the reward go unconfirmed.

"And still you are going about in public as if all the hue and cry meant nothing to you? The beard is an improvement—it makes you look older and more determined—but it doesn't disguise you. I should have known you anywhere, and other people will."

Again his shoulders went up.

"What's the use?" he said. "I couldn't dig deep enough nor fly high enough to dodge everybody. You have found me, and if you hadn't, somebody else would have. It would have been the same any time and anywhere."

"You knew we were here?" she inquired.

He made the sign of assent.

"And yet you didn't think it worth while to take your meals somewhere else?"

He made a virtue of necessity. "I should certainly have taken the small precaution you suggest if the clerk hadn't told me that your father had gone up to the Gloria district. I took it for granted that you had gone with him."

The lazy smile came again in the brown eyes, and it irritated him.

"I am going to believe that you wouldn't have tried to hide from me," she said slowly. "You'll give my conceit that much to live on, won't you?"

"You mean that I ought to have been willing to trust you? Perhaps I was. But I could hardly think of you as apart from your father. I knew very well what he would do."

"I was intending to go on up to the mines with him," she said evenly. "But last evening, while I was waiting for him to finish his talk with some mining men, I was standing in the mezzanine, looking down into the lobby. I saw you go to the desk and leave your key; I was sure I couldn't be mistaken; so I told father that I had changed my mind about going out to the mines and he seemed greatly relieved. He had been trying to persuade me that I would be much more comfortable if I should wait for him here."

It was no stirring of belated sentiment that made Smith say: "You—you cared enough to wish to see me?"

"Naturally," she replied. "Some people forget easily: others don't. I suppose I am one of the others."

Smith remembered the proverb about a woman scorned and

saw a menace more to be feared than all the terrors of the law lurking in the even-toned rejoinder. It was with some foolish idea of thrusting the menace aside at any cost that he said: "You have only to send a ten-word telegram to Sheriff Macauley, you know. I'm not sure that it isn't your duty to do so."

"Why should I telegraph Barton Macauley?" she asked placidly. "I'm not one of his deputies."

"But you believe me guilty, don't you?"

The handsome shoulders twitched in the barest hint of indifference. "As I have said, I am not in Bart Macauley's employ—nor in Mr. Watrous Dunham's. Neither am I the judge and jury to put you in the prisoner's box and try you. I suppose you knew what you were doing, and why you did it. But I do think you might have written me a line, Montague. That would have been the least you could have done."

The serving of the salad course broke in just here, and for some time afterward the talk was not resumed. Miss Richlander was apparently enjoying her dinner. Smith was not enjoying his, but he ate as a troubled man often will; mechanically and as a matter of routine. It was not until the dessert had been served that the young woman took up the thread of the conversation precisely as if it had never been dropped.

"I think you know that you have no reason to be afraid of me, Montague; but I can't say as much for father. He will be back in a few days, and when he comes it will be prudent for you to vanish. That is a future, however."

Smith's laugh was brittle.

"We'll leave it a future, if you like. 'Sufficient unto the day is the evil thereof.'"

"Oh; so you class me as an evil, do you?"

"No; you know I didn't mean that; I merely mean that it's no use crossing the bridges before we come to them. I've been living from day to day so long now, that I am becoming hardened to it."

Again there was a pause, and again it was Miss Richlander who broke it.

"You don't want to go back to Lawrenceville?" she suggested.

"Hardly—in the circumstances."

"What will you do?—go away from Brewster and stay until father has finished buying his mine?"

"No; I can't very well go away—for business reasons."

The slow smile was dimpling again at the corners of the perfect mouth.

"You are going to need a little help, Montague—my help—

aren't you? It occurs to me that you can well afford to show me some little friendly attention while I am Robinson-Crusoed here waiting for father to come back."

"Let me understand," he broke in, frowning across the table at her. "You are willing to ignore what has happened—to that extent? You are not forgetting that in the eyes of the law I am a criminal?"

She made a faint little gesture of impatience.

"Why do you persist in dragging that in? I am not supposed to know anything about your business affairs, with Watrous Dunham or anybody else. Besides, no one knows me here, and no one cares. Besides, again, I am a stranger in a strange city and we are—or we used to be—old friends."

Her half-cynical tone made him frown again, thoughtfully, this time.

"Women are curious creatures," he commented. "I used to think I knew a little something about them, but I guess it was a mistake. What do you want me to do?"

"Oh, anything you like; anything that will keep me from being bored to death."

Smith laid his napkin aside and glanced at his watch.

"There is a play of some kind on at the opera-house, I believe," he said, rising and going around to draw her chair aside. "If you'd care to go, I'll see if I can't hold somebody up for a couple of seats."

"That is more like it. I used to be afraid that you hadn't a drop of sporting blood in you, Montague, and I am glad to learn, even at this late day, that I was mistaken. Take me up-stairs, and we'll go to the play."

They left the dining-room together, and there was more than one pair of eyes to follow them in frank admiration. "What a strikingly handsome couple," said a bejewelled lady who sat at the table nearest the door; and her companion, a gentleman with restless eyes and thin lips and a rather wicked jaw, said: "Yes; I don't know the woman, but the man is Colonel Baldwin's new financier; the fellow who calls himself 'John Smith.'"

The bediamonded lady smiled dryly. "You say that as if you had a mortal quarrel with his name, Crawford. If I were the girl, I shouldn't find fault with the name. You say you don't know her?"

Stanton had pushed his chair back and was rising. "Take your time with the ice-cream, and I'll join you later up-stairs. I'm going to find out who the girl is, since you want to know."

On the progress through the lobby to the elevators there were others to make remarks upon the handsome pair; among them the ex-cowboy mine owner whose name was still "Billy" Starbuck to everybody in the Timanyoni region.

"Say! wouldn't that jar you, now?" he muttered to himself. And again: "This John Smith fellow sure does need a guardian—and for just this one time I reckon I might as well butt in and be it. If he's fixing to shake that little Corona girl he's sure going to earn what's coming to him. That's my ante."

XVI
Broken Threads

Mr. Crawford Stanton's attempt to find out who Smith's dinner companion was began with a casual question shot at the hotel clerk; with that, and a glance at the register. From the clerk he learned Miss Richlander's name and the circumstances under which she had become a waiting transient in the hotel. From the register he got nothing but the magnate's name and the misleading address, "Chicago."

"Is Mr. Richlander a Chicago man?" he asked of the clerk.

"No. He merely registered from his last stop—as a good many people do. His home town is Lawrenceville."

"Which Lawrenceville is that?" Stanton inquired; but the clerk shook his head.

"You may search me, Mr. Stanton. I didn't ask. It's in Indiana, isn't it? You might find out from Miss Richlander."

Stanton became thoughtful for a moment and then crossed the lobby to his business office, which had an entrance from the hotel ground floor. Behind the closed door, which he took the precaution to lock, he turned on the light and opened a large atlas. A glance at the town listings revealed some half-dozen Lawrencevilles, in as many different States, one State offering two, for good measure. That ended the search for the moment, and a little later he went up-stairs to rejoin the resplendent lady, who was taking her after-dinner ease in the most comfortable lounging-chair the mezzanine parlors afforded.

"No good," he reported. "The girl's name is Richlander, and she—or her father—comes from one of half a dozen 'Lawrencevilles'—you can take your choice among 'em."

"Money?" queried the comfortable one.

"Buying mines in the Topaz," said the husband mechanically. He was not thinking specially of Mr. Josiah Richlander's possible or probable rating with the commercial agencies; he was wondering how well Miss Richlander knew John Smith, and in what manner she could be persuaded to tell what she might know. While he was turning it over in his mind the two in question, Smith and the young woman, passed through the lobby on their way to the theatre. Stanton, watching them narrowly from the vantage-point afforded by the galleried mezzanine, drew his own conclusions. By all the little signs they were not merely chance acquaintances or even casual friends. Their relations were closer—and of longer standing.

Stanton puzzled over his problem a long time, long after Mrs. Stanton had forsaken the easy chair and had disappeared from the scene. His Eastern employers were growing irascibly impatient, and the letters and telegrams were beginning to have an abrasive quality disagreeably irritating to a hard-working field captain. Who was this fellow Smith, and what was his backing? they were beginning to ask; and with the asking there were intimations that if Mr. Crawford Stanton were finding his task too difficult, there was always an alternative.

As a business man Stanton was usually able to keep irritating personalities at a proper distance. But the Timanyoni-Escalante war was beginning to get on his nerves. At first, it had presented itself as the simplest of business campaigns. A great land grab had been carried through, and there was an ample water-supply to transform the arid desert into ranch acres with enormous increases in values. A farmers' ditch company, loosely organized and administered, was the sole obstacle in the way, and upon his arrival in Brewster, Stanton had set blithely about removing it.

Just when all was going well, when the farmers were almost in sight of their finish, and the actual stock absorption had fairly begun, the new factor had broken in; a young man capable and daring to a degree that was amazing, even in the direct and courageous West. Where and how Smith would strike, Stanton never knew until after the blow had been sent home. Secrecy, the most difficult requirement in any business campaign, had been so strictly maintained that up to the present evening of cogitations in the Hophra House mezzanine, Stanton was still unable to tell his New York and Washington employers positively whether Smith had money—Eastern money—behind him, or was engineering the big coup alone. Kinzie was steadfastly refusing to talk, and the sole significant fact, thus far, was that practically all of the new High Line stock had been taken up by local purchasers.

Stanton was still wrestling with his problem when the "handsome couple" returned from the play. The trust field captain saw them as they crossed the lobby to the elevator and again marked the little evidences of familiarity. "That settles it," he mused, with an outthrust of the pugnacious jaw. "She knows more about Smith than anybody else in this neck of woods—and she's got it to tell!"

Stanton began his inquisition for better information the following day, with the bejewelled lady for his ally. Miss Richlander was alone and unfriended in the hotel—and also a little bored. Hence she was easy of approach; so easy that by luncheon time the sham promoter's wife was able to introduce her husband. Stanton lost no moment investigative. For the inquiring purpose, Smith was made to figure as a business acquaintance, and Stanton was generous in his praises of the young man's astounding financial ability.

"He's simply a wonder, Miss Richlander!" he confided over the luncheon-table. "Coming here a few weeks ago, absolutely unknown, he has already become a prominent man of affairs in Brewster. And so discreetly reticent! To this good day nobody knows where he comes from, or anything about him."

"No?" said Miss Verda. "How singular!" But she did not volunteer to supply any of the missing biographical facts.

"Absolutely nothing," Stanton went on smoothly. "And, of course, his silence about himself has been grossly misinterpreted. I have even heard it said that he is an escaped convict."

"How perfectly absurd!" was the smiling comment.

"Isn't it? But you know how people will talk. They are saying now that his name isn't Smith; that he has merely taken the commonest name in the category as an alias."

"I can contradict that, anyway," Miss Richlander offered. "His name is really and truly John Smith."

"You have known him a long time, haven't you?" inquired the lady with the headlight diamonds.

"Oh, yes; for quite a long time, indeed."

"That was back in New York State?" Stanton slipped in.

"In the East, yes. He comes of an excellent family. His father's people were well-to-do farmers, and one of his great-uncles on his mother's side was on the supreme bench in our State; he was chief justice during the later years of his life."

"What State did you say?" queried Stanton craftily. But Miss Verda was far too wide-awake to let him surprise her.

"Our home State, of course. I don't believe any member of

Mr. Smith's immediate family on either side has ever moved out of it."

Stanton gave it up for the time being, and was convinced upon two points. Miss Richlander's reticence could have but one meaning: for some good reason, Smith would not, or dare not, give any home references. That was one point, and the second was that Miss Richlander knew, and knew that others wanted to know—and refused to tell. Stanton weighed the probabilities thoughtfully in the privacy of his office. There were two hypotheses: Smith might have business reasons for the secrecy—he might have backers who wished to remain completely unknown in their fight against the big land trust; but if he had no backers the other hypothesis clinched itself instantly—he was in hiding; he had done something from which he had run away.

It was not until after office hours that Stanton was able to reduce his equation to its simplest terms, and it was Shaw, dropping in to make his report after his first day's work as clerk and stenographer in the High Line headquarters, who cleared the air of at least one fog bank of doubts.

"I've been through the records and the stock-books," said the spy, when, in obedience to orders, he had locked the office door. "Smith is playing a lone hand. He flimflammed Kinzie for his first chunk of money, and after that it was easy. Every dollar invested in High Line has been dug up right here in the Timanyoni. Here's the list of stockholders."

Stanton ran his eye down the string of names and swore when he saw Maxwell's subscription of $25,000. "Damn it!" he rasped; "and he's Fairbairn's own son-in-law!"

"So is Starbuck, for that matter; and he's in for twenty thousand," said Shaw. "And, by the way, Billy is a man who will bear watching. He's hand-in-glove with Smith, and he's onto all of our little crooks and turns. I heard him telling Smith to-day that he owed it to the company to carry a gun."

Stanton's smile showed his teeth.

"I wish he would; carry one and kill somebody with it. Then we'd know what to do with him."

The spy was rolling a cigarette and his half-closed eyes had a murderous glint in them.

"Me, for instance?" he inquired cynically.

"Anybody," said Stanton absently. He was going over the list of stockholders again and had scarcely heard what Shaw had said.

"That brings us down to business, Mr. Stanton," said the ex-railroad clerk slowly. "I'm not getting money enough out of this to cover the risk—my risk."

The man at the desk looked up quickly.

"What's that you say? By heavens, Shaw, have I got to send you over the road before you'll come to your senses? I've spoken once, and I'll do it just this one time more: you sing small if you want to keep out of jail!"

Shaw had lighted his cigarette and was edging toward the door.

"Not this trip, Mr. Stanton," he said coolly. "If you've got me, I've got you. I can find two men who will go into court and swear that you paid Pete Simms money to have Smith sandbagged, that day out at Simms's place at the dam! I may have to go to jail, as you say; but I'll bet you five to one that you'll beat me to it!" And with that he snapped the catch on the locked door and went away.

Some three hours after this rather hostile clash with the least trustworthy, but by far the most able, of his henchmen, Crawford Stanton left his wife chatting comfortably with Miss Richlander in the hotel parlors and went reluctantly to keep an appointment which he had been dreading ever since the early afternoon hour when a wire had come from Copah directing him to meet the "Nevada Flyer" upon its arrival at Brewster. The public knew the name signed to the telegram as that of a millionaire statesman; but Stanton knew it best as the name of a hard and not over-scrupulous master.

The train was whistling for the station when Stanton descended from his cab and hurried down the long platform. He assumed that the great personage would be travelling in a private car which would be coupled to the rear end of the "Flyer," and his guess was confirmed. A white-jacketed porter was waiting to admit him to the presence when the train came to a stand, and as he climbed into the vestibule of the luxurious private car, Stanton got what comfort he could out of the thought that the interview would necessarily be limited by the ten minutes' engine-changing stop of the fast train.

The presence chamber was the open compartment of the palace on wheels, and it held a single occupant when Stanton entered; a big-bodied man with bibulous eyes and a massive square-angled head and face, a face in which the cartoonists emphasized the heavy drooping mustache and the ever-present black cigar growing out of it.

"Hello, Crawford," the great man grunted, making no move to

lift his huge body out of the padded lounging-chair. "You got my wire?"

"Yes," returned the promoter, limiting himself to the one word.

"What's the matter with you here on this land deal? Why don't you get action?"

Stanton tried to explain as fully as might be, holding in view the necessity for haste. The big man in the easy chair was frowning heavily when the explanation was finished.

"And you say this one man has blocked the game? Why the devil don't you get rid of him—buy him, or run him off, or something?"

"I don't believe he can be bought."

"Well, then, chase him out. We can't afford to be hung up this way indefinitely by every little amateur that happens to come along and sit in the game. Get action and do something. From what you say, this fellow is probably some piker who has left his country for his country's good. Get the detectives after him and run him down."

"That will take time, and time is what we haven't got."

The big man pulled himself up in his chair and glared savagely at the protester.

"Stanton, you make me tired—very tired! You know what we have at stake in this deal, and thus far you're the only man in it who hasn't made good. You've had all the help you've asked for, and all the money you wanted to spend. If you've lost your grip, say so plainly, and get down and out. We don't want any 'has-been' on this job. If you are at the end of your resources——"

The conductor's shout of "All aboard!" dominated the clamor of the station noises, and the air-brakes were singing as the engineer of the changed locomotives tested the connections. Stanton saw his chance to duck and took it.

"I have been trying to stop short of anything that might make talk," he said. "This town might easily be made too hot to hold us, and——"

"You're speaking for yourself, now," rapped out the tyrant. "What the devil do we care for the temperature of Brewster? I've only one word for you, Crawford: you get busy and give us results. Skip out, now, or you'll get carried by. And, say; let me have a wire at Los Angeles, not later than Thursday. Get that?"

Stanton got it: also, he escaped, making a flying leap from the moving train. At the cab rank he found the motor-cab which he had hired for the drive down from the hotel. Climbing in, he gave a brittle order to the chauffeur. Simultaneously a man wearing the softest of Stetsons lounged away from his post of observation under a near-by electric pole and ran across the railroad plaza to unhitch and mount a wiry little cow-pony. Once in the saddle, however, the mounted man did not hurry his horse. Having overheard Stanton's order-giving, there was no need to keep the motor-cab in sight as it sputtered through the streets and out upon the backgrounding mesa, its ill-smelling course ending at a lonely road-house in the mesa hills on the Topaz trail.

When the hired vehicle came to a stand in front of the lighted bar-room of the road-house, Stanton gave a waiting order to the driver and went in. Of the dog-faced barkeeper he asked an abrupt question, and at the man's jerk of a thumb toward the rear, the promoter passed on and entered the private room at the back.

The private room had but one occupant—the man Lanterby, who was sitting behind a round card-table and vainly endeavoring to make one of the pair of empty whiskey-glasses spin in a complete circuit about a black bottle standing on the table.

Stanton pulled up a chair and sat down, and Lanterby poured libations for two from the black bottle. The promoter, ordinarily as abstemious as a Trappist, drained his portion at a gulp.

"Well?" he snapped, pushing the bottle aside. "What did you find out?"

"I reckon it can be done, if it has to be," was the low-toned reply.

"Done and well covered up?"

"Yep. It'll be charged up to the high water—maybe."

"Is the river still rising?"

"A little bit higher every night now. That's the way it comes up. The snow on the mountain melts in the day and the run-off comes in the night."

"You can handle it by yourself, can't you?"

"Me and Boogerfield can."

"All right. Get everything ready and wait for the word from me. You didn't let Pegleg in on it, did you?"

"I had to. We'd have to work from his joint."

"That was a bad move. Simms would sell you out if anybody wanted to buy. He'd sell his best friend," frowned Stanton.

Lanterby showed the whites of his eyes and a set of broken teeth in a wolfish grin.

"Pete can't run fast enough to sell me out," he boasted. "I'll have somethin' in my clothes that'll run faster than he can, with that wooden leg o' his."

Stanton nodded and poured himself another drink—a larger

one than the first; and then thought better of it and spilled the liquor on the floor.

"That will do for the dynamite part of it. It's a last resort, of course. We don't want to have to rebuild the dam, and I have one more string that I want to pull first. This man Smith: I've got a pointer on him, at last. Is Boogerfield still feeling sore about the man-handling Smith gave him?"

"You bet your life he is."

"Good. Keep him stirred up along that line." Stanton got up and looked thirstily at the bottle, but let it alone. "That's all for to-night. Stay out of sight as much as you can, and go easy on the whiskey. I may not come here again. If I don't, I'll send you one of two words. 'Williams' will mean that you're to strike for the dam. 'Jake' will mean that you are to get Boogerfield fighting drunk and send him after Smith. Whichever way it comes out, you'll find the money where I've said it will be, and you and Boogerfield had better fade away—and take Pegleg with you, if you can."

The hired car was still waiting when Stanton went out through the bar-room and gave the driver his return orders. And, because the night was dark, neither of the two at the car saw the man in the soft Stetson straighten himself up from his crouching place under the back-room window and vanish silently in the gloom.

XVII
A Night of Fiascos

Smith had seen nothing of Miss Richlander during the day of the Stanton plottings, partly because there was a forenoon meeting of the High Line stockholders called for the purpose of electing him secretary and treasurer in fact of the company, and partly because the major portion of the afternoon was spent in conference with Williams at the dam.

The work of construction had now reached its most critical stage, and Williams was driving it strenuously. Each twenty-four hours, with the recurring night rise from the melting snows, the torrenting river reached a higher water-mark, and three times in as many weeks the engineer had changed from a quick-setting cement to a still quicker, time-saving and a swift piling-up of the great dike wall being now the prime necessities.

Returning from the dam site quite late in the evening, Smith spent a hard-working hour or more at his desk in the Kinzie Building offices; and it was here that Starbuck found him.

"What?" said the new secretary, looking up from his work when Starbuck's wiry figure loomed in the doorway, "I thought you were once more a family man, and had cut out the night prowling."

Starbuck jack-knifed himself comfortably in a chair.

"I was. But the little girl's run away again; gone with her sister—Maxwell's wife, you know—to Denver to get her teeth fixed; and I'm foot-loose. Been butting in a little on your game, this evening, just to be doing. How's tricks with you, now?"

"We're strictly in the fight," declared Smith enthusiastically. "We closed the deal to-day for the last half-mile of the main ditch right of way, which puts us up on the mesa slope above the Escalante Grant. If they knock us out now, they'll have to do it with dynamite."

"Yes," said the ex-cow-man, thoughtfully; "with dynamite." Then: "How is Williams getting along?"

"Fine! The water is crawling up on him a little every night, but with no accidents, he'll be able to hold the flood rise when it comes. The only thing that worries me now is the time limit."

"The time limit?" echoed Starbuck. "What's that?"

"It's the handicap we inherit from the original company. Certain State rights to the water were conveyed in the old charter, on condition that the project should be completed, or at least be far enough along to turn water into the ditches, by a given date. This time limit, which carries over from Timanyoni Ditch to Timanyoni High Line, expires next week. We're petitioning for an extension, but if we don't get it we shall still be able to back the water up so that it will flow into the lower level of ditches by next Thursday; that is, barring accidents."

"Yes; with no accidents," mused Starbuck. "Can't get shut of the 'if,' no way nor shape, can we? So that's why the Stanton people have been fighting so wolfishly for delay, is it? Wanted to make the High Line lose its charter? John, this is a wicked, wicked world, and I can sympathize with the little kiddie who said he was going out in the garden to eat worms." Then he switched abruptly. "Where did you corral all those good looks you took to the opera-house last night, John?"

Smith's laugh was strictly perfunctory.

"That was Miss Verda Richlander, an old friend of mine from back home. She is out here with her father, and the father has gone up into the Topaz country to buy him a gold brick."

"Not in the Topaz," Starbuck struck in loyally. "We don't make the bricks up there—not the phony kind. But let that go and tell me something else. A while back, when you were giving me a little song and dance about the colonel's daughter, you mentioned another woman—though not by name, if you happen to recollect. I was just wondering if this Miss Rich-people, or whatever her name is, might be the other one."

Again the new secretary laughed—this time without embarrassment. "You've called the turn, Billy. She is the other one."

"H'm; chasing you up?"

"Oh, no; it was just one of the near-miracles. She didn't know I was here, and I had no hint that she was coming."

"I didn't know," commented the reformed cowboy. "Sometimes when you think it's a cold trail, it's a warm one; and then again when you think it's warm, it fools you."

"Oh, pshaw!" scoffed the trail-maker, "you make me weary, Billy. We are merely good friends. No longer ago than last night I had the strongest possible proof of Miss Richlander's friendship."

"Did, eh? All right; it's your roast; not mine. But I'm going to pull one chestnut out of the fire for you, even if I do get my fingers burned. This Miss Rich-folks has had only one day here in Brewster, but she's used it in getting mighty chummy with the Stantons. Did you know that?"

"What!" ejaculated Smith.

"Jesso," smiled Starbuck. "She had her luncheon with 'em to-day, and for an hour or so this evening the three of 'em sat together up in the Hophra inside-veranda parlor. Does that figure as news to you?"

"It does," said Smith simply; and he added: "I don't understand it."

"Funny," remarked the ex-cow-man. "It didn't ball me up for more than a minute or two. Stanton fixed it some way—because he needed to. Tell me something, John; could this Miss Rich-garden help Stanton out in any of his little schemes, if she took a notion?"

Smith turned away and stared at the blackened square of outer darkness lying beyond the office window.

"She could, Billy—but she won't," he answered.

"You can dig up your last dollar and bet on that, can you?"

"Yes, I think I can."

"H'm; that's just what I was most afraid of."

"Don't be an ass, Billy."

"I'm trying mighty hard not to be, John, but sometimes the ears will grow on the best of us—in spite of the devil. What I mean is this: when a woman thinks enough of a man to keep his secrets, she's mighty likely to think too much of him to keep those same secrets from spreading themselves on the bill-boards when the pinch comes."

"I'm no good at conundrums," said Smith. "Put it in plain words."

"So I will," snapped Starbuck, half morosely. "Two nights ago, when you were telling me about this Miss Rich-acres, you said there was nothing to it, and I said you never could tell, when there was a woman in it. I saw you two when you came out of the Hophra dining-room together last night, and I saw the look in that girl's eyes. Do you know what I said to myself right then, John? I said: 'Oh, you little girl out at the Hillcrest ranch—good-by, you!'"

Smith's grin was half antagonistic. "You are an ass, Billy," he asserted. "I never was in love with Verda Richlander, nor she with me."

"Speak for yourself and let it hang there, John. You can't speak for the woman—no man ever can. What I'm hoping now is that she doesn't know anything about you that Stanton could make use of."

Again the High Line's new secretary turned to stare at the black backgrounded window.

"You mean that she might hear of—of Miss Corona?" he suggested.

"You've roped it down, at last," said the friendly enemy. "Stanton'll tell her—he'll tell her anything and everything that might make her turn loose any little bit of information she may have about you. As I said a minute ago, I'm hoping she hasn't got anything on you, John."

Smith was still facing the window when he replied. "I'm sorry to have to disappoint you, Starbuck. What Miss Richlander could do to me, if she chooses, would be good and plenty."

The ex-cowboy mine owner drew a long breath and felt for his tobacco-sack and rice-paper.

"All of which opens up more talk trails," he said thoughtfully. "Since you wouldn't try to take care of yourself, and since your neck happens to be the most valuable asset Timanyoni High Line has, just at present, I've been butting in, as I told you. Listen to my tale of woe, if you haven't anything better to do. Besides the Miss Rich-ranches episode there are a couple of others. Want to hear about 'em?"

Smith nodded.

"All right. A little while past dinner this evening, Stanton had a hurry call to meet the 'Nevada Flyer.' Tailed onto the train there was a private luxury car, and in the private car sat a gentleman whose face you've seen plenty of times in the political cartoons, usually with cuss-words under it. He is one of Stanton's bosses; and Stanton was in for a wigging—and got it. I couldn't hear, but I could see—through the car window. He had Stanton standing on one foot before the train pulled out and let Crawford make his get-away. You guess, and I'll guess, and we'll both say it was about this Escalante snap which is aiming to be known as the Escalante fizzle. Ain't it the truth?"

Again Smith nodded, and said: "Go on."

"After Number Five had gone, Stanton broke for his auto-cab, looking like he could bite a nail in two. I happened to hear the order he gave the shover, and I had my cayuse hitched over at Bob Sharkey's joint. Naturally, I ambled along after Crawford, and while I didn't beat him to it, I got there soon enough. It was out at Jeff Barton's road-house on the Topaz trail, and Stanton was shut up in the back room with a sort of tin-horn 'bad man' named Lanterby."

"You listened?" said Smith, still without eagerness.

"Right you are. And they fooled me. Two schemes were on tap; one pointing at Williams and the dam, and the other at you. These were both 'last resorts'; Stanton said he had one more string to pull first. If that broke—well, I've said it half a dozen times already, John: you'll either have to hire a body-guard or go heeled. I'm telling you right here and now, that bunch is going to get you, even if it costs money!"

"You say Stanton said he had one more string to pull: he didn't give it a name, did he?"

"No, but I've got a notion of my own," was the ready answer. "He's trying to get next to you through the women, with this Miss Rich-pasture for his can-opener. But when everything else fails, he is to send a password to Lanterby, one of two passwords. 'Williams' means dynamite and the dam: 'Jake' means the removal from the map of a fellow named Smith. Nice prospect, isn't it?"

Smith was jabbing his paper-knife absently into the desk-blotter. "And yet we go on calling this a civilized country!" he said meditatively. Then with a sudden change of front: "I'm in this fight to stay until I win out or die out, Billy; you know that. As I have said, Miss Verda can kill me off if she chooses to; but she won't choose to. Now let's get to work. It's pretty late to rout a justice of the peace out of bed to issue a warrant for us, but we'll do it. Then we'll go after Lanterby and make him turn state's evidence. Come on; let's get busy."

But Starbuck, reaching softly for a chair-righting handhold

upon Smith's desk, made no reply. Instead, he snapped his lithe body out of the chair and launched it in a sudden tiger-spring at the door. To Smith's astonishment the door, which should have been latched, came in at Starbuck's wrenching jerk of the knob, bringing with it, hatless, and with the breath startled out of him, the new stenographer, Shaw.

"There's your state's evidence," said Starbuck grimly, pushing the half-dazed door-listener into a chair. "Just put the auger a couple of inches into this fellow and see what you can find."

Measured by any standard of human discomfort, Richard Shaw had an exceedingly bad quarter of an hour to worry through when Smith and Starbuck applied the thumbscrews and sought by every means known to modern inquisitorial methods to force a confession out of him.

Caring nothing for loyalty to the man who was paying him, Shaw had, nevertheless, a highly developed anxiety for his own welfare; and knowing the dangerous ground upon which he stood, he evaded and shuffled and prevaricated under the charges and questionings until it became apparent to both of his inquisitors that nothing short of bribery or physical torture would get the truth out of him. Smith was not willing to offer the bribe, and since the literal thumbscrews were out of the question, Shaw was locked into one of the vacant rooms across the corridor until his captors could determine what was to be done with him.

"That is one time when I fired and missed the whole side of the barn," Starbuck admitted, when Shaw had been remanded to the makeshift cell across the hall. "I know that fellow is on Stanton's pay-roll; and it's reasonably certain that he got his job with you so that he could keep cases on you. But we can't prove anything that we say, so long as he refuses to talk."

"No," Smith agreed. "I can discharge him, and that's about all that can be done with him. We can't even tax him with listening. You heard what he said—that he saw the light up here from the street, and came up to see if I didn't need him."

"He is a pretty smooth article," said Starbuck reflectively. "He used to be a clerk in Maxwell's railroad office, and he was mixed up in some kind of crookedness, I don't remember just what."

Smith caught quickly at the suggestion.

"Wait a minute, Billy," he broke in; and then: "There's no doubt in your mind that he's a spy?"

"Sure, he is," was the prompt rejoinder.

"I was just thinking—he has heard what was said here to-night—which is enough to give Stanton a pretty good chance to outfigure us again."

"Right you are."

"In which case it would be little short of idiotic in us to turn him loose. We've got to hold him, proof or no proof. Where would we be apt to catch Maxwell at this time of night?"

"At home and in bed, I reckon."

"Call him up on the 'phone and state the case briefly. Tell him if he has any nip on Shaw that would warrant us in turning him over to the sheriff, we'd like to know it."

"You're getting the range now," laughed the ex-cow-man, and instead of using the desk set, he went to shut himself into the sound-proof telephone-closet.

When he emerged a few minutes later he was grinning exultantly. "That was sure a smooth one of yours, John. Dick gave me the facts. Shaw's a thief; but he has a sick sister on his hands—or said he had—and the railroad didn't prosecute. Dick says for us to jug him to-night and to-morrow morning he'll swear out the necessary papers."

"Good. We'll do that first; and then we'll go after this fellow Lanterby. I want to get Stanton where I can pinch him, Billy; no, there's nothing personal about it; but when a great corporation like the Escalante Land Company gets down to plain anarchy and dynamiting, it's time to make somebody sweat for it. Let's go and get Shaw."

Together they went across the corridor, and Smith unlocked the door of the disused room. The light switch was on the door-jamb and Starbuck found and pressed the button. The single incandescent bulb hanging from the ceiling sprang alive—and showed the two men at the door an empty room and an open window. The bird had flown.

Starbuck was grinning again when he went to look out of the window. The roof of the adjoining building was only a few feet below the sill level, and there was a convenient fire-escape ladder leading to the ground.

"It's us for that road-house out on the Topaz trail before the news gets around to Stanton and Lanterby," he said definitely; and they lost no time in securing an auto for the dash.

But that, too, proved to be a fiasco. When they reached Barton's all-night place on the hill road, the bar was still open and a card game was running in an up-stairs room. Starbuck did the necessary cross-questioning of the dog-faced bartender.

"You know me, Pug, and what I can do to you if I have to. We want Hank Lanterby. Pitch out and show us where."

The barkeeper threw up one hand as if he were warding off a blow.

"You c'd have him in a holy minute, for all o' me, Billy; you sure could," he protested. "But he's gone."

"On the level?" snapped Starbuck.

"That's straight; I wouldn't lie to you, Billy. Telephone call came from town a little spell ago, and I got Hank outa bed t' answer it. He borra'd Barton's mare an' faded inside of a pair o' minutes."

"Which way?" demanded the questioner.

"T' the hills; leastways he ain't headin' f'r town when he breaks from here."

Starbuck turned to Smith with a wry smile.

"Shaw beat us to it and he scores on us," he said. "We may as well hike back, 'phone Williams to keep his eye on things up at the dam, and go to bed. There'll be nothing more doing to-night."

XVIII
A Chance to Hedge

With all things moving favorably for Timanyoni High Line up to the night of fiascos, the battle for the great water-right seemed to take a sudden slant against the local promoters, after the failure to cripple Stanton by the attempt to suppress two of his subordinates. Early the next day there were panicky rumors in the air, all pointing to a possible eleventh-hour failure of the local enterprise, and none of them traceable to any definite starting-point.

One of the stories was to the effect that the Timanyoni dam had faulty foundations and that the haste in building had added to its insecurity. By noon bets were freely offered in the pool-rooms that the dam would never stand its first filling; and on the heels of this came clamorous court petitions from ranch owners below the dam site, setting forth the flood dangers to which they were exposed and praying for an injunction to stop the work.

That this was a new move on Stanton's part, neither Smith nor Stillings questioned for a moment; but they had no sooner got the nervous ranchmen pacified by giving an indemnity bond for any damage that might be done, before it became evident that the rumors were having another and still more serious effect. It was a little past one o'clock when Kinzie sent up-stairs for Smith, and Smith wondered why, with the telephone at his elbow, the banker had sent the summons by the janitor.

When the newly elected secretary had himself shot down the elevator, he was moved to wonder again at the number of people who were waiting to see the president. The anteroom was crowded with them; and when the janitor led him around through the working room of the bank to come at the inside door to Kinzie's room, Smith thought the détour was made merely to dodge the waiting throng.

There was a crude surprise lying in wait for Smith when the door of the president's room swung open to admit him. Sitting at ease on Kinzie's big leather-covered lounge, with a huge book of engraving samples on his knees, was a round-bodied man with a face like a good-natured full moon. Instantly he tossed the book aside and sprang up.

"Why, Montague!" he burst out, "if this doesn't beat the band! Is it really you, or only your remarkably healthy-looking ghost? By George! but I'm glad to see you!"

Smith shook hands with Debritt, and if the salesman's hearty greeting was not returned in kind, the lack was due more to the turmoil of emotions he had stirred up than to any studied coolness on the part of the trapped fugitive. Fortunately, the salesman had finished showing Kinzie his samples and was ready to go, so there was no time for any awkward revelations.

"I'm at the Hophra, for just a little while, Montague, and you must look me up," was Debritt's parting admonition; and Smith was searching the salesman's eyes keenly for the accusation which ought to be in them; searching and failing to find it.

"Yes; I'll look you up, of course, Boswell. I'm at the Hophra, myself," he returned mechanically; and the next moment he was alone with Kinzie.

"You sent for me?" he said to the banker; and Kinzie pointed to a chair.

"Yes; sit down and tell me what has broken loose. I've been trying to get Baldwin or Williams on the wire—they're both at the dam, I understand—but the 'phone seems to be out of service. What has gone wrong with you people?"

Smith spread his hands. "We were never in better shape to win out than we are at this moment, Mr. Kinzie. This little flurry about newer and bigger damage suits to be brought by the valley truck-gardeners doesn't amount to anything."

"I know all about that," said the president, with a touch of impatience. "But there is a screw loose somewhere. How about that time limit in your charter? Are you going to get water into the ditches within your charter restrictions?"

"We shall clear the law, all right, within the limit," was the prompt reply. But the banker was still unsatisfied.

"Did you notice that roomful of people out there waiting to see me?" he asked. "They are High Line investors, a good many of them, and they are waiting for a chance to ask me if they hadn't better get rid of their stock for whatever it will bring. That's why I sent for you. I want to know what's happened. And this time, Mr. Smith, I want the truth."

Smith accepted the implied challenge promptly, though in his heart he knew that a net of some kind was drawing around him.

"Meaning that I haven't been telling you the truth, heretofore?" he asked hardily.

"Meaning just that," responded the banker.

"Name the time and place, if you please."

"It was the first time you came here—with Baldwin."

"No," said Smith. "I gave you nothing but straight facts at that time, Mr. Kinzie. It was your own deductions that were at fault. You jumped to the conclusion that I was here as the representative of Eastern capital, and I neither denied nor affirmed. But that is neither here nor there. We have made good in the financing, and, incidentally, we've helped the bank. You have no kick coming."

Kinzie wheeled in his chair and pointed an accusing finger at Smith.

"Mr. Smith, before we do any more business together, I want to know who you are and where you come from. If you can't answer a few plain questions I shall draw my own inferences."

Smith leaped up and towered over the thick-set elderly man in the pivot-chair.

"Mr. Kinzie, do you want me to tell you what you are? You're a trimmer—a fence-climber! Do you suppose I don't know what has happened? Stanton has started this new scare, and he has been here with you! You've thought it all over, and now you want to welsh and go over to what you think is going to be the winning side! Do it, if you feel like it—and I'll transfer our account to the little Savings concern up-town!"

There was fire in his eye and hot wrath in his tone; and once more Kinzie found his conclusions warping.

"Oh, don't fly off the handle so brashly, young man," he protested. "You've been in the banking business, yourself—you needn't deny it—and you know what a banker's first care should be.

Sit down again and let's thresh this thing out. I don't want to have to drop you."

Being fairly at bay, with Debritt in town and Josiah Richlander due to come back to Brewster at any moment, Smith put his back to the wall and ignored the chair.

"You are at liberty to do anything you see fit, so far as I am concerned," he rapped out, "and whatever you do, I'll try to hand it back to you, with interest."

"That is good strong talk," retorted the banker, "but it doesn't tell me who you are, or why you are so evidently anxious to forget your past, Mr. Smith. I'm not asking much, if you'll stop to consider. And you'll give me credit for being fair and aboveboard with you. I might have held that engraving salesman and questioned him; he knows you—knows your other name."

Smith put the entire matter aside with an impatient gesture. "Leave my past record out of it, if you please, Mr. Kinzie. At the present moment I am the financial head of Timanyoni High Line. What I want to know is this: do you continue to stand with us? or do you insist upon the privilege of seesawing every time Stanton turns up with a fresh scare? Let me have it, yes or no; and then I shall know what to do."

The gray-haired man in the big chair took time to think about it, pursing his lips and making a quick-set hedge of his cropped mustache. In the end he capitulated.

"I don't want to break with you—or with Dexter Baldwin," he said, at length. "But I'm going to talk straight to you. Your little local crowd of ranchmen and mining men will never be allowed to hold that dam and your ditch right of way; never in this world, Smith."

"If you are our friend, you'll tell us why," Smith came back smartly.

"Because you have got too big a crowd to fight; a crowd that can spend millions to your hundreds. I didn't know until to-day who was behind Stanton, though I had made my own guess. You mustn't be foolish, and you mustn't pull Dexter Baldwin in over his head—which is what you are doing now."

Smith thrust his hands into his pockets and looked away.

"What do you advise, Mr. Kinzie?" he asked.

"Just this. At the present moment you seem to have a strangle-hold on the New York people that it will take a good bit of money to break. They'll break it, never fear. A Scotch terrier may be the bravest little dog that ever barked, but he can't fight a mastiff with any hope of saving his life. But there is still a chance for a compromise. Turn this muddle of yours over to me and let me make terms with the New Yorkers. I'll come as near to getting par for you as I can."

Smith, still with his hands in his pockets, took a turn across the room. It was a sharp temptation. No one knew better than he what it would mean to be involved in a long fight, with huge capital on one side and only justice and a modest bank balance on the other. To continue would be to leave Colonel Baldwin and Maxwell and Starbuck and their local following a legacy of strife and shrewd battlings. He knew that Kinzie's offer was made in good faith. It was most probably based on a tentative proposal from Stanton, who, in turn, spoke for the great syndicate. By letting go he might get the local investors out whole, or possibly with some small profit.

Against the acceptance of this alternative every fibre of the new-found manhood in him rose up in stubborn protest. Had it indeed come to a pass at which mere money could dominate and dictate, rob, steal, oppress, and ride roughshod over all opposition? Smith asked himself the question, and figured the big Missouri colonel's magnificent anger if it should be asked of him. That thought and another—the thought of what Corona would say and think if he should surrender—turned the scale.

"No, Mr. Kinzie; we'll not compromise while I have anything to say about it; we'll fight it to a finish," he said abruptly; and with that he went out through the crowded anteroom and so back to his desk in the up-stairs offices.

XIX
Two Women

For one day and yet another after the minatory interview with David Kinzie, Smith fought mechanically, developing the machine-like doggedness of the soldier who sees the battle going irresistibly against him and still smites on in sheer desperation.

As if the night of fiascos had been the turning-point, he saw the carefully built reorganization structure, reared by his own efforts upon the foundation laid by Colonel Baldwin and his ranchmen associates, falling to pieces. In spite of all he could do, the panic of stock-selling continued; the city council, alarmed by the persistent story of the unsafety of the dam, was threatening to cancel the lighting contract with Timanyoni High Line; and Kinzie, though he was doing nothing openly, had caused the word about the proposed compromise with the Escalante people to be passed far and wide among the Timanyoni stockholders, together with the intimation that disaster could be averted now only by prompt action and the swift effacement of their rule-or-ruin secretary and treasurer.

"They're after you, John," was the way the colonel put it at the close of the second day of back-slippings. "They say you're fiddlin' while Rome's a-burnin'. Maybe you know what they mean by that; I don't."

Smith did know. During the two days of stress, Miss Verda had been very exacting. There had been another night at the theatre and much time-killing after meals in the parlors of the Hophra House. Worse still, there had been a daylight auto trip about town and up to the dam. The victim was writhing miserably under the price-paying, but there seemed to be no help for it. With Kinzie and Stanton working together, with Debritt gone only as far as Red Butte and promising to return, and with Josiah Richlander still within easy reach at the Topaz mines, he stood in hourly peril of the explosion, and a single written line from Verda to her father would light the match. Smith could find no word bitter enough to fitly characterize the depths into which he had sunk. It was the newest phase of the metamorphosis. Since the night of Verda Richlander's arrival in Brewster, he had not seen Corona; he was telling himself that he had forfeited the right to see her. Out of the chaotic wreck of things but one driving motive had survived, and it had grown to the stature of an obsession: the determination to wring victory out of defeat for Timanyoni High Line; to fall, if he must fall, fighting to the last gasp and with his face to the enemy.

"I know," he said, replying, after the reflective pause, to the charge passed on by Colonel Dexter. "There is a friend of mine here from the East, and I have been obliged to show her some attention, so they say I am neglecting my job. They are also talking it around that I am your Jonah, and saying that your only hope is to pitch me overboard."

"That's Dave Kinzie," growled the Missourian. "He seems to have it in for you, some way. He was trying to tell me this afternoon that I ought not to take you out to the ranch any more until you loosen up and tell us where you came from. I told him to go and soak his addled old head in a bucket of water!"

"Nevertheless, he was right," Smith returned gloomily. Then: "I am about at the end of my rope, Colonel—the rope I warned you about when you brought me here and put me into the saddle; and I'm trying desperately to hang on until my job's done. When it is done, when Timanyoni High Line can stand fairly on its own feet and fight its own battles, I'm gone."

"Oh, no, you're not," denied the ranchman-president in generous protest. "I don't know—you've never told us—what sort of a kettle of hot water you've got into, but you have made a few solid friends here in the Timanyoni, John, and they are going to stand by you. And—just to show Dave Kinzie that nobody cares a whoop for what he says—you come on out home with me to-night and get away from this muddle for a few minutes. It'll do you a heap of good; you know it always does."

Smith shook his head reluctantly but firmly.

"Never again, Colonel. It can only be a matter of a few days now, and I'm not going to pull you, and your wife and daughter, into the limelight if I can help it."

Colonel Dexter got out of his chair and walked to the office window. When he came back it was to say: "Are they sure-enough chasing you, John?—for something that you have done? Is that what you're trying to tell me?"

"That is it—and they are nearly here. Now you know at least one of the reasons why I can't go with you to-night."

"I'll be shot if I do!" stormed the generous one. "I promised the Missus I'd bring you."

"You must make my excuses to her; and to Corona you may say that I am once more carrying a gun. She will understand."

"Which means, I take it, that you've been telling Corry more than you've told the rest of us. That brings on more talk, John. I haven't said a word before, have I?"

"No."

"Well, I'm going to say it now: I've got only just one daughter in the wide, wide world, John."

Smith stood up and put his hands behind him, facing the older man squarely.

"Colonel, I'd give ten years of my life, this minute, if I might go with you to Hillcrest this evening and tell Corona what I have been wanting to tell her ever since I have come to know what her love might make of me. The fact that I can't do it is the bitterest thing I have ever had to face, or can ever be made to face."

Colonel Baldwin fell back into his swing-chair and thrust his hands into his pockets.

"It beats the Dutch how things tangle themselves up for us poor mortals every little so-while," he commented, after a frowning pause. And then: "You haven't said anything like that to Corry, have you?"

"No."

"That was white, anyway. And now I suppose the other woman—this Miss Rich-some-thing-or-other over at the hotel—has come and dug you up and got you on the end of her trail-rope. That's the way it goes when a man mixes and mingles too much. You never can tell—"

"Hold on," Smith interposed. "Whatever else I may be, I'm not that kind of a scoundrel. I don't owe Miss Richlander anything that I can't pay without doing injustice to the woman I love. But in another way I am a scoundrel, Colonel. For the past two days I have been contemptible enough to play upon a woman's vanity merely for the sake of keeping her from talking too much."

The grizzled old ranchman shook his head sorrowfully.

"I didn't think that of you, John; I sure didn't. Why, that's what you might call a low-down, tin-horn sort of a game."

"It is just that, and I know it as well as you do. But it's the price I have to pay for my few days of grace. Miss Richlander knows the Stantons; they've made it their business to get acquainted with her. One word from her to Crawford Stanton, and a wire from him to my home town in the Middle West would settle me."

The older man straightened himself in his chair, and his steel-gray eyes blazed suddenly.

"Break away from 'em, John!" he urged. "Break it off short, and let 'em all do their damnedest! Away along at the first, Williams and I both said you wasn't a crooked crook, and I'm believing it yet. When it comes to the show-down, we'll all fight for you, and they'll have to bring a derrick along if they want to snatch you out of the Timanyoni. You go over yonder to the Hophra House and tell that young woman that the bridle's off, and she can talk all she wants to!"

"No," said Smith shortly. "I know what I am doing, and I shall go on as I have begun. It's the only way. Matters are desperate enough with us now, and if I should drop out——"

The telephone-bell was ringing, and Baldwin twisted his chair to bring himself within reach of the desk set. The message was a brief one and at its finish the ranchman-president was frowning heavily.

"By Jupiter! it does seem as if the bad luck all comes in a bunch!" he protested. "Williams was rushing things just a little too fast, and they've lost a whole section of the dam by stripping the forms before the concrete was set. That puts us back another twenty-four hours, at least. Don't that beat the mischief?"

Smith reached for his hat. "It's six o'clock," he said; "and

Williams's form-strippers have furnished one more reason why I shouldn't keep Miss Richlander waiting for her dinner." And with that he cut the talk short and went his way.

Brewster being only a one-night stand on the long playing circuit between Denver and the Pacific coast, there was an open date at the opera-house, and with a blank evening before her, the Olympian beauty, making the tête-à-tête dinner count for what it would, tightened her hold upon the one man available, demanding excitement. Nothing else offering, she suggested an evening auto drive, and Smith dutifully telephoned Maxwell, the railroad superintendent, and borrowed a runabout.

Being left to his own choice of routes after the start was made, he headed the machine up the river road, and the drive paused at the dam. Craving a new sensation, Miss Richlander had it in full measure when the machine had been braked to a stop at the construction camp. Williams, hoarse from much shouting and haggard-eyed for want of sleep, was driving his men fiercely in a fight against time. The night rise in the river had already set in, and the slumped section of concrete had left a broad gap through which the water threatened to pour, endangering not only the power-house directly beneath it, but also the main structure of the dam itself.

The stagings were black with men hurrying back and forth under the glare of the electrics, and the concrete gangs were laboring frantically to clear the wreck made by the crumbling mass, to the end that the carpenters might bulkhead the gap with timbers and planks to hold back the rising flood. The mixers had stopped temporarily, but the machinery was held in readiness to go into action the moment the débris should be removed and the new forms locked into place. Every now and then one of Williams's assistants, a red-headed young fellow with a voice like a fog-horn, took readings of the climbing river level from a gauge in the slack water, calling out the figures in a singsong chant: "Nineteen six! Nineteen six and a quarter! Nineteen six and a half!"

"Get a move, you fellows there on the stage!" yelled Williams. "She's coming up faster than usual to-night! Double pay if you get that bulkhead in before the tide wets your feet!"

Smith felt as if he ought to get out of the car and help, but there was nothing he could do. Miss Richlander had been silent for the better part of the drive from town, but now she began to talk.

"So this is what you left Lawrenceville for, is it, Montague?" she said, knitting her perfect brows at the hubbub and strife. "If I were not here, I believe you would be down there, struggling with the rest of them."

"I certainly should," he answered briefly, adding: "not that I should be of much use."

"There are a good many easier ways of making money," she offered, including the entire industrial strife in the implied detraction.

"This is a man's way, asking for all—and the best—there is in a man," he asserted. "You can't understand, of course; you have eaten the bread of profits and discount and interest all your life. But here is something really creative. The world will be the richer for what is being done here; more mouths can be filled and more backs clothed. That is the true test of wealth, and the only test."

"And you are willing to live in a raw wilderness for the sake of having a part in these crudities?"

"I may say that I had no choice, at first; it was this or nothing. But I may also say that whatever the future may do to me, I shall always have it to remember that for a little time I was a man, and not a tailor's model."

"Is that the way you are thinking now of your former life?" she gibed.

"It is the truth. The man you knew in Lawrenceville cared more for the set of a coat, for the color of a tie, for conventional ease and the little luxuries, than he did for his soul. And nobody thought enough of him to kick him alive and show him that he was strangling the only part of him that was at all worth saving."

"If your point of view appeals to me, as perhaps it does—as possibly it would to any woman who can appreciate masculinity in a man, even though it be of the crudest—the life that is giving it to you certainly does not," she replied, with a little lip-curling of scorn. Then: "You couldn't bring your wife to such a place as Brewster, Montague."

He had no answer for this, and none was needed. Williams had caught sight of the auto, and he came up, wiping his face with a red handkerchief.

"I thought it must be you," he said to Smith. "Thank the Lord, we're going to escape, this one more time! The bulkhead's in, and we'll be dumping concrete in another fifteen minutes. But it was a narrow squeak—an awful narrow squeak!"

Smith turned to his companion, saw permission in her eyes, and introduced Williams. Somewhat to Smith's surprise, Miss Verda evinced a suddenly awakened interest in the engineer and in his work, making him tell the story of the near-disaster. While he was telling it, the roar of another auto rose above the clamor on the stagings and Colonel Baldwin's gray roadster drew up beside the borrowed runabout. Smith gave one glance at the small, trimly coated figure in the mechanician's seat and ground his teeth in helpless fury.

In what followed he had little part or lot. Miss Richlander wished to see the construction battle at shorter range, and Williams was opening the door of the runabout. The colonel was afoot and was helping his daughter to alight. Smith swore a silent oath to keep his place, and he did it; but Williams was already introducing Baldwin and Corona to Miss Richlander. There was a bit of commonplace talk, and then the quartet walked down the embankment and out upon the finished portion of the dam, Williams explaining the near-disaster as they went.

Smith sat back behind the pilot-wheel of the runabout and waited. Not for a king's ransom would he have joined the group on the dam. He suspected shrewdly that Verda had already heard of Corona through the Stantons; that she was inwardly rejoicing at the new hold upon him which chance had flung in her way. At the end of Williams's fifteen minutes the rattle and grind of the mixers began. When the stream of concrete came pouring through the high-tilted spouts, Smith looked to see the colonel and Williams bringing the two women back to the camp level. What the light of the masthead arcs showed him was the figure of one of the women returning alone, while the two men and the other woman went on across the stagings to the farther river bank where the battery of mixers fed the swiftly moving lift.

Smith did not get out to go and meet the returning figure; his courage was not of that quality. But he could not pretend to be either asleep or dead when Corona came up between the two cars and spoke to him.

"You have nothing whatever to take back," she said, smiling up at him from her seat on the running-board of the roadster. "She is all you said she was—and more. She is gorgeously beautiful!"

Smith flung his freshly lighted cigar away and climbed out to sit beside her.

"What do you think of me?" he demanded bluntly.

"What should I think? Didn't I scold you for running away from her that first evening? I am glad you thought better of it afterward."

"I am not thinking better of it at all—in the way you mean."

"But Miss Richlander is," was the quiet reply.

"You have a right to say anything you please; and after it is all said, to say it again. I am not the man you have been taking me for; not in any respect. Your father knows now, and he will tell you."

"Colonel-daddy has told me one thing—the thing you told him to tell me. And I am sorry—sorry and disappointed."

He smiled morosely. "Billy Starbuck calls the Timanyoni a half-reformed gun-country, and from the very first he has been urging me to 'go heeled,' as he phrases it."

"It isn't the mere carrying of a gun," she protested. "With most men that would be only a prudent precaution for the leader in a fight like this one you are making. But it means more than that to you; it means a complete change of attitude toward your kind. Tell me if I am wrong."

"No; you are right. The time is coming when I shall be obliged to kill somebody. And I think I shall rather welcome it."

"Now you have gone so far away that I can hardly see you," she said softly. "'Once in a blue moon,' you said, the impossible might happen. It did happen in your case, didn't it?—giving you a chance to grow and expand and to break with all the old traditions, whatever they were. And the break left you free to make of yourself what you should choose. You have all the abilities; you can reach out and take what other men have to beg for. Once you thought you would take only the best, and then you grew so fast that we could hardly keep you in sight. But now you are meaning to take the worst."

"I don't understand," he said soberly.

"You will understand some day," she asserted, matching his sober tone. "When that time comes, you will know that the only great men are those who love their fellow men; who are too big to be little; who can fight without hatred; who can die, if need be, that others may live."

"My God!" said the man, and though he said it under his breath there was, pent up in the two words, the cry of a soul in travail; a soul to whom its own powers have suddenly been revealed, together with its lost opportunities and its crushing inability to rise to the heights supernal.

"It came too soon—if I could only have had a little more time," he was saying; but at that, the colonel and Williams came up, bringing Miss Richlander, and the heart-mellowing moment was gone.

Smith drove the borrowed runabout back to town in sober silence, and the glorious beauty in the seat beside him did not try to make him talk. Perhaps she, too, was busy with thoughts of her own. At all events, when Smith had helped her out of the car at the hotel entrance and had seen her as far as the elevator, she thanked him half absently and took his excuse, that he must return the runabout to Maxwell's garage, without laying any further commands upon him.

Just as he was turning away, a bell-boy came across from the clerk's desk with a telegram for Miss Richlander. Smith had no excuse for lingering, but with the air thick with threats he made the tipping of the boy answer for a momentary stop-gap. Miss Verda tore the envelope open and read the enclosure with a fine-lined little frown coming and going between her eyes.

"It's from Tucker Jibbey," she said, glancing up at Smith. "Some one has told him where we are, and he is following us. He says he'll be here on the evening train. Will you meet him and tell him I've gone to bed?"

At the mention of Jibbey, the money-spoiled son of the man who stood next to Josiah Richlander in the credit ratings, and Lawrenceville's best imitation of a flâneur, Smith's first emotion was one of relief at the thought that Jibbey would at least divide time with him in the entertainment of the bored beauty; then he remembered that Jibbey had once considered him a rival, and that the sham "rounder's" presence in Brewster would constitute a menace more threatening than all the others put together.

"I can't meet Tucker," he said bluntly. "You know very well I can't."

"That's so," was the quiet reply. "Of course, you can't. What will you do when he comes?—run away?"

"No; I can't do that, either. I shall keep out of his way, if I can. If he finds me and makes any bad breaks, he'll get what's coming to him. If he's worth anything to you, you'll put him on the stage in the morning and send him up into the mountains to join your father."

"The idea!" she laughed. "He's not coming out here to see father. Poor Tucker! If he could only know what he is in for!" Then: "It is beginning to look as if you might have to go still deeper in debt to me, Montague. There is one more thing I'd like to do before I leave Brewster. If I'll promise to keep Tucker away from you, will you drive me out to the Baldwins' to-morrow afternoon? I want to see the colonel's fine horses, and he has invited me, you know."

Smith's eyes darkened.

"There is a limit, Verda, and you've reached it," he said quickly. "If the colonel invited you to Hillcrest, it was because you didn't leave him any chance not to. I resign in favor of Jibbey," and with that he handed her into the waiting elevator and said: "Good night."

XX
Tucker Jibbey

Though it was a working man's bedtime when Smith put Miss Richlander into the elevator at the Hophra House and bade her good night, he knew that there would be no sleep for him until he had made sure of the arrival or non-arrival of the young man who, no less certainly than Josiah Richlander or Debritt, could slay him with a word. Returning the borrowed runabout to its garage, he went to the railroad station and learned that the "Flyer" from the East was over four hours late. With thirty minutes to spare, he walked the long train platform, chewing an extinct cigar and growing more and more desperate at each pacing turn.

With time to weigh and measure the probabilities, he saw what would come to pass. Verda Richlander might keep her own counsel, or she might not; but in any event, Stanton would be quick to identify Jibbey as a follower of Verda's, and so, by implication, a man who would be acquainted with Verda's intimates. Smith recalled Jibbey's varied weaknesses. If Verda should get hold of him first, and was still generous enough to warn him against Stanton, the blow might be delayed. But if Stanton should be quick enough, and cunning enough to play upon Jibbey's thirst, the liquor-loosened tongue would tell all that it knew.

In such a crisis the elemental need rises up to thrust all other promptings, ethical or merely prudent, into the background. Smith had been profoundly moved by Corona Baldwin's latest appeal to such survivals of truth and honor and fair-dealing as the strange metamorphosis and the culminating struggle against odds had left him. But in any new birth it is inevitable that the offspring of the man that was shall be at first—like all new-born beings—a pure savage, guided only by instinct. And of the instincts, that of self-preservation easily overtops all others.

Smith saw how suddenly the pit of disaster would yawn for him upon Jibbey's arrival, and the compunctions stirred by Corona's plea for the higher ideals withdrew or were crushed in the turmoil. He had set his hand to the plough and he would not turn back. It was Jibbey's effacement in some way, or his own, he told himself, for he had long since determined that he would never be taken alive to be dragged back to face certain conviction in the Lawrenceville courts and a living death in the home State penitentiary.

With this determination gripping him afresh, he glanced at his watch. In fifteen minutes more his fate would be decided. The station baggage and express handlers were beginning to trundle their loaded trucks out across the platform to be in readiness for the incoming train. There was still time enough, but none to spare. Smith passed through the station quickly and on the town side of the building took a cab. "Benkler's," was his curt order to the driver; and three minutes later he was telling the night man at the garage that he had come back to borrow Maxwell's runabout again, and urging haste in the refilling of the tanks.

The delayed "Flyer" was whistling in when Smith drove the runabout to the station, and he had barely time to back the machine into place in the cab rank and to hurry out to the platform before the train came clattering down over the yard switches. Since all the debarking passengers had to come through the archway exit from the track platform, Smith halted at a point from which he could pass them in review. The day-coach people came first, and after them a smaller contingent from the sleepers. At the tail of the straggling procession Smith saw his man, a thin-faced, hollow-eyed young fellow with an unlighted cigarette hanging from his loose lower lip. Smith marked all the little details: the rakish hat, the flaming-red tie, the russet-leather suitcase with its silver identification tag. Then he placed himself squarely in the young man's way.

Jibbey's stare was only momentary. With a broad-mouthed grin he dropped the suitcase and thrust out a hand.

"Well, well—Monty, old sport! So this is where you ducked to, is it? By Jove, it's no wonder Bart Macauley couldn't get a line on you! How are tricks, anyway?"

Smith was carefully refusing to see the out-stretched hand. And it asked for a sudden tightening of the muscles of self-possession to keep him from looking over his shoulder to see if any of Stanton's shadow men were at hand.

"Verda got your telegram, and she asked me to meet you," he rejoined crisply. "Also, to make her excuses for to-night: she has gone to bed."

"So that's the way the cat's jumping, is it?" said the imitation black sheep, the grin twisting itself into a leer. "She got a line on you, even if Macauley couldn't. By Gad! I guess I didn't get out here any too soon."

Smith ignored the half-jealous pleasantry. "Bring your grip," he directed. "I have an auto here and we'll drive."

Being a stranger in a strange city, Jibbey could not know that the hotel was only three squares distant. For the same cause he was entirely unsuspicious when Smith turned the car to the right out of the cab rank and took a street leading to the western suburb. But when the pavements had been left behind, together with all the town lights save an occasional arc-lamp at a crossing, and he was trying for the third time to hold a match to the hanging cigarette, enough ground had been covered to prompt a question.

"Hell of a place to call itself a city, if anybody should ask you," he chattered. "Much of this to worry through?"

Smith bent lower over the tiller-wheel, advancing the spark and opening the throttle for more gas.

"A good bit of it. Didn't you know that Mr. Richlander is out in the hills, buying a mine?"

Tucker Jibbey was rapid only in his attitude toward the world of decency; the rapidity did not extend to his mental processes. The suburb street had become a country road, the bridge over the torrenting Gloria had thundered under the flying wheels, and a great butte, black in its foresting from foot to summit, was rising slowly among the western stars before his small brain had grasped the relation of cause to effect.

"Say, here, Monty—dammit all, you hold on! Verda isn't with Old Moneybags; she's staying at the hotel in town. I wired and found out before I left Denver. Where in Sam Hill are you taking me to?"

Smith made no reply other than to open the cut-out and to put his foot on the accelerator. The small car leaped forward at racing speed and Jibbey clutched wildly at the wheel.

"Stop her—stop her!" he shrilled. "Lemme get out!"

Smith had one hand free and it went swiftly to his hip pocket. A second later Jibbey's shrilling protest died away in a gurgle of terror.

"For—for God's sake, Monty—don't kill me!" he gasped, when he saw the free hand clutching a weapon and uplifted as if to strike. "Wh—what've I done to you?"

"I'll tell you—a little later. Keep quiet and let this wheel alone, if you want to live long enough to find out where you're going. Quiet down, I say, or I'll beat your damned head off!—oh, you would, would you? All right—if you will have it!"

It lacked only a few minutes of midnight when Smith returned the borrowed runabout for the second time that night, sending it jerkily through the open door of Benkler's garage and swinging stiffly from behind the steering-wheel to thrust a bank-note into the hand of the waiting night man.

"Wash the car down good, and be sure it's all right before Mr.

Maxwell sends around in the morning," he commanded gruffly; and then: "Take your whisk and dust me off."

The night man had seen the figure of his tip and was nothing loath.

"Gosh!" he exclaimed, with large Western freedom; "you sure look as if you'd been drivin' a good ways, and tol'able hard. What's this on your sleeve? Say! it looks like blood!"

"No; it's mud," was the short reply; and after the liberal tipper had gone, the garage man was left to wonder where, on the dust-dry roads in the Timanyoni, the borrower of Mr. Maxwell's car had found mud deep enough to splash him, and, further, why there was no trace of the mud on the dust-covered car itself.

XXI
At Any Cost

Brewster, drawing its business profit chiefly from the mines in the Topaz and upper Gloria districts, had been only moderately enthusiastic over the original irrigation project organized by Colonel Dexter Baldwin and the group of ranchmen who were to be directly benefited. But when the scope of the plan was enlarged to include a new source of power and light for the city, the scheme had become, in a broader sense, a public utility, and Brewster had promptly awakened to the importance of its success as a local enterprise.

The inclusion of the hydro-electric privilege in the new charter had been a bit of far-sighted business craft on the part of the young man whose name was now in everybody's mouth. As he had pointed out to his new board of directors, there was an abundant excess of water, and a modest profit on the electric plant would pay the operating expenses of the entire system, including the irrigating upkeep and extension work. In addition to this, a reasonable contract price for electric current to be furnished to the city would give the project a quasi-public character, at least to the extent of enlisting public sympathy on the side of the company in the fight with the land trust.

This piece of business foresight found itself amply justified as the race against time was narrowed down to days and hours. Though there was spiteful opposition offered by one of the two daily newspapers—currently charged with being subsidized by the land trust—public sentiment as a whole, led by the other newspaper, was strongly on the side of the local corporation. Baldwin, Maxwell, Starbuck, and a few more of the leading spirits in Timanyoni High Line had many friends, and Crawford Stanton found his task growing increasingly difficult as the climax drew near.

But to a man with an iron jaw difficulties become merely incentives to greater effort. Being between the devil, in the person of an employer who knew no mercy, on the one hand, and the deep blue sea of failure on the other, the promoter left no expedient untried, and the one which was yielding the best results, thus far, was the steady undercurrent of detraction and calamitous rumor which he had contrived to set in motion. As we have seen, it was first whispered, and then openly asserted, that the dam was being built too hurriedly; that its foundations were insecure; that, sooner or later, it would be carried away in high water, and the city and the intervening country would be flood-swept and devastated.

Beyond this, the detractive gossip attacked the personnel of the new company. Baldwin was all right as a man, and he knew how to raise fine horses; but what did he, or any of his associates, know about building dams and installing hydro-electric plants? Williams, the chief engineer, was an ex-government man, and—government projects being anathema in the Timanyoni by reason of the restrictive rules and regulations of the Hophra Forest Reserve—everybody knew what that meant: out-of-date methods, red-tape detail, general inefficiency. And Smith, the young plunger who had dropped in from nobody knew where: what could be said of him more than that he had succeeded in temporarily hypnotizing an entire city? Who was he? and where had the colonel found him? Was his name really Smith, or was that only a convenient alias?

Having set these queries afoot in Brewster, Stanton was unwearied in keeping them alive and pressing them home. And since such askings grow by what they feed upon, the questions soon began to lose the interrogatory form and to become assertions of fact. Banker Kinzie was quoted as saying, or at least as intimating, that he had lost faith, not only in the High Line scheme, but particularly in its secretary and treasurer; and to this bit of gossip was added another to the effect that Smith had grossly deceived the bank by claiming to be the representative of Eastern capital when he was nothing more than an adventurer trading upon the credulity and good nature of an entire community.

To these calumniating charges it was admitted on all sides that Smith, himself, was giving some color of truth. To those who had opposed him he had shown no mercy, and there were plenty of defeated litigants, and some few dropped stockholders, among the obstructors to claim that the new High Line promoter was a bully and a browbeater; that a poor man stood no chance in a fight with the Timanyoni Company.

On the sentimental side the charges were still graver—in the Western point of view. In its social aspect Brewster was still in the country-village stage, and Smith's goings and comings at Hillcrest had been quickly marked. From that to assuming the sentimental status, with the colonel's daughter in the title rôle, was a step that had already been taken by the society editress of the Brewster Banner in a veiled hint of a forthcoming "announcement" in which "the charming daughter of one of our oldest and most respected families" and "a brilliant young business man from the East" were to figure as the parties in interest. Conceive, therefore, the shock that had been given to these kindlier gossips when Smith's visits to the Baldwin ranch ceased abruptly between two days, and the "brilliant young business man" was seen everywhere and always in the company of the beautiful stranger who was stopping at the Hophra House. In its palmier day the Timanyoni had hanged a man for less.

On the day following the hindering concrete failure at the dam, Smith gave still more color to the charges of his detractors in the business field. Those whose affairs brought them in contact with him found a man suddenly grown years older and harder, moody and harshly dictatorial, not to say quarrelsome; a man who seemed to have parted, in the short space of a single night, with all of the humanizing affabilities which he had shown to such a marked degree in the re-organizing and refinancing of the irrigation project.

"We've got our young Napoleon of finance on the toboggan-slide, at last," was the way in which Mr. Crawford Stanton phrased it for the bejewelled lady at their luncheon in the Hophra café. "Kinzie is about to throw him over, and all this talk about botch work on the dam is getting his goat. They're telling it around town this morning that you can't get near him without risking a fight. Old Man Backus went up to his office in behalf of a bunch of the scared stockholders, and Smith abused him first and then threw him out bodily—hurt him pretty savagely, they say."

The large lady's accurately pencilled eyebrows went up in mild surprise.

"Bad temper?" she queried.

"Bad temper, or an acute attack of 'rattle-itis'; you can take your choice. I suppose he hasn't, by any chance, quarrelled with Miss Richlander overnight?—or has he?"

The fat lady shook her diamonds. "I should say not. They were at luncheon together in the ladies' ordinary as I came down a few minutes ago."

Thus the partner of Crawford Stanton's joys and sorrows. But an invisible onlooker in the small dining-room above-stairs might have drawn other conclusions. Smith and the daughter of the Lawrenceville magnate had a small table to themselves, and if the talk were not precisely quarrelsome, it leaned that way at times.

"I have never seen you quite so brutal and impossible as you are to-day, Montague. You don't seem like the same man. Was it something the little ranch girl said to you last night when she calmly walked away from us and went back to you at the autos?"

"No; she said nothing that she hadn't a perfect right to say."

"But it, or something else, has changed you—very much for the worse. Are you going to reconsider and take me out to the Baldwin ranch this afternoon?"

"And let you parade me there as your latest acquisition?—never in this world!"

"More of the brutality. Positively, you are getting me into a frame of mind in which Tucker Jibbey will seem like a blessed relief. Whatever do you suppose has become of Tucker?"

"How should I know?"

"If he had come in last night, and you had met him—as I asked you to—in any such heavenly temper as you are indulging now, I might think you had murdered him."

It was doubtless by sheer accident that Smith, reaching at the moment for the salad-oil, overturned his water-glass. But the small accident by no means accounted for the sudden graying of his face under the Timanyoni wind tan—for that or for the shaking hands with which he seconded the waiter's anxious efforts to repair the damage. When they were alone again, the momentary trepidation had given place to a renewed hardness that lent a biting rasp to his voice.

"Kinzie, the suspicious old banker that I've been telling you about, is determined to run me down," he said, changing the subject abruptly. "I've got it pretty straight that he is planning to send one of his clerks to the Topaz district to try and find your father."

"In the hope that father will tell what he knows about you?"

"Just that."

"Does this Mr. Kinzie know where father is to be found?"

"He doesn't; that's the only hitch."

Miss Verda's smile across the little table was level-eyed.

"I could be lots of help to you, Montague, in this fight you are making, if you'd only let me," she suggested. "For example, I might tell you that Mr. Stanton has exhausted his entire stock of ingenuity in trying to make me tell him where father has gone."

"I'll fight for my own hand," was the grating rejoinder. "I can assure you, right now, that Kinzie's messenger will never reach your father—alive."

"Ooh!" shuddered the beauty, with a little lift of the rounded shoulders. "How utterly and hopelessly primitive! Let me show you a much simpler and humaner alternative. Contrive to get word to Mr. Kinzie in some way that he might send his messenger direct to me. Can you do that?"

"You mean that you'd send the clerk on a wild-goose chase?"

"If you insist on putting it in the baldest possible form," said the young woman, with a low laugh. "I have a map of the mining district, you know. Father left it with me—in case I should want to communicate with him."

Smith looked up with a smile which was a mere baring of the teeth.

"You wouldn't get in a man's way with any fine-spun theories of the ultimate right and wrong, would you? You wouldn't say that the only great man is the man who loves his fellow men, and all that?"

Again the handsome shoulders were lifted, this time in cool scorn.

"Are you quoting the little ranch person?" she inquired. Then she answered his query: "The only great men worth speaking of are the men who win. For the lack of something better to do, I'm willing to help you win, Montague. Contrive in some way to have that clerk sent to me. It can come about quite casually if it is properly suggested. Most naturally, I am the one who would know where my father is to be found. And I have changed my mind about wanting to drive to the Baldwins'. We'll compromise on the play—if there is a play."

Two things came of this talk over the luncheon table. Smith went back to his office and shut himself up, without going near the Brewster City National. None the less, the expedient suggested by Verda Richlander must have found its means of communication in some way, since at two o'clock David Kinzie summoned the confidential clerk who had been directed to provide himself with a livery mount and gave him his instructions.

"I'm turning this over to you, Hoback, because you know enough to keep a still tongue in your head. Mr. Stanton doesn't know where Mr. Richlander is, but Mr. Richlander's daughter does know. Go over to the hotel and introduce yourself as coming from me. Say to the daughter that it is necessary for us to communicate with her father on a matter of important business, and ask her if she can direct you. That's all; only don't mention Stanton in the matter. Come back and report after you've seen her."

This was one of the results of the luncheon-table talk; and the other came a short half-hour further along, when the confidential clerk returned to make his report.

"I don't know why Miss Richlander wouldn't tell Mr. Stanton," he said. "She was mighty nice to me; made me a pencil sketch of the Topaz country and marked the mines that her father is examining."

"Good!" said David Kinzie, with his stubbly mustache at its most aggressive angle. "It's pretty late in the day, but you'd better make a start and get as far as you can before dark. When you find Mr. Richlander, handle him gently. Tell him who you are, and then ask him if he knows anything about a man named 'Montague,' or 'Montague Smith'; ask him who he is, and where he comes from. If you get that far with him, he'll probably tell you the rest of it."

Smith saw no more of Miss Richlander until eight o'clock in the evening, at which time he sent his card to her room and waited for her in the mezzanine parlors. When she came down to him, radiant in fine raiment, he seemed not to see the bedeckings or the beauty which they adorned.

"There is a play, and I have the seats," he announced briefly.

"Merci!" she flung back. "Small favors thankfully received, and larger ones in proportion; though it's hardly a favor, this time, because I have paid for it in advance. Mr. Kinzie's young man came to see me this afternoon."

"What did you do?"

"I gave him a tracing of my map, and he was so grateful that it made me want to tell him that it was all wrong; that he wouldn't find father in a month if he followed the directions."

"But you didn't!"

"No; I can play the game, when it seems worth while."

Smith was frowning thoughtfully when he led her to the elevator alcove.

"My way would have been the surer," he muttered, half to himself.

"Barbarian!" she laughed; and then: "To think that you were once a 'débutantes' darling'! Oh, yes; I know it was Carter Westfall who said it first, but it was true enough to name you instantly for all Lawrenceville."

Smith made no comment, and Miss Richlander did not speak

again until they were waiting in the women's lobby for the house porter to call a cab. Then, as if she had just remembered it:

"Oh! I forgot to ask you: is the Eastern train in?"

He nodded. "It was on time this evening—for a wonder."

"And no Tucker yet! What in the world do you suppose could have happened to him, Montague?"

The porter was announcing the theatre cab and Smith reserved his answer until the motor hackney was rolling jerkily away toward the opera-house.

"Jibbey has probably got what was coming to him," he said grittingly. "I don't know whether you have ever remarked it or not, but the insect of the Jibbey breed usually finds somebody to come along and step on it, sooner or later."

XXII
The Megalomaniac

On a day which was only sixty-odd hours short of the expiration of the time limit fixed by the charter conditions under which the original Timanyoni Ditch Company had obtained its franchise, Bartley Williams, lean and sombre-eyed from the strain he had been under for many days and nights, saw the president's gray roadster ploughing its way through the mesa sand on the approach to the construction camp, and was glad.

"I've been trying all the morning to squeeze out time to get into town," he told Baldwin, when the roadster came to a stand in front of the shack commissary. "Where is Smith?"

The colonel threw up his hand in a gesture expressive of complete detachment.

"Don't ask me. John has gone plumb loco in these last two or three days. It's as much as your life's worth to ask him where he has been or where he is going or what he means to do next."

"He hasn't stopped fighting?" said the engineer, half aghast at the bare possibility.

"Oh, no; he's at it harder than ever—going it just a shaving too strong, is what I'd tell him, if he'd let me get near enough to shout at him. Last night, after the theatre, he went around to the Herald office, and the way they're talking it on the street, he was aiming to shoot up the whole newspaper joint if Mark Allen, the editor, wouldn't take back a bunch of the lies he's been publishing about the High Line. It wound up in a scrap of some sort. I don't know who got the worst of it, but John isn't crippled up any, to speak of, this morning—only in his temper."

"Smith puzzles me more than a little," was Williams's comment. "It's just as you say; for the last few days he's been acting as if he had a grouch a mile long. Is it the old sore threatening to break out again?—the 'lame duck' business?"

"I shouldn't wonder," said the colonel evasively. Loyal to the last, he was not quite ready to share with Williams the half-confidence in which Smith had admitted, by implication at least, that the waiting young woman at the Hophra House held his future between her thumb and finger.

Williams shook his head. "I guess we'll have to stand for the grouch, if he'll only keep busy. He has the hot end of it, trying to stop the stampede among the stockholders, and hold up the money pinch, and keep Stanton from springing any new razzle on us. We couldn't very well get along without him, right now, Colonel. With all due respect to you and the members of the board, he is the fighting backbone of the whole outfit."

"He is that," was Baldwin's ready admission. "He is just what we've been calling him from the first, Bartley—a three-ply, dyed-in-the-wool wonder in his specialty. Stanton hasn't been able to make a single move yet that Smith hasn't foreseen and discounted. He is fighting now like a man in the last ditch, and I believe he thinks he is in the last ditch. The one time lately when I have had anything like a straight talk with him, he hinted at that and gave me to understand that he'd be willing to quit and take his medicine if he could hold on until Timanyoni High Line wins out."

"That will be only two days more," said the engineer, saying it as one who has been counting the days in keen anxiety. And then: "Stillings told me yesterday that we're not going to get an extension of the time limit from the State authorities."

"No; that little fire went out, blink, just as Smith said it would. Stanton's backers have the political pull—in the State, as well as in Washington. They're going to hold us to the letter of the law."

"Let 'em do it. We'll win out yet—if we don't run up against one or both of the only two things I'm afraid of now: high water, or the railroad call down."

"The water is pushing you pretty hard?"

"It's touch and go every night now. A warm rain in the mountains—well, I won't say that it would tear us up, because I don't believe it would, or could; but it would delay us, world without end."

"And the railroad grab? Have you heard anything more about that?"

"That is what I was trying to get to town for; to talk the railroad business over with you and Stillings and Smith. They've had a gang here this morning; a bunch of engineers, with a stranger, who gave his name as Hallowell, in charge. They claimed to be verifying the old survey, and Hallowell notified me formally that our dam stood squarely in their right of way for a bridge crossing of the river."

"They didn't serve any papers on you, did they?" inquired the colonel anxiously.

"No; the notice was verbal. But Hallowell wound up with a threat. He said, 'You've had due warning, legally and otherwise, Mr. Williams. This is our right of way, bought and paid for, as we can prove when the matter gets into the courts. You mustn't be surprised if we take whatever steps may be necessary to recover what belongs to us.'"

"Force?" queried the Missourian, with a glint of the border-fighter's fire in his eyes.

"Maybe. But we're ready for that. Did you know that Smith loaded half a dozen cases of Winchesters on a motor-truck yesterday, and had them sent out here?"

"No!"

"He did—and told me to say nothing about it. It seems that he ordered them some time ago from an arms agency in Denver. That fellow foresees everything, Colonel."

Dexter Baldwin had climbed into his car and was making ready to turn it for the run back to town.

"If I were you, Bartley, I believe I'd open up those gun boxes and pass the word among as many of the men as you think you can trust with rifles in their hands. I'll tell Smith—and Bob Stillings."

Colonel Baldwin made half of his promise good, the half relating to the company's attorney, as soon as he reached Brewster. But the other half had to remain in abeyance. Smith was not in his office, and no one seemed to know where he had gone. The colonel shrewdly suspected that Miss Richlander was making another draft upon the secretary's time, and he said as much to Starbuck, later in the day, when the mine owner sauntered into the High Line headquarters and proceeded to roll the inevitable cigarette.

"Not any, this time, Colonel," was Starbuck's rebuttal. "You've missed it by a whole row of apple-trees. Miss Rich-dollars is over at the hotel. I saw her at luncheon with the Stantons less than an hour ago."

"You haven't seen Smith, have you?"

"No; but I know where he is. He's out in the country, somewhere, taking the air in Dick Maxwell's runabout. I wanted to borrow the wagon myself, and Dick told me he had already lent it to Smith."

"We're needing him," said the colonel shortly, and then he told Starbuck of the newest development in the paper-railroad scheme of obstruction.

From that the talk drifted to a discussion of Kinzie's latest attitude. By this time there had been an alarming number of stock sales by small holders, all of them handled by the Brewster City National, and it was plainly evident that Kinzie had finally gone over to the enemy and was buying—as cheaply as possible—for some unnamed customer. This had been Stanton's earliest expedient; to "bear" the stock and to buy up the control; and he was apparently trying it again.

"If they keep it up, they can wear us out by littles, and we'll break our necks finishing the dam and saving the franchise only to turn it over to them in the round-up," said the colonel dejectedly. "I've talked until I'm hoarse, but you can't talk marrow into an empty bone, Billy. I used to think we had a fairly good bunch of men in with us, but in these last few days I've been changing my mind at a fox-trot. These hedgers'll promise you anything on top of earth to your face, and then go straight back on you the minute you're out of sight."

The remainder of the day, up to the time when the offices were closing and the colonel was making ready to go home, passed without incident. In Smith's continued absence, Starbuck had offered to go to the dam to stand a night-watch with Williams against a possible surprise by the right-of-way claimants; and Stillings, who had been petitioning for an injunction, came up to report progress just as Baldwin was locking his desk.

"The judge has taken it under advisement, but that is as far as he would go to-day," said the lawyer. "It's simply a bald steal, of course, and unless they ring in crooked evidence on us, we can show it up in court. But that would mean more delay, and delay is the one thing we can't stand. I'm sworn to uphold the law, and I can't counsel armed resistance. Just the same, I hope Williams has his nerve with him."

"He has; and I haven't lost mine, yet," snapped a voice at the door; and Smith came in, dust-covered and swarthy with the grime of the wind-swept grass-lands. Out of the pocket of his driving coat he drew a thick packet of papers and slapped it upon the drawn-down curtain of Baldwin's desk. "There you are," he went on gratingly. "Now you can tell Mr. David Kinzie to go straight to hell with his stock-pinching, and the more money he puts into it, the more somebody's going to lose!"

"My Lord, John!—what have you done?" demanded Baldwin.

"I've shown 'em what it means to go up against a winner!" was the half-triumphant, half-savage exultation. "I have put a crimp in that fence-climbing banker of yours that will last him for one while! I've secured thirty-day options, at par, on enough High Line stock to swing a clear majority if Kinzie should buy up every other share there is outstanding. It has taken me all day, and I've driven a thousand miles, but the thing is done."

"But, John! If anything should happen, and we'd have to make good on those options.... The Lord have mercy! It would break the last man of us!"

"We're not going to let things happen!" was the gritting rejoinder. "I've told you both a dozen times that I'm in this thing to win! You take care of those options, Stillings; they're worth a million dollars to somebody. Lock 'em up somewhere and then forget where they are. Now I'm going to hunt up Mr. Crawford Stanton—before I eat or sleep!"

"Easy, John; hold up a minute!" the colonel broke in soothingly; and Stillings, more practical, closed the office door silently and put his back against it. "This is a pretty sudden country, but there is some sort of a limit, you know," the big Missourian went on. "What's your idea in going to Stanton?"

"I mean to give him twelve hours in which to pack his trunk and get out of Brewster and the Timanyoni. If he hasn't disappeared by to-morrow morning——"

Stillings was signalling in dumb show to Baldwin. He had quietly opened the door and was crooking his finger and making signs over his shoulder toward the corridor. Baldwin saw what was wanted, and immediately shot his desk cover open and turned on the lights.

"That last lot of steel and cement vouchers was made out yesterday, John," he said, slipping the rubber band from a file of papers in the desk. "If you'll take time to sit down here and run 'em over, and put your name on 'em, I'll hold Martin long enough to let him get the checks in to-night's mail. Those fellows in St. Louis act as if they are terribly scared they won't get their money quick enough, and I've been holding the papers for you all day. I'll be back after a little."

Smith dragged up the president's big swing-chair and planted himself in it, and an instant later he was lost to everything save the columns of figures on the vouchers. Stillings had let himself out, and when the colonel followed him, the lawyer cautiously closed the door of the private office, and edged Baldwin into the corridor.

"We've mighty near got a madman to deal with in there, Colonel," he whispered, when the two were out of ear-shot. "I was watching his eyes when he said that about Stanton, and they fairly blazed. I meant to tell you more about that racket last night in the Herald office; I heard the inside of it this afternoon from Murphey. Smith went in and held the whole outfit up with a gun, and Murphey says he beat Allen over the head with it. He's going to kill somebody, if we don't look out."

Baldwin was shaking his head dubiously.

"He's acting like a locoed thoroughbred that's gone outlaw," he said. "Do you reckon he's sure-enough crazy, Bob?"

"Only in the murder nerve. This deal with the options shows that he's all to the good on the business side. That was the smoothest trick that's been turned in any stage of this dodging fight with the big fellows. It simply knocks Kinzie's rat-gnawing game dead. If there were only somebody who could calm Smith down a little and bring him to reason—somebody near enough to him to dig down under his shell and get at the real man that used to be there when he first took hold with us——"

"A woman?" queried Baldwin, frowning disapproval in anticipation of what Stillings might be going to suggest.

"A woman for choice, of course. I was thinking of this young woman over at the Hophra House; the one he has been running around with so much during the past few days. She is evidently an old flame of his, and anybody can see with half an eye that she has a pretty good grip on him. Suppose we go across the street and give her an invitation to come and do a little missionary work on Smith. She looks level-headed and sensible enough to take it the way it's meant."

It is quite possible that the colonel's heart-felt relief at Stillings's suggestion of Miss Richlander instead of another woman went some little distance toward turning the scale for the transplanted Missourian. Stillings was a lawyer and had no scruples, but the colonel had them in just proportion to his Southern birth and breeding.

"I don't like to drag a woman into it, any way or shape, Bob," he protested; and he would have gone on to say that he had good reason to believe that Miss Richlander's influence over Smith might not be at all of the meliorating sort, but Stillings cut him short.

"There need be no 'dragging.' The young woman doubtless knows the business situation as well as we do—he has probably told her all about it—and if she cares half as much for Smith as she seems to, she'll be glad to chip in and help to cool him down. We can be perfectly plain and outspoken with her, I'm sure; she evidently knows Smith a whole lot better than we do. It's a chance, and we'd better try it. He's good for half an hour or so with those vouchers."

Two minutes later, Colonel Dexter Baldwin, with Stillings at his elbow, was at the clerk's desk in the Hophra House sending a card up to Miss Richlander's rooms. Five minutes beyond that, the boy came back to say that Miss Richlander was out auto-driving with Mr. and Mrs. Stanton. The clerk, knowing Baldwin well, eyebrowed his regret and suggested a wait of a few minutes.

"They'll certainly be in before long," he said. "Mrs. Stanton has never been known to miss the dinner hour since she came to us. She is as punctual as the clock."

Baldwin, still ill at ease and reluctant, led the way to a pair of chairs in the writing alcove of the lobby; two chairs commanding a clear view of the street entrance. Sitting down to wait with what patience they could summon, neither of the two men saw a gray automobile, driven by a young woman, come to a stand before the entrance of the Kinzie Building on the opposite side of the street. And, missing this, they missed equally the sight of the young woman alighting from the machine and disappearing through the swinging doors opening into the bank building's elevator lobby.

XXIII
The Arrow to the Mark

Smith, concentrating abstractedly, as his habit was, upon the work in hand, was still deep in the voucher-auditing when the office door was opened and a small shocked voice said: "Oh, wooh! how you startled me! I saw the light, and I supposed, of course, it was Colonel-daddy. Where is he?"

Smith pushed the papers aside and looked up scowling.

"Your father? He was here a minute ago, with Stillings. Isn't he out in the main office?"

"No, there is no one there."

"Martin is there," he said, contradicting her bluntly. And then: "Your father said he'd be back. You've come to take him home?"

She nodded and came to sit in a chair at the desk-end, saying: "Don't let me interrupt you, please. I'll be quiet."

"I don't mean to let anything interrupt me until I have finished what I have undertaken to do; I'm past all that, now."

"So you told me two evenings ago," she reminded him gently, adding: "And I have heard about what you did last night."

"About the newspaper fracas? You don't approve of anything like that, of course. Neither did I, once. But you were right in what you said the other evening out at the dam; there is no middle way. You know what the animal tamers tell us about the beasts. I've had my taste of blood. There are a good many men in this world who need killing. Crawford Stanton is one of them, and I'm not sure that Mr. David Kinzie isn't another."

"I can't hear what you say when you talk like that," she objected, looking past him with the gray eyes veiled.

"Do you want me to lie down and let them put the steam-roller over me?" he demanded irritably. "Is that your ideal of the perfect man?"

"I didn't say any such thing as that, did I?"

"Perhaps not, in so many words. But you meant it."

"What I said, and what I meant, had nothing at all to do with Timanyoni High Line and its fight for life," she said calmly, recalling the wandering gaze and letting him see her eyes. "I was thinking altogether of one man's attitude toward his world."

"That was night before last," he put in soberly. "I've gone a long way since night before last, Corona."

"I know you have. Why doesn't daddy come back?"

"He'll come soon enough. You're not afraid to be here alone with me, are you?"

"No; but anybody might be afraid of the man you are going to be."

His laugh was as mirthless as the creaking of a rusty door-hinge.

"You needn't put it in the future tense. I have already broken with whatever traditions there were left to break with. Last night I threatened to kill Allen, and, perhaps, I should have done it if he hadn't begged like a dog and dragged his wife and children into it."

"I know," she acquiesced, and again she was looking past him.

"And that isn't all. Yesterday, Kinzie set a trap for me and baited it with one of his clerks. For a little while it seemed as if the only way to spring the trap was for me to go after the clerk and put a bullet through him. It wasn't necessary, as it turned out, but if it had been——"

"Oh, you couldn't!" she broke in quickly. "I can't believe that of you!"

"You think I couldn't? Let me tell you of a thing that I have done. Night before last, in less than an hour after you sat and talked with me at the dam, Verda Richlander had a wire from a young fellow who wants to marry her. He had found out that she was here in Brewster, and the wire was to tell her that he was coming in that night on the delayed 'Flyer.' She asked me to meet him and tell him she had gone to bed. He is a miserable little wretch; a sort of sham reprobate; and she has never cared for him, except to keep him dangling with a lot of others. I told her I wouldn't meet him, and she knew very well that I couldn't meet him—and stay out of jail. Are you listening?"

"I'm trying to."

"It was the pinch, and I wasn't big enough—in your sense of the word—to meet it. I saw what would happen. If Tucker Jibbey came here, Stanton would pounce upon him at once; and Jibbey, with a drink or two under his belt, would tell all he knew. I fought it all out while I was waiting for the train. It was Jibbey's effacement, or the end of the world for me, and for Timanyoni High Line."

Dexter Baldwin's daughter was not of those who shriek and faint at the apparition of horror. But the gray eyes were dilating and her breath was coming in little gasps when she said:

"I can't believe it! You are not going to tell me that you met this man as a friend, and then——"

"No; it didn't quite come to a murder in cold blood, though I thought it might. I had Maxwell's runabout, and I got Jibbey into it. He thought I was going to drive him to the hotel. After we got out of town he grew suspicious, and there was a struggle in the auto. I—I had to beat him over the head to make him keep quiet; I thought for the moment that I had killed him, and I knew, then, just how far I had gone on the road I've been travelling ever since a certain night in the middle of last May. The proof was in the way I felt; I wasn't either sorry or horror-stricken; I was merely relieved to think that he wouldn't trouble me, or clutter up the world with his worthless presence any longer."

"But that wasn't your real self!" she expostulated.

"What was it, then?"

"I don't know—I only know that it wasn't you. But tell me: did he die?"

"No."

"What have you done with him?"

"Do you know the old abandoned Wire-Silver mine at Little Butte?"

"I knew it before it was abandoned, yes."

"I was out there one Sunday afternoon with Starbuck. The mine is bulkheaded and locked, but one of the keys on my ring fitted the lock, and Starbuck and I went in and stumbled around for a while in the dark tunnels. I took Jibbey there and locked him up. He's there now."

"Alone in that horrible place—and without food?"

"Alone, yes; but I went out yesterday and put a basket of food where he could get it."

"What are you going to do with him?"

"I am going to leave him there until after I have put Stanton and Kinzie and the other buccaneers safely out of business. When that is done, he can go; and I'll go, too."

She had risen, and at the summing-up she turned from him and went aside to the one window to stand for a long minute gazing down into the electric-lighted street. When she came back her lips were pressed together and she was very pale.

"When I was in school, our old psychology professor used to try to tell us about the underman; the brute that lies dormant inside of us and is kept down only by reason and the super-man. I never believed it was anything more than a fine-spun theory—until now. But now I know it is true."

He spread his hands.

"I can't help it, can I?"

"The man that you are now can't help it; no. But the man that you could be—if he would only come back—" she stopped with a little uncontrollable shudder and sat down again, covering her face with her hands.

"I'm going to turn Jibbey loose—after I'm through," he vouchsafed.

She took her hands away and blazed up at him suddenly, with her face aflame.

"Yes! after you are safe; after there is no longer any risk in it for you! That is worse than if you had killed him—worse for you, I mean. Oh, can't you see? It's the very depth of cowardly infamy!"

He smiled sourly. "You think I'm a coward? They've been calling me everything else but that in the past few days."

"You are a coward!" she flashed back. "You have proved it. You daren't go out to Little Butte to-night and get that man and bring him to Brewster while there is yet time for him to do whatever it is that you are afraid he will do!"

Was it the quintessence of feminine subtlety, or only honest rage and indignation, that told her how to aim the armor-piercing arrow? God, who alone knows the secret workings of the woman heart and brain, can tell. But the arrow sped true and found its mark. Smith got up stiffly out of the big swing-chair and stood glooming down at her.

"You think I did it for myself?—just to save my own worthless hide? I'll show you; show you all the things that you say are now impossible. Did you bring the gray roadster?"

She nodded briefly.

"Your father is coming back; I hear the elevator-bell. I am going to take the car, and I don't want to meet him. Will you say what is needful?"

She nodded again, and he went out quickly. It was only a few steps down the corridor to the elevator landing, and the stair circled the caged elevator-shaft to the ground floor. Smith halted in the darkened corner of the stairway long enough to make sure that the colonel, with Stillings and a woman in an automobile coat and veil—a woman who figured for him in the passing glance as Corona's mother—got off at the office floor. Then he ran down to the street level, cranked the gray roadster and sprang in to send the car rocketing westward.

XXIV
A Little Leaven

The final touch of sunset pink had long since faded from the high western sky-line, and the summer-night stars served only to make the darkness visible along the road which had once been the stage route down the Timanyoni River and across to the mining-camp of Red Butte. Smith, slackening speed for the first time in the swift valley-crossing flight, twisted the gray roadster sharply to the left out of the road, and eased it across the railroad track to send it lurching and bumping over the rotting ties of an old branch-line spur from which the steel had been removed, and which ran in a course roughly paralleling the eastward-facing front of a forested mountain.

Four miles from the turn out of the main road, at a point on the spur right of way where a washed-out culvert made farther progress with the car impossible, he shut off the power and got down to continue his journey afoot. Following the line of the abandoned spur, he came, at the end of another mile, to the deserted shacks of the mining plant which the short branch railroad had been built to serve; a roofless power-house, empty ore platforms dry-rotting in disuse, windowless bunk shanties, and the long, low bulk of a log-built commissary. The mine workings were tunnel-driven in the mountainside, and a crooked ore track led out to them. Smith followed the ore track until he came to the bulkheaded entrance flanked by empty storage bins, and to the lock of a small door framed in the bulkheading he applied a key.

It was pitch dark beyond the door, and the silence was like that of the grave. Smith had brought a candle on his food-carrying visit of the day before, and, groping in its hiding-place just outside of the door, he found and lighted it, holding it sheltered in his cupped hand as he stepped into the black void beyond the bulkhead. With the feeble flame making little more than a dim yellow nimbus in the gloom, he looked about him. There was no sign of occupancy save Jibbey's suitcase lying where it had been flung on the night of the assisted disappearance. But of the man himself there was no trace.

Smith stumbled forward into the black depths and the chill of the place laid hold upon him and shook him like the premonitory shiver of an approaching ague. What if the darkness and solitude had been too much for Jibbey's untried fortitude and the poor wretch had crawled away into the dismal labyrinth to lose himself and die? The searcher stopped and listened. In some far-distant ramification of the mine he could hear the drip, drip, of underground water, but when he shouted there was no response save that made by the echoes moaning and whispering in the stoped-out caverns overhead.

Shielding the flickering candle again, Smith went on, pausing at each branching side-cutting to throw the light into the pockets of darkness. Insensibly he quickened his pace until he was hastening blindly through a maze of tunnels and cross driftings, deeper and still deeper into the bowels of the great mountain. Coming suddenly at the last into the chamber of the dripping water, he found what he was searching for, and again the ague chill shook him. There were no apparent signs of life in the sodden, muck-begrimed figure lying in a crumpled heap among the water pools.

"Jibbey!" he called: and then again, ignoring the unnerving, awe-inspiring echoes rustling like flying bats in the cavernous overspaces: "Jibbey!"

The sodden heap bestirred itself slowly and became a man sitting up to blink helplessly at the light and supporting himself on one hand.

"Is that you, Monty?" said a voice tremulous and broken; and then: "I can't see. The light blinds me. Have you come to fi-finish the job?"

"I have come to take you out of this; to take you back with me to Brewster. Get up and come on."

The victim of Smith's ruthlessness struggled stiffly to his feet. Never much more than a physical weakling, and with his natural strength wasted by a life of dissipation, the blow on the head with the pistol butt and the forty-eight hours of sharp hardship and privation had cut deeply into his scanty reserves.

"Did—did Verda send you to do it?" he queried.

"No; she doesn't know where you are. She thinks you stopped over somewhere on your way west. Come along, if you want to go back with me."

Jibbey stumbled away a step or two and flattened himself against the cavern wall. His eyes were still staring and his lips were drawn back to show his teeth.

"Hold on a minute," he jerked out. "You're not—not going to wipe it all out as easy as that. You've taken my gun away from me, but I've got my two hands yet. Stick that candle in a hole in the wall and look out for yourself. I'm telling you, right now, that one or the other of us is going to stay here—and stay dead!"

"Don't be a fool!" Smith broke in. "I didn't come here to scrap with you."

"You'd better—and you'd better make a job of it while you're about it!" shrieked the castaway, lost now to everything save the biting sense of his wrongs. "You've put it all over me—knocked my chances with Verda Richlander and shut me up here in this hellhole to go mad-dog crazy! If you let me get out of here alive I'll pay you back, if it's the last thing I ever do on top of God's green earth! You'll go back to Lawrenceville with the bracelets on! You'll—" red rage could go no farther in mere words and he flung himself in feeble fierceness upon Smith, clutching and struggling and waking the grewsome echoes again with frantic, meaningless maledictions.

Smith dropped the candle to defend himself, but he did not strike back; wrapping the madman in a pinioning grip, he held him helpless until the vengeful ecstasy had exhausted itself. When it was over, and Jibbey had been released, gasping and sobbing, to stagger back against the tunnel wall, Smith groped for the candle and found and relighted it.

"Tucker," he said gently, "you are more of a man than I took you to be—a good bit more. And you needn't break your heart because you can't handle a fellow who is perfectly fit, and who weighs half as much again as you do. Now that you're giving me a chance to say it, I can tell you that Verda Richlander doesn't figure in this at all. I'm not going to marry her, and she didn't come out here in the expectation of finding me."

"Then what does figure in it?" was the dry-lipped query.

"It was merely a matter of self-preservation. There are men in Brewster who would pay high for the information you might give them about me."

"You might have given me a hint and a chance, Monty. I'm not all dog!"

"That's all past and gone. I didn't give you your chance, but I'm going to give it to you now. Let's go—if you're fit to try it."

"Wait a minute. If you think, because you didn't pull your gun just now and drop me and leave me to rot in this hole, if you think that squares the deal——"

"I'm not making any conditions," Smith interposed. "There are a number of telegraph offices in Brewster, and for at least two days longer I shall always be within easy reach."

Jibbey's anger flared up once more.

"You think I won't do it? You think I'll be so danged glad to get to some place where they sell whiskey that I'll forget all about it and let you off? Don't you make any mistake, Monty Smith! You can't knock me on the head and lock me up as if I were a yellow dog. I'll fix you!"

Smith made no reply. Linking his free arm in Jibbey's, he led the way through the mazes, stopping at the tunnel mouth to blow out the candle and to pick up Jibbey's suitcase. In the open air the freed captive flung his arms abroad and drank in a deep breath of the clean, sweet, outdoor air. "God!" he gasped; "how good it is!" and after that he tramped in sober silence at Smith's heels until they reached the automobile.

It took some little careful manœuvring to get the roadster successfully turned on the railroad embankment, and Jibbey stood aside while Smith worked with the controls. Past this, he climbed into the spare seat, still without a word, and the rough four miles over the rotting cross-ties were soon left behind. At the crossing of the railroad main track and the turn into the highway, the river, bassooning deep-toned among its bowlders, was near at hand, and Jibbey spoke for the first time since they had left the mine mouth.

"I'm horribly thirsty, Monty. That water in the mine had copper or something in it, and I couldn't drink it. You didn't know that, did you?—when you put me in there, I mean? Won't you stop the car and let me go stick my face in that river?"

The car was brought to a stand and Jibbey got out to scramble down the river bank in the starlight. Obeying some inner prompting which he did not stop to analyze, Smith left his seat behind the wheel and walked over to the edge of the embankment where Jibbey had descended. The path to the river's margin was down the steep slope of a rock fill made in widening the highway to keep it clear of the railroad track. With the glare of the roadster's acetylenes turned the other way, Smith could see Jibbey at the foot of the slope lowering himself face downward on his propped arms to reach the water. Then, for a single instant, the murderous underman rose up and laughed. For in that instant, Jibbey, careless in his thirst, lost his balance and went headlong into the torrent.

A battling eon had passed before Smith, battered, beaten, and half-strangled, succeeded in landing the unconscious thirst-quencher on a shelving bank three hundred yards below the stopped automobile. After that there was another eon in which he completely forgot his own bruisings while he worked desperately over the drowned man, raising and lowering the limp arms while he strove to recall more of the resuscitative directions given in the Lawrenceville Athletic Club's first-aid drills.

In good time, after an interval so long that it seemed endless to the despairing first-aider, the breath came back into the reluctant lungs. Jibbey coughed, choked, gasped, and sat up. His teeth were chattering, and he was chilled to the bone by the sudden plunge into the cold snow water, but he was unmistakably alive.

"What—what happened to me, Monty?" he shuddered. "Did I lose my grip and tumble in?"

"You did, for a fact."

"And you went in after me?"

"Of course."

"No, by Gad! It wasn't 'of course'—not by a long shot! All you had to do was to let me go, and the score—your score—would have been wiped out for good and all. Why didn't you do it?"

"Because I should have lost my bet."

"Your bet?"

"Well, yes. It wasn't exactly a bet; but I promised somebody that I would bring you back to Brewster to-night, alive and well, and able to send a telegram. And if I had let you drown yourself, I should have lost out."

"You promised somebody?—not Verda?"

"No; somebody else."

Jibbey tried to get upon his feet, couldn't quite compass it, and sat down again.

"I don't believe a word of it," he mumbled, loose-lipped. "You did it because you're not so danged tough and hard-hearted as you thought you were." And then: "Give me a lift, Monty, and get me to the auto. I guess—I'm about—all in."

Smith half led, half carried his charge up to the road and then left him to go and back the car over the three hundred-odd yards of the interspace. A final heave lifted Jibbey into his place, and it is safe to say that Colonel Dexter Baldwin's roadster never made better time than it did on the race which finally brought the glow of the Brewster town lights reddening against the eastern sky.

At the hotel Smith helped his dripping passenger out of the car, made a quick rush with him to an elevator, and so up to his own rooms on the fourth floor.

"Strip!" he commanded; "get out of those wet rags and tumble into the bath. Make it as hot as you can stand it. I'll go down and register you and have your trunk sent up from the station. You have a trunk, haven't you?"

Jibbey fished a soaked card baggage-check out of his pocket and passed it over.

"You're as bad off as I am, Monty," he protested. "Wait and get some dry things on before you go."

"I'll be up again before you're out of the tub. I suppose you'd like to put yourself outside of a big drink of whiskey, just about now, but that's one thing I won't buy for you. How would a pot of hot coffee from the café strike you?"

"You could make it Mellin's Food and I'd drink it if you said so," chattered the drowned one from the inside of the wet undershirt he was trying to pull off over his head.

Smith did his various errands quickly. When he reached the fourth-floor suite again, Jibbey was out of the bath; was sitting on the edge of the bed wrapped in blankets, with the steaming pot of coffee sent up on Smith's hurry order beside him on a tray.

"It's your turn at the tub," he bubbled cheerfully. "I didn't have any glad rags to put on, so I swiped some of your bedclothes. Go to it, old man, before you catch cold."

Smith was already pointing for the bath. "Your trunk will be up in a few minutes, and I've told them to send it here," he said.

"When you want to quit me, you'll find your rooms five doors to the right in this same corridor: suite number four-sixteen."

It was a long half-hour before Smith emerged from his bathroom once more clothed and in his right mind. In the interval the reclaimed trunk had been sent up, and Jibbey was also clothed. He had found one of Smith's pipes and some tobacco and was smoking with the luxurious enjoyment of one who had suffered the pangs imposed by two days of total abstinence.

"Just hangin' around to say good night," he began, when Smith showed himself in the sitting-room. Then he returned the borrowed pipe to its place on the mantel and said his small say to the definite end. "After all that's happened to us two to-night, Monty, I hope you're going to forget my crazy yappings and not lose any sleep about that Lawrenceville business. I'm seventeen different kinds of a rotten failure; there's no manner of doubt about that; and once in a while—just once in a while—I've got sense enough to know it. You saved my life when it would have been all to the good for you to let me go. I guess the world wouldn't have been much of a loser if I had gone, and you knew that, too. Will you—er—would you shake hands with me, Monty?"

Smith did it, and lo! a miracle was wrought: in the nervous grasp of the joined hands a quickening thrill passed from man to man;, a thrill humanizing, redemptory, heart-mellowing. And, oddly enough, one would say, it was the weaker man who gave and the stronger who received.

XXV
The Pace-Setter

Smith made an early breakfast on the morning following the auto drive to the abandoned mine, hoping thereby to avoid meeting both Miss Richlander and Jibbey. The Hophra café was practically empty when he went in and took his accustomed place at one of the alcove tables, but he had barely given his order when Starbuck appeared and came to join him.

"You're looking a whole heap better this morning, John," said the mine owner quizzically, as he held up a finger for the waiter. "How's the grouch?"

Smith's answering grin had something of its former good nature in it. "To-day's the day, Billy," he said. "To-morrow at midnight we must have the water running in the ditches or lose our franchise. It's chasing around in the back part of my mind that Stanton will make his grand-stand play to-day. I'm not harboring any grouches on the edge of the battle. They are a handicap, anyway, and always."

"That's good medicine talk," said the older man, eying him keenly. And then: "You had us all guessing, yesterday and the day before, John. You sure was acting as if you'd gone plumb locoed."

"I was locoed," was the quiet admission.

"What cured you?"

"It's too long a story to tell over the breakfast-table. What do you hear from Williams?"

"All quiet during the night; but the weather reports are scaring him up a good bit this morning."

"Storms on the range?"

"Yes. The river gained four feet last night, and there is flood water and drift coming down to beat the band. Just the same, Bartley says he is going to make good."

Smith nodded. "Bartley is all right; the right man in the right place. Have you seen the colonel since he left the offices last evening?"

"Yes. I drove him and Corona out to the ranch in my new car. He said he'd lost his roadster; somebody had sneaked in and borrowed it."

"I suppose he told you about the latest move—our move—in the stock-selling game?"

"No, he didn't; but Stillings did. You played it pretty fine, John; only I hope to gracious we won't have to redeem those options. It would bu'st our little inside crowd wide open to have to buy in all that stock at par."

Smith laughed. "'Sufficient unto the day,' Billy. It was the only way to block Stanton. It's neck or nothing with him now, and he has only one more string that he can pull."

"The railroad right-of-way deal?"

"Yes; he has been holding that in reserve—that, and one other thing."

"What was the other thing?"

"Me," said Smith, cheerfully disregardful of his English. "You haven't forgotten his instructions to the man Lanterby, that night out at the road-house on the Topaz pike?—the talk that you overheard?"

"No; I haven't forgotten."

"His idea, then, was to have me killed off in a scrap of some sort—as a last resort, of course; but later on he found a safer expedient, and he has been trying his level best to work it ever since."

Starbuck was absently fishing for a second cube of sugar in the sugar-bowl. "Has it got anything to do with the bunch of news that you won't tell us—about yourself, John?"

"It has. Two days ago, Stanton had his finger fairly on the trigger, but a friend of mine stepped in and snapped the safety-catch. Last night, again, he stood to win out; to have the pry-hold he has been searching for handed to him on a silver platter, so to speak. But a man fell into the river, and Stanton lost out once more."

Starbuck glanced up soberly. "You're talking in riddles now, John. I don't sabe."

"It isn't necessary for you to sabe. Results are what count. Barring accidents, you Timanyoni High Line people can reasonably count on having me with you for the next few critical days; and, I may add, you never needed me more pointedly."

Starbuck's smile was face-wide.

"I hope I don't feel sorry," he remarked. "Some day, when you can take an hour or so off, I'm going to get you to show me around in your little mu-zeeum of self-conceit, John. Maybe I can learn how to gather me up one."

Smith matched the mine owner's good-natured smile. For some unexplainable reason the world, his particular world, seemed to have lost its malignance. He could even think of Stanton without bitterness; and the weapon which had been weighting his hip pocket for the past few days had been carefully buried in the bottom of the lower dressing-case drawer before he came down to breakfast.

"You may laugh, Billy, but you'll have to admit that I've been outfiguring the whole bunch of you, right from the start," he retorted brazenly. "It's my scheme, and I'm going to put it through with a whoop. You'll see—before to-morrow night."

"I reckon, when you do put it through, you can ask your own fee," said Starbuck quietly.

"I'm going to; and the size of it will astonish you, Billy. I shall turn over the little block of stock you folks have been good enough to let me carry, give you and the colonel and the board of directors a small dinner in the club-room up-stairs and—vanish. But let's get down to business. This is practically Stanton's last day of grace. If he can't get some legal hold upon us before midnight to-morrow night, or work some scheme to make us lose our franchise, his job is gone."

"Show me," said the mine owner succinctly.

"It's easy. With the dam completed and the water running in the ditches, we become at once a going concern, with assets a long way in advance of our liabilities. The day after to-morrow—if we pull through—you won't be able to buy a single share of Timanyoni High Line at any figure. As a natural consequence, public sentiment, which, we may say, is at present a little doubtful, will come over to our side in a land-slide, and Stanton's outfit, if it wants to continue the fight, will have to fight the entire Timanyoni, with the city of Brewster thrown in for good measure. Am I making it plain?"

"Right you are, so far. Go on."

"On the other hand, if Stanton can block us before to-morrow night; hang us up in some way and make us lose our rights under the charter; we're gone—snuffed out like a candle. Listen, Billy, and I'll tell you something that I haven't dared to tell anybody, not even Colonel Baldwin. I've been spending the company's money like water to keep in touch. The minute we fail, and long before we could hope to reorganize a second time and apply for a new charter, Stanton's company will be in the field, with its charter already granted. From that to taking possession of our dam, either by means of an enabling act of the Legislature, or by purchase from the paper railroad, will be only a step. And we couldn't do a thing! We'd have no legal rights, and no money to fight with!"

Starbuck pushed his chair away from the table and drew a long breath.

"Good Lord!" he sighed; "I wish to goodness it was day after to-morrow! Can you carry it any further, John?"

"Yes; a step or two. For a week Stanton has been busy on the paper-railroad claim, and that is what made me buy a few cases of Winchesters and send them out to Williams: I was afraid Stanton might try force. He won't do that if he can help it; he'll go in with some legal show, if possible, because our force at the dam far outnumbers any gang he could hire, and he knows we are armed."

"He can't work the legal game," said Starbuck definitively. "I've known Judge Warner ever since I was knee-high to a hop-toad, and a squarer man doesn't breathe."

"That is all right, but you're forgetting something. The paper railroad is—or was once—an interstate corporation, and so may ask for relief from the federal courts, thus going over Judge Warner's head. I'm not saying anything against Lorching, the federal judge at Red Butte. I've met him, and he is a good jurist and presumably an honest man. But he is well along in years, and has an exaggerated notion of his own importance. Stanton, or rather his figurehead railroad people, have asked him to intervene, and he has taken the case under advisement. That is where we stand this morning."

Starbuck was nodding slowly. "I see what you mean, now," he said. "If Lorching jumps the wrong way for us, you're looking to see a United States marshal walk up to Bartley Williams some time to-day and tell him to quit. That would put the final kibosh on us, wouldn't it?"

Smith was rising in his place.

"I'm not dead yet, Billy," he rejoined cheerfully. "I haven't let it get this far without hammering out a few expedients for our side. If I can manage to stay in the fight to-day and to-morrow——"

A little new underclerk had come in from the hotel office and was trying to give Starbuck a note in a square envelope, and Starbuck was saying: "No; that's Mr. Smith, over there."

Smith took the note and opened it, and he scarcely heard the clerk's explanation that it had been put in his box the evening before, and that the day clerk had been afraid he would get away without finding it. It was from Verda Richlander, and it had neither superscription nor signature. This is what Smith read:

"My little ruse has failed miserably. Mr. K's. messenger found my father in spite of it, and he—the messenger—returned this evening: I know, because he brought a note from father to me. Come to me as early to-morrow morning as you can, and we'll plan what can be done."

Smith crushed the note in his hand and thrust it into his pocket. Starbuck was making a cigarette, and was studiously refraining from breaking in. But Smith did not keep him waiting.

"That was my knock-out, Billy," he said with a quietness that was almost overdone. "My time has suddenly been shortened to hours—perhaps to minutes. Get a car as quickly as you can and go to Judge Warner's house. I have an appointment with him at nine o'clock. Tell him I'll keep it, if I can, but that he needn't wait for me if I am not there on the minute."

XXVI
The Colonel's "Defi"

Though it was only eight o'clock, Smith sent his card to Miss Richlander's rooms at once and then had himself lifted to the mezzanine floor to wait for her. She came in a few minutes, a strikingly beautiful figure of a woman in the freshness of her morning gown, red-lipped, bright-eyed, and serenely conscious of her own resplendent gifts of face and figure. Smith went quickly to meet her and drew her aside into the music parlor. Already the need for caution was beginning to make itself felt.

"I have come," he said briefly.

"You got my note?" she asked.

"A few minutes ago—just as I was leaving the breakfast-table."

"You will leave Brewster at once—while the way is still open?"

He shook his head, "I can't do that; in common justice to the men who have trusted me, and who are now needing me more than ever, I must stay through this one day, and possibly another."

"Mr. Kinzie will not be likely to lose any time," she prefigured thoughtfully. "He has probably telegraphed to Lawrenceville before this." Then, with a glance over her shoulder to make sure that there were no eavesdroppers: "Of course, you know that Mr. Stanton is at the bottom of all this prying and spying?"

"It is Stanton's business to put me out of the game, if he can. I've told you enough of the situation here so that you can understand why it is necessary for him to efface me. His time has grown very short now."

Again the statuesque beauty glanced over her shoulder.

"Lawrenceville is a long way off, and Sheriff Macauley is enough of a politician—in an election year—to want to be reasonably certain before he incurs the expense of sending a deputy all the way out here, don't you think?" she inquired.

"Certainty? There isn't the slightest element of uncertainty in it. There are hundreds of people in Brewster who can identify me."

"But not one of these Brewsterites can identify you as John Montague Smith, of Lawrenceville—the man who is wanted by Sheriff Macauley," she put in quickly. Then she added: "My father foresaw that difficulty. As I told you in my note, he sent me a letter by Mr. Kinzie's messenger. After telling me that he will be detained in the mountains several days longer, he refers to Mr. Kinzie's request and suggests——"

The fugitive was smiling grimly. "He suggests that you might help Mr. Kinzie out by telling him whether or not he has got hold of the right John Smith?"

"Not quite that," she rejoined. "He merely suggests that I may be asked to identify you; in which case I am to be prudent, and—to quote him exactly—'not get mixed up in the affair in any way so that it would make talk.'"

"I see," said Smith. And then: "You have a disagreeable duty ahead of you, and I'd relieve you of the necessity by running away, if I could. But that is impossible, as I have explained."

She was silent for a moment; then she said: "When I told you a few days ago that you were going to need my help, Montague, I didn't foresee anything like this. Have you any means of finding out whether or not Mr. Kinzie has sent his wire to Lawrenceville?"

"Yes, I think I can do that much."

"Suppose you do it and then let me know. I shall breakfast with the Stantons in a few minutes; and after nine o'clock ... if you could contrive to keep out of the way until I can get word to you; just so they won't be able to bring us face to face with each other——"

Smith saw what she meant; saw, also, whereunto his wretched fate was dragging him. It was the newest of all the reincarnations, the one which had begun with Jibbey's silent hand-clasp the night before, which prompted him to say:

"If they should ask you about me, you must tell them the truth, Verda."

Her smile was mildly scornful.

"Is that what the plain-faced little ranch person would do?" she asked.

"I don't know; yes, I guess it is."

"Doesn't she care any more for you than that?"

Smith did not reply. He was standing where he could watch the comings and goings of the elevators. Time was precious and he was chafing at the delay, but Miss Richlander was not yet ready to let him go.

"Tell me honestly, Montague," she said; "is it anything more than a case of propinquity with this Baldwin girl?—on your part, I mean."

"It isn't anything," he returned soberly. "Corona Baldwin will never marry any man who has so much to explain as I have."

"You didn't know this was her home, when you came out here?"

"No."

"But you had met her somewhere, before you came?"

"Once; yes. It was in Guthrieville, over a year ago. I had driven over to call on some people that I knew, and I met her there at a house where she was visiting."

"Does she remember that she had met you?"

"No, not yet." He was certain enough of this to answer without reservations.

"But you remembered her?"

"Not at first."

"I see," she nodded, and then, without warning: "What was the matter with you last night—about dinner-time?"

"Why should you think there was anything the matter with me?"

"I was out driving with the Stantons. When I came back to the hotel I found Colonel Baldwin and another man—a lawyer, I think he was—waiting for me. They said you were needing a friend who could go and talk to you and—'calm you down,' was the phrase the lawyer used. I was good-natured enough to go with them, but when we reached your offices you had gone, and the ranch girl was there alone, waiting for her father."

"That was nonsense!" he commented; "their going after you as if I were a maniac or a drunken man, I mean."

This time Miss Richlander's smile was distinctly resentful. "I suppose the colonel's daughter answered the purpose better," she said. "There was an awkward little contretemps, and Miss Baldwin refused, rather rudely, I thought, to tell her father where you had gone."

Smith broke away from the unwelcome subject abruptly, saying: "There is something else you ought to know. Jibbey is here, at last."

"Here in the hotel?"

"Yes."

"Does he know you are here?"

"He does."

"Why didn't you tell me before? That will complicate things dreadfully. Tucker will talk and tell all he knows; he can't help it."

"This is one time when he will not talk. Perhaps he will tell you why when you see him."

Miss Richlander glanced at the face of the small watch pinned on her shoulder.

"You must not stay here any longer," she protested. "The Stantons may come down any minute, now, and they mustn't find us together. I am still forgiving enough to want to help you, but you must do your part and let me know what is going on."

Smith promised and took his dismissal with a mingled sense of relief and fresh embarrassment. In the new development which was threatening to drag him back once more into the primitive savageries, he would have been entirely willing to eliminate Verda Richlander as a factor, helpful or otherwise. But there was good reason to fear that she might refuse to be eliminated.

William Starbuck's new car was standing in front of Judge

Warner's house in the southern suburb when Smith descended from the closed cab which he had taken at the Hophra House side entrance. The clock in the court-house tower was striking the quarter of nine. The elevated mesa upon which the suburb was built commanded a broad view of the town and the outlying ranch lands, and in the distance beyond the river the Hillcrest cottonwoods outlined themselves against a background of miniature buttes.

Smith's gaze took in the wide, sunlit prospect. He had paid and dismissed his cabman, and the thought came to him that in a few hours the wooded buttes, the bare plains, the mighty mountains, and the pictured city spreading map-like at his feet would probably exist for him only as a memory. While he halted on the terrace, Starbuck came out of the house.

"The judge is at breakfast," the mine owner announced. "You're to go in and wait. What do you want me to do next?"

Smith glanced down regretfully at the shining varnish and resplendent metal of the new automobile. "If your car wasn't so new," he began; but Starbuck cut him off.

"Call the car a thousand years old and go on."

"All right. When I get through with the judge I shall want to go out to the dam. Will you wait and take me?"

"Surest thing on earth,"—with prompt acquiescence. And then: "Is it as bad as you thought it was going to be, John?"

"It's about as bad as it can be," was the sober reply, and with that Smith went in to wait for his interview with the Timanyoni's best-beloved jurist.

As we have seen, this was at nine o'clock, or a few minutes before the hour, and as Starbuck descended the stone steps to take his seat in the car, David Kinzie, at his desk in the Brewster City National, was asking the telephone "central" to give him the Timanyoni High Line offices. Martin, the bookkeeper, answered, and he took a message from the bank president that presently brought Colonel Dexter Baldwin to the private room in the bank known to nervous debtors as "the sweat-box".

"Sit down, Dexter," said the banker shortly; "sit down a minute while I look at my mail."

It was one of David Kinzie's small subtleties to make a man sit idly thus, on one pretext or another; it rarely failed to put the incomer at a disadvantage, and on the present occasion it worked like a charm. Baldwin had let his cigar go out and had chewed the end of it into a pulp before Kinzie swung around in his chair and launched out abruptly.

"You and I have always been pretty good friends, Dexter," he began, "and I have called you down here this morning to prove to you that I am still your friend. Where is your man Smith?"

Baldwin shook his head. "I don't know," he answered. "I haven't seen him since last evening."

"Are you sure he is still in town?"

"I haven't any reason to think that he isn't."

"Hasn't run away, then?"

The Missouri colonel squared himself doggedly in the suppliant debtor's chair, which was the one Kinzie had placed for him. "What are you driving at, Dave?" he demanded.

"We'll tackle your end of it, first," said the banker curtly. "Do you know that you and your crowd have come to the bottom of the bag on that dam proposition?"

"No, I don't."

"Well, you have. You've got just this one more day to live."

The Missourian fell back upon his native phrase.

"I reckon you'll have to show me, Dave."

"I will. Have you seen the weather report this morning?"

"No."

"I thought not. I've had a trained observer up in the eastern hills for the past week. The river rose four feet last night, and there are predictions out for more cloudbursts and thunderstorms in the headwater region. The snow is melting fast in the higher gulches, and you know as well as I do that there is at least a strong probability that your dam won't hold the flood rise."

"I don't know it," asserted Baldwin stoutly. "But go on. You've got your gun loaded: what are you aiming it at?"

"Just this: there is a chance that you'll lose the dam by natural causes before the concrete hardens; but if you don't, you're sure to lose it the other way. I told you weeks ago that the other people were carrying too many big guns for you. I don't want to see you killed off, Dexter."

"I'm no quitter; you ought to know that, Dave," was the blunt rejoinder.

"I know; but there are times when it is simply foolhardy to hold on. The compromise proposition that I put up to you people a while back still holds good. But to-day is the last day, Dexter. You must accept it now, if you are going to accept it at all."

"And if we still refuse?"

"You'll go smash, the whole kit of you. As I've said, this is the last call."

By this time Baldwin's cigar was a hopeless wreck.

"You've got something up your sleeve, Dave: what is it?" he inquired.

The banker pursed his lips and the bristling mustache assumed its most aggressive angle.

"There are a number of things, but the one which concerns you most, just now, is this: we've got Smith's record, at last. He is an outlaw, with a price on his head. We've dug out the whole story. He is a defaulting bank cashier, and before he ran away he tried to kill his president."

Baldwin was frowning heavily. "Who told you all this? Was it this Miss Richlander over at the Hophra House?"

"No; it was her father. I sent one of my young men out to the Topaz to look him up."

"And you have telegraphed to the chief of police, or the sheriff, or whoever it is that wants Smith?"

"Not yet. I wanted to give you one more chance, Dexter. Business comes first. The Brewster City National is a bank, not a detective agency. You go and find Smith and fire him; tell him he is down and out; get rid of him, once for all. Then come back here and we'll fix up that compromise with Stanton."

Baldwin found a match and tried to relight the dead cigar. But it was chewed past redemption.

"Let's get it plumb straight, Dave," he pleaded, in the quiet tone of one who will leave no peace-keeping stone unturned. "You say you've got John dead to rights. Smith is a mighty common name. I shouldn't wonder if there were half a million 'r so John Smiths—taking the country over. How do you know you've got the right one?"

"His middle name is 'Montague'," snapped the banker, "and the man who is wanted called himself 'J. Montague Smith'. But we can identify him positively. There is one person in Brewster who knew Smith before he came here; namely, Mr. Richlander's daughter. She can tell us if he is the right Smith, and she probably will if the police ask her to."

Baldwin may have had his own opinion about that, but if so, he kept it to himself and spoke feelingly of other things.

"Dave," he said, rising to stand over the square-built man in the swing-chair, "we've bumped the bumps over a good many miles of rough road together since we first hit the Timanyoni years ago, and it's like pulling a sound tooth to have to tell you the plain truth. You've got a mighty bad case of money-rot. The profit account has grown so big with you that you can't see out over the top of it. You've horsed back and forth between Stanton's outfit and ours until you can't tell the difference between your old friends and a bunch of low-down, conscienceless land-pirates. You pull your gun and go to shooting whenever you get ready. We'll stay with you and try to hold up our end—and John's. And you mark my words, Dave; you're the man that's going to get left in this deal; the straddler always gets left." And with that he cut the interview short and went back to the High Line offices on the upper floor.

XXVII
Two Witnesses

Driven by Starbuck in the brand-new car, Smith reached the dam at half-past ten and was in time to see the swarming carpenters begin the placing of the forms for the pouring of the final section of the great wall. Though the high water was lapping at the foot timbers of the forming, and the weather reports were still portentous, Williams was in fine fettle. There had been no further interferences on the part of the railroad people, every man on the job was spurting for the finish, and the successful end was now fairly in sight.

"We'll be pouring this afternoon," he told Smith, "and with a twenty-four-hour set for the concrete, and the forms left in place for additional security, we can shut the spillway gates and back the water into the main ditch. Instead of being a hindrance then, the flood-tide will help. Under slack-water conditions it would take a day or two to finish filling the reservoir lake, but now we'll get the few feet of rise needed to fill the sluices almost while you wait."

"You have your guards out, as we planned?" Smith inquired.

"Twenty of the best men I could find. They are patrolling on both sides of the river, with instructions to report if they see so much as a rabbit jump up."

"Good. I'm going to let Starbuck drive me around the lake limits to see to it personally that your pickets are on the job. But first, I'd like to use your 'phone for a minute or two," and with that Smith shut himself up in the small field-office and called Martin, the bookkeeper, at the town headquarters.

The result of the brief talk with Martin seemed satisfactory, for when it was concluded, Smith rang off and asked for the Hophra House. Being given the hotel exchange, he called the number of

Miss Richlander's suite, and the answer came promptly in the full, throaty voice of the Olympian beauty.

"Is that you, Montague?"

"Yes. I'm out at the dam. Nothing has been done yet. No telegraphing, I mean. You understand?"

"Perfectly. But something is going to be done. Mr. K. has had Colonel B. with him in the bank. I saw the colonel go in while I was at breakfast. When are you coming back to town?"

"Not for some time; I have a drive to make that will keep me out until afternoon."

"Very well; you'd better stay away as long as you can, and then you'd better communicate with me before you show yourself much in public. I'll have Jibbey looking out for you."

Smith said "good-by" and hung up the receiver with a fresh twinge of dissatisfaction. Every step made his dependence upon Verda Richlander more complete. To be sure, he told himself, they had both forsworn sentiment in the old days, but was that any guaranty that it was not now awakening in Josiah Richlander's daughter? And Corona Baldwin: what would she say to this newest alliance? Would she not say again, and this time with greater truth, that he was a coward of the basest sort; of the type that makes no scruple of hiding behind a woman's skirts?

Happily, there was work to do, and he went out and did it. With the new car to cover the longer interspaces, a complete round of Williams's sentries was made, with détours up and down the line of the abandoned Red Butte Southwestern, whose right-of-way claims had been so recently revived. Smith tried to tell himself that he was only making a necessary reconnaissance thoroughly; that he was not delaying his return to town because Verda had told him to. But when the real motive could no longer be denied, he brought himself up with a jerk. If it had come to this, that he was afraid to face whatever might be awaiting him in Brewster, it was time to take counsel once more of the elemental things.

"Back to Brewster, Billy, by way of the camp," he directed, and the overworked car was turned and headed accordingly.

It was some little time before this, between the noon-hour and the one-o'clock Hophra House luncheon, to be exact, that Mr. David Kinzie, still halting between two opinions, left his desk and the bank and crossed the street to the hotel. Inquiry at the lobby counter revealing the fact that Miss Richlander was in her rooms, Kinzie wrote his name on a card and let the clerk send it up. The boy came back almost immediately with word that Miss Richlander was waiting in the mezzanine parlors.

The banker tipped the call-boy and went up alone. He had seen Miss Richlander, once when she was driving with Smith and again at the theatre in the same company. So he knew what to expect when he tramped heavily into the parlor overlooking the street. None the less, the dazzling beauty of the young woman who rose to shake hands with him and call him by name rather took him off his feet. David Kinzie was a hopeless bachelor, from choice, but there are women, and women.

"Do you know, Mr. Kinzie, I have been expecting you all day," she said sweetly, making him sit down beside her on one of the flaming red monstrosities billed in the hotel inventories as "Louis Quinze sofas". "My father sent me a note by one of your young men, and he said that perhaps you would—that perhaps you might want to—" Her rich voice was at its fruitiest, and the hesitation was of exactly the proper shade.

Kinzie, cold-blooded as a fish with despondent debtors, felt himself suddenly warmed and moved to be gentle with this gracious young woman.

"Er—yes, Miss Richlander—er—a disagreeable duty, you know. I wanted to ask about this young man, Smith. We don't know him very well here in Brewster, and as he has considerable business dealings with the bank, we—that is, I thought your father might be able to tell us something about his standing in his home town."

"And my father did tell you?"

"Well—yes; he—er—he says Smith is a—a grand rascal; a fugitive from justice; and we thought—" David Kinzie, well hardened in all the processes of dealing with men, was making difficult weather of it with this all-too-beautiful young woman.

Miss Richlander's laugh was well restrained. She seemed to be struggling earnestly to make it appear so.

"You business gentlemen are so funny!" she commented. "You know, of course, Mr. Kinzie, that this Mr. Smith and I are old friends; you've probably seen us together enough to be sure of that. Hasn't it occurred to you that however well I might know the Mr. Smith my father has written you about, I should hardly care to be seen in public with him?"

"Then there are two of them?" Kinzie demanded.

The young woman was laughing again. "Would that be so very wonderful?—with so many Smiths in the world?"

"But—er—the middle name, Miss Richlander: that isn't so infern—so very common, I'm sure."

"It is rather remarkable, isn't it? But there are a good many Montagues in our part of the world, too. The man my father wrote you about always signed himself 'J. Montague', as if he were a little ashamed of the 'John'."

"Then this Brewster Smith isn't the one who is wanted in Lawrenceville for embezzlement and attempted murder?"

"Excuse me," said the beauty, with another very palpable attempt to smother her amusement. "If you could only know this other Smith; the one my father wrote you about, and the one he thinks you were asking about: they are not the least bit alike. J. Montague, as I remember him, was a typical society man; a dancing man who was the pet of the younger girls—and of their mothers, for that matter; you know what I mean—the kind of man who wears dress clothes even when he dines alone, and who wouldn't let his beard grow overnight for a king's ransom. But wait a moment. There is a young gentleman here who came last evening direct from Lawrenceville. Let me send for him."

She rose and pressed the bell-push, and when the floor boy came, he was sent to the lobby to page Jibbey. During the little wait, David Kinzie was skilfully made to talk about other things. Jibbey was easily found, as it appeared, and he came at once. Miss Richlander did the honors graciously.

"Mr. Kinzie, this is Mr. Tucker Jibbey, the son of one of our Lawrenceville bankers. Tucker—Mr. Kinzie; the president of the Brewster City National." Then, before Kinzie could begin: "Tucker, I've sent for you in self-defense. You know both Mr. John Smith, at present of Brewster, and also J. Montague Smith, sometime of Lawrenceville and now of goodness only knows where. Mr. Kinzie is trying to make out that they are one and the same."

Jibbey laughed broadly. He stood in no awe of banks, bankers, or stubbly mustaches.

"I'll tell John, when I see him again—and take a chance on being able to run faster than he can," he chuckled. "Ripping good joke!"

"Then you know both men?" said Kinzie, glancing at his watch and rising.

"Like a book. They're no more alike than black and white. Our man here is from Cincinnati; isn't that where you met him, Verda? Yes, I'm sure it is—that night at the Carsons', if you remember. I believe I was the one who introduced him. And I recollect you didn't like him at first, because he wore a beard. They told me, the last time I was over in Cinci, that he'd gone West somewhere, but they didn't say where. He was the first man I met when I lit down here. Damn' little world, isn't it, Mr. Kinzie?"

David Kinzie was backing away, watch in hand. Business was

very pressing, he said, and he must get back to his desk. He was very much obliged to Miss Richlander, and was only sorry that he had troubled her. When her father should return to Brewster he would be glad to meet him, and so on and so on, to and beyond the portières which finally blotted him out, for the two who were left in the Louis Quinze parlor.

"Is that about what you wanted me to say?" queried Jibbey, when the click of the elevator door-latch told them that Mr. Kinzie was descending.

"Tucker, there are times when you are almost lovable," said the beauty softly, with a hand on Jibbey's shoulder.

"I'm glad it's what you wanted, because it's what I was going to say, anyway," returned the ne'er-do-well soberly, thus showing that he, too, had not yet outlived the influence of the overnight hand-grip.

An hour further along in the afternoon, Starbuck's new car, pausing momentarily at the construction camp to give its occupants a chance to witness the rapid fulfilment of Williams's prediction in the swiftly pouring streams of concrete, advertised its shining presence to the engineer, who came up for a word with Smith while Starbuck had his head under the hood of the new-paint-burning motor.

"Somebody's been trying to get you over the wire, John; some woman," he said, in tones as low as the thunderings of the rock-crushers would sanction. "She wouldn't give me her number, but she wanted me to tell you, if you came back here, that it was all right; that you had nothing to be afraid of. She said you'd understand."

XXVIII
The Straddler

Since Brewster was a full-fledged city, its banks closed at three o'clock. Ten minutes after the hour, which happened also to be about the same length of time after Starbuck and Smith had reached town, Mr. Crawford Stanton got himself admitted by the janitor at the side door of the Brewster City National. President Kinzie was still at his desk in his private room, and the promoter entered unannounced.

"I thought I'd hang off and give you the limit—all the time

there was," he said, dropping into the debtor's chair at the desk-end. And then, with a quarrelsome rasp in his tone: "Are you getting ready to switch again?"

Though his victims often cursed the banker for his shrewd caution and his ruthless profit-takings, no one had ever accused him of timidity in a stand-up encounter.

"You've taken that tone with me before, Stanton, and I don't like it," he returned brusquely. "I've been willing to serve you, as I could, in a business matter, and I am still willing to serve you; but you may as well keep it in mind that neither you, nor the people you represent, own the Brewster City National, or any part of it, in fee simple."

"We can buy you out any minute we think we need you," retorted Stanton. "But never mind about that. Your man came back from the Topaz last night; I know, because I make it my business to keep cases on you and everybody else. You've let the better part of the day go by without saying a word, and I've drawn the only conclusion there is to draw: you're getting ready to swap sides again."

Kinzie frowned his impatience. "If I have to do business with your people much longer, Mr. Stanton, I shall certainly suggest that they put a man in charge out here who can control his temper. I have acted in perfect good faith with you from the beginning. What you say is true; our man did return from the Topaz last night. But I thought it wise to make a few investigations on my own account before we should be committed to the course you advocated, and it is fortunate for us that I did. Here is Mr. Richlander's letter."

Stanton read the letter through hastily, punctuating its final sentence with a brittle oath.

"And you've muddled over this all day, when every hour is worth more to us than your one-horse bank could earn in a year?" he rapped out. "What have you done? Have you telegraphed this sheriff?"

"No; and neither will you when I tell you the facts. I was afraid you might go off at half-cock, as usual, if I turned the matter over to you. You see what Mr. Richlander says, and you will note his description of the man Smith who is wanted in Lawrenceville. It doesn't tally in any respect with Baldwin's treasurer, and the common name aroused my suspicions at once. We had nothing to go on unless we could identify our man definitely, so I took the straightforward course and went to Miss Richlander."

Stanton's laugh was a derisive shout.

"You need a guardian, Kinzie; you do, for a fact!" he sneered.

"You sit here, day in and day out, like a greedy old spider in the middle of a web, clawing in a man-fly every time the door opens, but what you don't know about women—Bah! you make my back ache! Of course, the girl pulled the wool over your eyes; any woman could do that!"

"You are not gaining anything by being abusive, Stanton. As I have said, it is fortunate for all of us that I took the matter into my own hands and used a little ordinary common sense. There are two Smiths, just as I suspected when I read Mr. Richlander's letter. Miss Richlander didn't ask me to take her word for it. She called in a young man named Jibbey, who arrived here, direct from Lawrenceville, as I understand, last evening. He is a banker's son, and he knows both Smiths. This man of Baldwin's is not the one Mr. Richlander is trying to describe in that letter."

Stanton bit the tip from a cigar and struck a light.

"Kinzie," he said, "you've got me guessing. If you are really the easy mark you are trying to tell me you are, you have no business running a bank. I'm going to be charitable and put it the other way around. You think we're going to lose out, and you are trying to throw me off the scent. You had a long talk with Colonel Baldwin this morning—I kept cases on that, too—and you figured that you'd make money by seesawing again. I'm glad to be able to tell you that you are just about twenty-four hours too late."

The round-bodied banker righted his pivot-chair with a snap and his lips were puffed out like the lips of a swimmer who sees the saving plank drifting out of reach.

"You are wrong, Stanton; altogether wrong!" he protested. "Baldwin was here because I sent for him to make a final attempt to swing him over to the compromise. You are doing me the greatest possible injustice!"

Stanton rose and made ready to go.

"I think that would be rather hard to do, Kinzie," he flung back. "Nobody loves a trimmmer. But in the present case you are not going to lose anything. We'll take your stock at par, as I promised you we would."

It was at this crisis that David Kinzie showed himself as the exponent of the saying that every man has his modicum of saving grace, by smiting upon the arm of his chair and glaring up at the promoter.

"There's another promise of yours that you've got to remember, too, Stanton," he argued hoarsely. "You've got to hold Dexter Baldwin harmless!"

Stanton's smile was a mask of pure malice. "I've made you no

172

definite promise as to that; but you shall have one now. I'll promise to break Baldwin in two and throw him and his ranchmen backers out of the Timanyoni. That's what you get for playing fast and loose with two people at the same time. When you look over your paying teller's statement for the day, you'll see that I have withdrawn our account from your tin-horn money shop. Good-day."

Five minutes later the promoter was squared before his own desk in the office across the street and was hastily scribbling a telegram while a messenger boy waited. It was addressed to Sheriff Macauley, at Lawrenceville, and the wording of it showed how completely Stanton was ignoring Banker Kinzie's investigations.

Your man Montague Smith is here, known as John Smith, secretary and treasurer Timanyoni High Line Company. Wire authority quick to chief police Brewster for his arrest and send deputy with requisition. Rush or you lose him.

Crawford Stanton.

He let the boy go with this, but immediately set to work on another which was addressed to the great man whose private car, returning from the Pacific Coast, was due to reach Denver by the evening Union Pacific train. This second message he translated laboriously into cipher, working it out word by word from a worn code book taken from the safe. But the copy from which he translated, and which, after the cipher was made, he carefully destroyed, read thus:

The obstacle is removed. M'Graw and his men will take possession to-night and hold until we can make the turn.

Stanton.

XXIX
The Flesh-Pots of Egypt

Convinced by Verda Richlander's telephone message to the construction camp that he stood in no immediate danger, Smith spent the heel of the afternoon in the High Line offices, keeping in wire touch with Stillings, whom he had sent on a secret mission to Red Butte, and with Williams at the dam.

Colonel Baldwin, as he learned from Martin, had gone to attend the funeral of one of his neighbors, and was thus, for the moment, out of reach. Smith told himself that the colonel's presence or absence made little difference. The High Line enterprise was on the knees of the gods. If Williams could pull through in time, if the river-swelling storms should hold off, if Stanton should delay his final raid past the critical hour—and there was now good reason to hope that all of these contingencies were probable—the victory was practically won.

But in another field the fighting secretary, denying himself in the privacy of his office to everybody but Martin, found small matter for rejoicing. It was one of life's ironies that the metamorphosis which had shown him, among other things, the heights and depths of a pure sentiment had apparently deprived him of the power to awaken it in the woman he loved.

It was thus that he was interpreting Corona Baldwin's attitude. She had recognized the transformation as a thing in process, and had been interested in it as a human experiment. Though it was chiefly owing to her beckoning that he had stepped out of the working ranks at the construction camp, he felt that he had never measured up to her ideals, and that her influence over him, so far as it was exerted consciously, was as impersonal as that of the sun on a growing plant. She had wished objectively to see the experiment succeed, and had been willing to use such means as had come to hand to make it succeed. For this cause, he concluded, with a curiously bitter taste in his mouth, her interest in the human experiment was his best warrant for shutting the door upon his love dream. Sentiment, the world over, has little sympathy with laboratory processes, and the woman who loves does not apply acid tests and call the object of her love a coward.

Letting the sting of the epithet have its full effect, he admitted that he was a coward. He had lacked the finer quality of courage when he had spirited Jibbey away, and he was lacking it again, now, in accepting the defensive alliance with Verda Richlander. He had not shown himself at the hotel since his return from the long drive with Starbuck, and the reason for it was that he knew his relations with Verda had now become an entanglement from which he was going to find it exceedingly difficult to release himself. She had served him, had most probably lied for him; and he assured himself, again with the bitter taste in his mouth, that there would be a price to pay.

It is through such doors of disheartenment that temptation finds its easiest entrance. For a dismal hour the old life, with its conventional enjoyments and limitations, its banalities, its entire freedom from the prickings of the larger ambitions and its total blindness on the side of broadening horizons and higher ideals, became a thing most ardently to be desired, a welcome avenue of escape from the toils and turmoils and the growing-pains of all the metamorphoses. What if a return to it should still be possible? What if, surrendering himself voluntarily, he should go back to Lawrenceville and fight it out with Watrous Dunham in the courts? Was there not more than an even chance that Dunham had offered the large reward for his apprehension merely to make sure that he would not return? Was it not possible that the thing the crooked president least desired was an airing of his iniquitous business methods in the courts?

Smith closed his desk at six o'clock and went across to the hotel to dress for dinner. The day of suspense was practically at an end and disaster still held aloof; was fairly outdistanced in the race, as it seemed. Williams's final report had been to the effect that the concrete-pouring was completed, and the long strain was off. Smith went to his rooms, and, as once before and for a similar reason, he laid his dress clothes out on the bed. He made sure that he would be required to dine with Verda Richlander, and he was stripping his coat when he heard a tap at the door and Jibbey came in.

"Glad rags, eh?" said the blasé one, with a glance at the array on the bed. "I've just run up to tell you that you needn't. Verda's dining with the Stantons, and she wants me to keep you out of sight until afterward. By and by, when she's foot-loose, she wants to see you in the mezzanine. Isn't there some quiet little joint where we two can go for a bite? You know the town, and I don't."

Smith put his coat on and together they circled the square to Frascati's, taking a table in the main café. While they were giving their dinner order, Starbuck came in and joined them, and Smith was glad. For reasons which he could scarcely have defined, he was relieved not to have to talk to Jibbey alone, and Starbuck played third hand admirably, taking kindly to the sham black sheep, and filling him up, in quiet, straight-faced humor, with many and most marvellous tales of the earlier frontier.

At the end of the meal, while Jibbey was still content to linger, listening open-mouthed to Starbuck's romancings, Smith excused himself and returned to the hotel. He had scarcely chosen his lounging-chair in a quiet corner of the mezzanine before Miss Richlander came to join him.

"It has been a long day, hasn't it?" she began evenly. "You have been busy with your dam, I suppose, but I—I have had nothing to do but to think, and that is something that I don't often allow myself to do. You have gone far since that night last May when you telephoned me that you would come up to the house later—and then broke your promise, Montague."

"In a way, I suppose I have," he admitted.

"You have, indeed. You are a totally different man."

"In what way, particularly?"

"In every conceivable way. If one could believe in transmigration, one would say that you had changed souls with some old, hard-hitting, rough-riding ancestor. Mr. Stanton has just been telling me the story of how, when you first came here, you fought barehanded with three miners somewhere back in the hills."

A bleak little smile of reminiscence wrinkled at the corners of the fighter's eyes.

"Did he tell you that I knocked them out—all three of them?" he asked.

"He said you beat them shamefully; and I tried to imagine you doing such a thing, and couldn't. Have your ambitions changed, too?"

"I am not sure now that I had any ambitions in that other life."

"Oh, yes, you had," she went on smoothly. "In the 'other life', as you call it, you would have been quite willing to marry a woman who could assure you a firm social standing and money enough to put you on a footing with other men of your capabilities. You wouldn't be willing to do that now, would you?—leaving the sentiment out as you used to leave it out then?"

"No, I hardly think I should."

Her laugh was musically low and sweet, and only mildly derisive.

"You are thinking that it is change of environment, wider horizons, and all that, which has changed you, Montague; but I know better. It is a woman, and, as you may remember, I have met her—twice." Then, with a faint glow of spiteful fire in the magnificent eyes: "How can you make yourself believe that she is pretty?"

He shrugged one shoulder in token of the utter uselessness of discussion in that direction.

"Sentiment?" he queried. "I think we needn't go into that, at this late day, Verda. It is a field that neither of us entered, or cared to enter, in the days that are gone. If I say that Corona Baldwin has—quite unconsciously on her part, I must ask you to believe—taught me what love means, that ought to be enough."

Again she was laughing softly.

"You seem to have broadly forgotten the old proverb about a woman scorned. What have you to expect from me after making such an admission as that?"

Smith pulled himself together and stood the argument firmly upon its unquestionable footing.

"Let us put all these indirections aside and be for the moment merely a man and a woman, as God made us, Verda," he said soberly. "You know, and I know, that there was never any question of love involved in our relations past and gone. We might have married, but in that case neither of us would have gotten or exacted anything more than the conventional decencies and amenities. We mustn't try to make believe at this late day. You had no illusions about me when I was Watrous Dunham's hired man; you haven't any illusions about me now."

"Perhaps not," was the calm rejoinder. "And yet to-day I have lied to save you from those who are trying to crush you."

"I told you not to do that," he rejoined quickly.

"I know you did; and yet, when you went away this morning you knew perfectly well that I was going to do it if I should get the opportunity. Didn't you, Montague?"

He nodded slowly; common honesty demanded that much.

"Very well; you accepted the service, and I gave it freely. Mr. Kinzie believes now that you are another Smith—not the one who ran away from Lawrenceville last May. Tell me: would the other woman have done as much if the chance had fallen to her?"

It was on the tip of his tongue to say, "I hope not," but he did not say it. Instead, he said: "But you don't really care, Verda; in the way you are trying to make me believe you do."

"Possibly not; possibly I am wholly selfish in the matter and am only looking for some loophole of escape."

"Escape? From whom?"

She looked away and shook her head. "From Watrous Dunham, let us say. You didn't suspect that, did you? It is so, nevertheless. My father desires it; and I suppose Watrous Dunham would like to have my money—you know I have something in my own right. Perhaps this may help to account for some other things— for your trouble, for one. You were in his way, you see. But never mind that: there are other matters to be considered now. Though Mr. Kinzie has been put off the track, Mr. Stanton hasn't. I have earned Mr. Stanton's ill-will because I wouldn't tell him about you, and this evening, at table, he took it out on me."

"In what way?"

"He gave me to understand, very plainly, that he had done something; that there was a sensation in prospect for all Brewster. He was so exultantly triumphant that it fairly frightened me. The fact that he wasn't afraid to show some part of his hand to me—

knowing that I would be sure to tell you—makes me afraid that the trap has already been set for you."

"In other words, you think he has gone over Kinzie's head and has telegraphed to Lawrenceville?"

"Montague, I'm almost certain of it!"

Smith stood up and put his hands behind him.

"Which means that I have only a few hours, at the longest," he said quietly. And then: "There is a good bit to be done, turning over the business of the office, and all that: I've been putting it off from day to day, saying that there would be time enough to set my house in order after the trap had been sprung. Now I am like the man who has put off the making of his will until it is too late. Will you let me thank you very heartily and vanish?"

"What shall you do?" she asked.

"Set my house in order, as I say—as well as I can in the time that remains. There are others to be considered, you know."

"Oh; the plain-faced little ranch girl among them, I suppose?"

"No; thank God, she is out of it entirely—in the way you mean," he broke out fervently.

"You mean that you haven't spoken to her—yet?"

"Of course I haven't. Do you suppose I would ask any woman to marry me with the shadow of the penitentiary hanging over me?"

"But you are not really guilty."

"That doesn't make any difference: Watrous Dunham will see to it that I get what he has planned to give me."

She was tapping an impatient tattoo on the carpet with one shapely foot.

"Why don't you turn this new leaf of yours back and go home and fight it out with Watrous Dunham, once for all?" she suggested.

"I shall probably go, fast enough, when Macauley or one of his deputies gets here with the extradition papers," he returned. "But as to fighting Dunham, without money——"

She looked up quickly, and this time there was no mistaking the meaning of the glow in the magnificent brown eyes.

"Your friends have money, Montague—plenty of it. All you have to do is to say that you will defend yourself. I am not sure that Watrous Dunham couldn't be made to take your place in the prisoner's dock, or that you couldn't be put in his place in the Lawrenceville Bank and Trust. You have captured Tucker Jibbey, and that means Tucker's father; and my father—well, when it comes to the worst, my father always does what I want him to. It's his one weakness."

For one little instant Smith felt the solid ground slipping from beneath his feet. Here was a way out, and his quick mentality was showing him that it was a perfectly feasible way. As Verda Richlander's husband and Josiah Richlander's son-in-law, he could fight Dunham and win. And the reward: once more he could take his place in the small Lawrenceville world, and settle down to the life of conventional good report and ease which he had once thought the acme of any reasonable man's aspirations. But at the half-yielding moment a word of Corona Baldwin's flashed into his brain and turned the scale: "It did happen in your case ... giving you a chance to grow and expand, and to break with all the old traditions ... and the break left you free to make of yourself what you should choose." It was the reincarnated Smith who met the look in the beautiful eyes and made answer.

"No," was the sober decision; and then he gave his reasons. "If I could do what you propose, I shouldn't be worth the powder it would take to drive a bullet through me, Verda, for now, you see, I know what love means. You say I have changed, and I have changed: I can imagine the past-and-gone J. Montague jumping at the chance you are offering. But the mill will never grind with the water that is past: I'll take what is coming to me, and try to take it like a man. Good-night—and good-by." And he turned his back upon the temptation and went away.

Fifteen minutes later he was in his office in the Kinzie Building, trying in vain to get Colonel Baldwin on the distance wire; trying also—and also in vain—to forget the recent clash and break with Verda Richlander. He had called it a temptation at the moment, but perhaps it was scarcely that. It was more like a final effort of the man who had been to retransform the man who was. For a single instant the doors of all his former ambitions had stood open. He saw how Josiah Richlander's money and influence, directed by Verda's compelling demands, could be used to break Dunham; and that done, all the rest would be easy, all the paths to the success he had once craved would be made smooth.

On the other hand, there was everything to lose, and nothing, as the world measures results, to be gained. In a few hours at the furthest the good name he had earned in Brewster would be hopelessly lost, and, so far as human foresight could prefigure, there was nothing ahead but loss and bitter disgrace. In spite of all this, while the long-distance "central" was still assuring him that the Hillcrest wire was busy, he found time to be fiercely glad that the choice had been only a choice offered and not a choice accepted. For love's sake, if for no higher motive, he would go down like a man, fighting to the end for the right to live and think and love as a man.

He was jiggling the switch of the desk 'phone for the twentieth time in the effort to secure the desired line of communication with Baldwin when a nervous step echoed in the corridor and the door opened to admit William Starbuck. There was red wrath in the mine owner's ordinarily cold eyes when he flung himself into a chair and eased the nausea of his soul in an outburst of picturesque profanity.

"The jig's up—definitely up, John," he was saying, when his speech became lucid enough to be understood. "We know now what Stanton's 'other string' was. A half-hour ago, a deputy United States marshal, with a posse big enough to capture a town, took possession of the dam and stopped the work. He says it's a court order from Judge Lorching at Red Butte, based on the claims of that infernal paper railroad!"

Smith pushed the telephone aside.

"But it's too late!" he protested. "The dam is completed; Williams 'phoned me before I went to dinner. All that remains to be done to save the charter is to shut the spillways and let the water back up so that it will flow into the main ditch!"

"Right there's where they've got us!" was the rasping reply. "They won't let Williams touch the spillway gates, and they're not going to let him touch them until after we have lost out on the time limit! Williams's man says they've put the seal of the court on the machinery and have posted armed guards everywhere. Wouldn't that make you run around in circles and yelp like a scalded dog?"

XXX

A Strong Man Armed

When the full meaning of Stanton's coup had thus set itself forth in terms unmistakable, Smith put his elbows on the desk and propped his head in his hands. It was not the attitude of dejection; it was rather a trance-like rigor of concentration, with each and all of the newly emergent powers once more springing alive to answer the battle-call. At the desk-end Starbuck sat with his hands locked over one knee, too disheartened to roll a cigarette, normal solace for all woundings less than mortal. After a minute or two Smith jerked himself around to face the news-bringer.

"Does Colonel Baldwin know?" he asked.

"Sure! That's the worst of it. Didn't I tell you? After he got back from Stuart's funeral he drove out to the dam, reaching the works just ahead of the trouble. When M'Graw and the posse outfit showed up, the colonel got it into his head that the whole thing was merely another trick of Stanton's—a fake. Ginty, the quarry boss, brought the news to town. He says there was a bloody mix-up, and at the end of it the colonel and Williams were both under arrest for resisting the officers."

Smith nodded thoughtfully. "Of course; that was just what was needed. With the president and the chief of construction locked up, and the wheels blocked for the next twenty-four hours, our charter will be gone."

"This world and another, and then the fireworks," Starbuck threw in. "With the property all roped up in a law tangle, and those stock options of yours due to fall in, it looks as if a few prominent citizens of the Timanyoni would have to take to the high grass and the tall timber. It sure does, John."

"The colonel was not entirely without his warrant for putting up a fight," Smith went on, after another reflective minute. "Do you know, Billy, I have been expecting something of this kind—and expecting it to be a fake. That's why I sent Stillings to Red Butte; to keep watch of Judge Lorching's court. Stillings was to 'phone me if Lorching issued an order."

"And he hasn't phoned you?"

"No; but that doesn't prove anything. The order may have been issued, and Stillings may have tried to let us know. There are a good many ways in which a man's mouth may be stopped—when there are no scruples on the other side."

"Then you think there is no doubt that the court order is straight, and that this man M'Graw is really a deputy marshal and has the law for what he is doing?"

"In the absence of any proof to the contrary, we are obliged to believe it—or at least to accept it. But we're not dead yet.... Billy, it's running in my mind that we've got to go out there and clean up Mr. M'Graw and his crowd."

Starbuck threw up his hands and made a noise like a dry wagon-wheel.

"Holy smoke!—go up against the whole United States?" he gasped.

Smith's grin showed his strong, even teeth.

"Starbuck, you remember what I told you one night?—the night I dragged you up to my rooms in the hotel and gave you a hint of the reason why I had no business to make love to Corona Baldwin?"

"Yep."

"Well, the time has come when I may as well fill out the blanks in the story for you. The night I left my home city in the Middle West I was called down to the bank of which I was the cashier and was shown how I was going to be dropped into a hole for a hundred thousand dollars of the bank's money; a loan which I had made as cashier in the absence of the president, but which had been authorized, verbally, by the president before he went away."

"A scapegoat, eh? There have been others. Go on."

"It was a frame-up, all around. The loan had been made to a friend of mine for the express purpose of smashing him—that was the president's object in letting it go through. Unluckily, I held a few shares of stock in my friend's company: and there you have it. Unless the president would admit that he had authorized the loan, I was in for an offense that could be easily twisted into embezzlement."

"The president stacked the cards on you?"

"He did. It was nine o'clock at night and we were alone together in the bank. He wanted me to shoulder the blame and run away; offered me money to go with. One word brought on another; and finally, when I dared him to press the police-alarm button, he pulled a gun on me. I hit him, just once, Billy, and he dropped like a stone."

"Great Moses!—dead?"

"I thought he was. His heart had stopped, and I couldn't get him up. Picture it, if you can—but you can't. I had never struck a man in anger before in all my life. My first thought was to go straight to the police station and make a clean breast of it. Then I saw how impossible it was going to be to dodge the penitentiary, and I bolted; jumped a freight-train and hoboed my way out of town. Two days later I got hold of a newspaper and found that I hadn't killed Dunham; but I was outlawed, just the same, and there was a reward offered."

Starbuck was nodding soberly. "You sure have been carrying a back-load all these weeks, John, never knowing what minute was going to be the next. Now I know what you meant when you hinted around about this Miss Rich-pastures. She knows you and she could give you away if she wanted to. Has she done it, John?"

"No; but her father has. Kinzie sent one of his clerks out to the Topaz to hunt up the old man. Kinzie hasn't done anything, himself, I guess; Miss Richlander told me that much; but Stanton has got hold of the end of the thread, and, while I don't know it definitely, it is practically certain he has sent a wire. If the Brewster police are not looking for me at this moment, they will be shortly. That brings us back to this High Line knock-out. As the matter stands, I'm the one man in our outfit who has absolutely nothing to lose. I am an officer of the company, and no legal notice has been served upon me. Can you fill out the remainder of the order?"

"No, I'll be switched if I can!"

"Then I'll fill it for you. So far as I know—legally, you understand—this raid has never been authorized by the courts; at least, that is what I'm going to assume until the proper papers have been served on me. Therefore I am free to strike one final blow for the colonel and his friends, and I'm going to do it, if I can dodge the police long enough to get action."

Starbuck's tilting chair righted itself with a crash.

"You've thought it all out?—just how to go at it?"

"Every move; and every one of them a straight bid for a second penitentiary sentence."

"All right," said the mine owner briefly. "Count me in."

"For information only," was the brusque reply. "You have a stake in the country and a good name to maintain. I have nothing. But you can tell me a few things. Are our workmen still on the ground?"

"Yes. Ginty said there were only a few stragglers who came to town with him. Most of the two shifts are staying on to get their pay—or until they find out that they aren't going to get it."

"And the colonel and Williams: the marshal is holding them out at the dam?"

"Uh-huh; locked up in the office shack, Ginty says."

"Good. I shan't need the colonel, but I shall need Williams. Now another question: you know Sheriff Harding fairly well, don't you? What sort of a man is he?"

"Square as a die, and as nervy as they make 'em. When he gets a warrant to serve, he'll bring in his man, dead or alive."

"That's all I'll ask of him. Now go and find me an auto, and then you can fade away and get ready to prove a good, stout alibi."

"Yes—like fits I will!" retorted the mine owner. "I told you once, John, that I was in this thing to a finish, and I meant it. Go on giving your orders."

"Very well; you've had your warning. The next thing is the auto. I want to catch Judge Warner before he goes to bed. I'll telephone while you're getting a car."

Starbuck had no farther to go than to the garage where he had put up his new car, and when he got it and drove to the Kinzie Building, Smith came out of the shadow of the entrance to mount beside him.

"Drive around to the garage again and let me try another 'phone," was the low-spoken request. "My wire isn't working."

The short run was quickly made, and Smith went to the garage office. A moment later a two-hundred-pound policeman strolled up to put a huge foot on the running-board of the waiting auto. Starbuck greeted him as a friend.

"Hello, Mac. How's tricks with you to-night?"

"Th' tricks are even, an' I'm tryin' to take th' odd wan," said the big Irishman. "'Tis a man named Smith I'm lookin' for, Misther Starbuck—J. Mon-tay-gue Smith; th' fi-nanshal boss av th' big ditch comp'ny. Have ye seen 'um?"

Starbuck, looking over the policeman's shoulder, could see Smith at the telephone in the garage office. Another man might have lost his head, but the ex-cow-puncher was of the chosen few whose wits sharpen handily in an emergency.

"He hangs out at the Hophra House a good part of the time in the evenings," he replied coolly. "Hop in and I'll drive you around."

Three minutes later the threatening danger was a danger pushed a little way into the future, and Starbuck was back at the garage curb waiting for Smith to come out. Through the window he saw Smith replacing the receiver on its hook, and a moment afterward he was opening the car door for his passenger.

"Did you make out to raise the judge?" he inquired, as Smith climbed in.

"Yes. He will meet me at his chambers in the court-house as soon as he can drive down from his house."

"What are you hoping to do, John? Judge Warner is only a circuit judge; he can't set an order of the United States court aside, can he?"

"No; but there is one thing that he can do. You may remember that I had a talk with him this morning at his house. I was trying then to cover all the chances, among them the possibility that Stanton would jump in with a gang of armed thugs at the last minute. We are going to assume that this is what has been done."

Starbuck set the car in motion and sent it spinning out of the side street, around the plaza, and beyond to the less brilliantly illuminated residence district—which was not the shortest way to the court-house.

"You mustn't pull Judge Warner's leg, John," he protested, breaking the purring silence after the business quarter had been left behind; "he's too good a man for that."

"I shall tell him the exact truth, so far as we know it," was the quick reply. "There is one chance in a thousand that we shall come out of this with the law—as well as the equities—on our side. I shall tell the judge that no papers have been served on us, and, so far as I know, they haven't. What are you driving all the way around here for?"

"This is one of the times when the longest way round is the shortest way home," Starbuck explained. "The bad news you were looking for 'has came'. While you were 'phoning in the garage I put one policeman wise—to nothing."

"He was looking for me?"

"Sure thing—and by name. We'll fool around here in the back streets until the judge has had time to show up. Then I'll drop you at the court-house and go hustle the sheriff for you. You'll want Harding, I take it?"

"Yes. I'm taking the chance that only the city authorities have been notified in my personal affair—not the county officers. It's a long chance, of course; I may be running my neck squarely into the noose. But it's all risk, Billy; every move in this night's game. Head up for the court-house. The judge will be there by this time."

Two minutes beyond this the car was drawing up to the curb on the mesa-facing side of the court-house square. There were two lighted windows in the second story of the otherwise darkened building, and Smith sprang to the sidewalk.

"Go now and find Harding, and have him bring one trusty deputy with him: I'll be ready by the time you get back," he directed; but Starbuck waited until he had seen Smith safely lost in the shadows of the pillared court-house entrance before he drove away.

XXXI
A Race to the Swift

Since Sheriff Harding had left his office in the county jail and had gone home to his ranch on the north side of the river some hours earlier, not a little precious time was consumed in hunting him up. Beyond this, there was another delay in securing the deputy. When Starbuck's car came to a stand for a second time before the mesa-fronting entrance of the court-house, Smith came quickly across the walk from the portal.

"Mr. Harding," he began abruptly, "Judge Warner has gone home and he has made me his messenger. There is a bit of sharp work to be done, and you'll need a strong posse. Can you deputize fifteen or twenty good men who can be depended upon in a fight and rendezvous them on the north-side river road in two hours from now?"

The sheriff, a big, bearded man who might have sat for the model of one of Frederic Remington's frontiersmen, took time to consider. "Is it a scrap?" he asked.

"It is likely to be. There are warrants to be served, and there will most probably be resistance. Your posse should be well armed."

"We'll try for it," was the decision. "On the north-side river road, you say? You'll want us mounted?"

"It will be better to take horses. We could get autos, but Judge Warner agrees with me that the thing had better be done quietly and without making too much of a stir in town."

"All right," said the man of the law. "Is that all?"

"No, not quite all. The first of the warrants is to be served here in Brewster—upon Mr. Crawford Stanton. Your deputy will probably find him at the Hophra House. Here is the paper: it is a bench warrant of commitment on a charge of conspiracy, and Stanton is to be locked up. Also you are to see to it that your jail telephone is out of order; so that Stanton won't be able to make any attempt to get a hearing and bail before to-morrow."

"That part of it is mighty risky," said Harding. "Does the judge know about that, too?"

"He does; and for the ends of pure justice, he concurs with me—though, of course, he couldn't give a mandatory order."

The sheriff turned to his jail deputy, who had descended from the rumble seat in the rear.

"You've heard the dope, Jimmie," he said shortly. "Go and get His Nobs and lock him up. And if he wants to be yelling 'Help!' and sending for his lawyer or somebody, why, the telephone's takin' a lay-off. Savvy?"

The deputy nodded and turned upon his heel, stuffing the warrant for Stanton's arrest into his pocket as he went. Smith swung up beside Starbuck, saying: "In a couple of hours, then, Mr. Harding; somewhere near the bridge approach on the other side of the river."

Starbuck had started the motor and was bending forward to adjust the oil feed when the sheriff left them.

"You seem to have made a ten-strike with Judge Warner," the ex-cow-puncher remarked, replacing the flash-lamp in its seat pocket.

"Judge Warner is a man in every inch of him; but there is something behind this night's work that I don't quite understand," was the quick reply. "I had hardly begun to state the case when the judge interrupted me. 'I know,' he said. 'I have been waiting for you people to come and ask for relief.' What do you make of that, Billy?"

"I don't know; unless somebody in Stanton's outfit has welshed. Shaw might have done it. He has been to Bob Stillings, and Stillings says he is sore at Stanton for some reason. Shaw was trying to get Stillings to agree to drop the railroad case against him, and Bob says he made some vague promise of help in the High Line business if the railroad people would agree not to prosecute."

"There is a screw loose somewhere; I know by the way Judge Warner took hold. When I proposed to swear out the warrant for Stanton's arrest, he said, 'I can't understand, Mr. Smith, why you haven't done this before,' and he sat down and filled out the blank. But we can let that go for the present. How are you going to get me across the river without taking me through the heart of the town and giving the Brewster police a shy at me?"

Starbuck's answer was wordless. With a quick twist of the pilot wheel he sent the car skidding around the corner, using undue haste, as it seemed, since they had two hours before them. A few minutes farther along the lights of the town had been left behind and the car was speeding swiftly westward on a country road paralleling the railway track; the road over which Smith had twice driven with the kidnapped Jibbey.

"I'm still guessing," the passenger ventured, when the last of the railroad distance signals had flashed to the rear. And then: "What's the frantic hurry, Billy?"

Starbuck was running with the muffler cut out, but now he cut it in and the roar of the motor sank to a humming murmur.

"I thought so," he remarked, turning his head to listen. "You didn't notice that police whistle just as we were leaving the courthouse, did you?—nor the answers to it while we were dodging through the suburbs? Somebody has marked us down and passed the word, and now they're chasing us with a buzz-wagon. Don't you hear it?"

By this time Smith could hear the sputtering roar of the following car only too plainly.

"It's a big one," he commented. "You can't outrun it, Billy; and, besides, there is nowhere to run to in this direction."

Again Starbuck's reply translated itself into action. With a skilful touch of the controls he sent the car ahead at top speed, and for a matter of ten miles or more held a diminishing lead in the race through sheer good driving and an accurate knowledge of the road and its twistings and turnings. Smith knew little of the westward half of the Park which they were approaching, and the little was not encouraging. Beyond Little Butte and the old Wire Silver mine the road they were traversing would become a cart track in the mountains; and there was no outlet to the north save by means of the railroad bridge at Little Butte station.

Throughout the race the pursuers had been gradually gaining, and by the time the forested bulk of Little Butte was outlining itself against the clouded sky on the left, the headlights of the oncoming police car were in plain view to the rear. Worse still, there were three grade crossings of the railroad track just ahead in the stretch of road which rounded the toe of the mountain; and from somewhere up the valley and beyond the railroad bridge came the distance-softened whistle of a train.

Starbuck set a high mark for himself as a courageous driver of motor-cars when he came to the last of the three road crossings. Jerking the car around sharply at the instant of track-crossing, he headed straight out over the ties for the railroad bridge. It was a courting of death. To drive the bridge at racing speed was hazardous enough, but to drive it thus in the face of a down-coming train seemed nothing less than madness.

It was after the car had shot into the first of the three bridge spans that the pursuers pulled up and opened fire. Starbuck bent lower over his wheel, and Smith clutched for handholds. Far up the track on the north side of the river a headlight flashed in the darkness, and the hoarse blast of a locomotive, whistling for the bridge, echoed and re-echoed among the hills.

Starbuck, tortured because he could not remember what sort of an approach the railway track made to the bridge on the farther side, drove for his life. With the bridge fairly crossed he found himself on a high embankment; and the oncoming train was now less than half a mile away. To turn out on the embankment was to hurl the car to certain destruction. To hold on was to take a hazardous chance of colliding with the train. Somewhere beyond the bridge approach there was a road; so much Starbuck could recall. If they could reach its crossing before the collision should come——

They did reach it, by what seemed to Smith a margin of no more than the length of the heavy freight train which went jangling past them a scant second or so after the car had been wrenched aside into the obscure mesa road. They had gone a mile or more on the reverse leg of the long down-river détour before Starbuck cut the speed and turned the wheel over to his seat-mate.

"Take her a minute while I get the makings," he said, dry-lipped, feeling in his pockets for tobacco and the rice-paper. Then he added: "Holy Solomon! I never wanted a smoke so bad in all my life!"

Smith's laugh was a chuckle.

"Gets next to you—after the fact—doesn't it? That's where we split. I had my scare before we hit the bridge, and it tasted like a mouthful of bitter aloes. Does this road take us back up the river?"

"It takes us twenty miles around through the Park and comes in at the head of Little Creek. But we have plenty of time. You told Harding two hours, didn't you?"

"Yes; but I must have a few minutes at Hillcrest before we get action, Billy."

Starbuck took the wheel again and said nothing until the roundabout race had been fully run and he was easing the car down the last of the hills into the Little Creek road. There had been three-quarters of an hour of skilful driving over a bad road to come between Smith's remark and its reply, but Starbuck apparently made no account of the length of the interval.

"You're aiming to go and see Corry?" he asked, while the car was coasting to the hill bottom.

"Yes."

With a sudden flick of the controls and a quick jamming of the brakes, Starbuck brought the car to a stand just as it came into the level road.

"We're man to man here under the canopy, John; and Corry Baldwin hasn't got any brother," he offered gravely. "I'm backing you in this business fight for all I'm worth—for Dick Maxwell's sake and the colonel's, and maybe a little bit for the sake of my own ante of twenty thousand. And I'm ready to back you in this old-home scrap with all the money you'll need to make your fight. But when it comes to the little girl it's different. Have you any good and fair right to hunt up Corry Baldwin while things are shaping themselves up as they are?"

Since Smith had made the acquaintance of the absolute ego he had acquired many things new and strange, among them a great ruthlessness in the pursuit of the desired object, and an equally large carelessness for consequences past the instant of attainment. None the less, he met the shrewd inquisition fairly.

"Give it a name," he said shortly.

"I will: I'll give it the one you gave it a while back. You said you were an outlaw, on two charges: embezzlement and assault. We'll let the assault part of it go. Even a pretty humane sort of fellow may have to kill somebody now and then and call it all in the day's work. But the other thing doesn't taste good."

"I didn't embezzle anything, Billy. I thought I made that plain."

"So you did. But you also made it plain that the home court would be likely to send you up for it, guilty or not guilty. And with a thing like that hanging over you ... you see, I know Corry Baldwin, John. If you put it up to her to-night, and she happens to fall in with your side of it—which is what you're aiming to make her do—all hell won't keep her from going back home with you and seeing you through!"

"Good God, Billy! If I thought she loved me well enough to do that! But think a minute. It may easily happen that this is my last chance. I may never see her again. I said I wouldn't tell her—that I loved her too well to tell her ... but now the final pinch has come, and I——"

"And that isn't all," Starbuck went on relentlessly. "There's this Miss Rich-acres. You say there's nothing to it, there, but you've as good as admitted that she's been lying to Dave Kinzie for you. Your hands ain't clean, John; not clean enough to let you go to Hillcrest to-night."

Smith groped in his pockets, found a cigar and lighted it. Perhaps he was recalling his own words spoken to Verda Richlander only a few hours earlier: "Do you suppose I would ask any woman to marry me with the shadow of the penitentiary hanging over me?" And yet that was just what he was about to do—or had been about to do.

"Pull out to the side of the road and we'll kill what time there is to kill right here," he directed soberly. And then: "What you say is right as right, Billy. Once more, I guess, I was locoed for the minute. Forget it; and while you're about it, forget Miss Richlander, too. Luckily for her, she is out of it—as far out of it as I am."

XXXII
Freedom

The Timanyoni, a mountain torrent in its upper and lower reaches, becomes a placid river of the plain at Brewster, dividing its flow among sandy islets, and broadening in its bed to make the long bridge connecting the city with the grass-land mesas a low, trestled causeway. On the northern bank of the river the Brewster street, of which the bridge is a prolongation, becomes a country road, forking a few hundred yards from the bridge approach to send one of its branchings northward among the Little Creek ranches and another westward up the right bank of the stream.

At this fork of the road, between eleven and twelve o'clock of the night of alarms, Sheriff Harding's party of special deputies began to assemble; mounted ranchmen for the greater part, summoned by the rural telephones and drifting in by twos and threes from the outlying grass-lands. Under each man's saddle-flap was slung the regulation weapon of the West—a scabbarded repeating rifle; and the small troop bunching itself in the river road looked serviceably militant and businesslike.

While Harding was counting his men and appointing his lieutenants an automobile rolled silently down the mesa road from the north and came to a stand among the horses. The sheriff drew rein beside the car and spoke to one of the two occupants of the double seat, saying:

"Well, Mr. Smith, we're all here."

"How many?" was the curt question.

"Twenty."

"Good. Here is your authority"—handing the legal papers to the officer. "Before we go in you ought to know the facts. A few hours ago a man named M'Graw, calling himself a deputy United States marshal and claiming to be acting under instructions from Judge Lorching's court in Red Butte, took possession of our dam and camp. On the even chance that he isn't what he claims to be, we are going to arrest him and every man in his crowd. Are you game for it?"

"I'm game to serve any papers that Judge Warner's got the nerve to issue," was the big man's reply.

"That's the talk; that's what I hoped to hear you say. We may have the law on our side, and we may not; but we certainly have the equities. Was Stanton arrested?"

"He sure was. Strothers found him in the Hophra House bar, and the line of talk he turned loose would have set a wet blanket afire. Just the same, he had to go along with Jimmie and get himself locked up."

"That is the first step; now if you're ready, we'll take the next."

Harding rode forward to marshal his troop, and when the advance began Starbuck shut off his car lamps and held his place at the rear of the straggling column, juggling throttle and spark until the car kept even pace with the horses and the low humming of the motor was indistinguishable above the muffled drumming of hoof-beats.

For the first mile or so the midnight silence was unbroken save by the subdued progress noises and the murmurings of the near-by river in its bed. Once Smith took the wheel while Starbuck rolled and lighted a cigarette, and once again, in obedience to a word from the mine owner, he turned the flash-light upon the gasolene pressure-gauge. In the fulness of time it was Starbuck who harked back to the talk which had been so abruptly broken off at the waiting halt in the Little Creek road.

"Let's not head into this ruction with an unpicked bone betwixt us, John," he began gently. "Maybe I said too much, back yonder at the foot of the hill."

"No; you didn't say too much," was the low-toned reply. And then: "Billy, I've had a strange experience this summer; the strangest a man ever lived through, I believe. A few months ago I was jerked out of my place in life and set down in another place where practically everything I had learned as a boy and man had to be forgotten. It was as if my life had been swept clean of everything that I knew how to use—like a house gutted of its well-worn and familiar furniture, and handed back to its tenant to be refitted with whatever could be found and made to serve. I don't know that I'm making it understandable to you, but——"

"Yes, you are," broke in the man at the wheel. "I've had to turn two or three little double somersaults myself in the years that are gone."

"They used to call me 'Monty-Boy,' back there in Lawrenceville, and I fitted the name," Smith went on. "I was neither better nor worse than thousands of other home-bred young fellows just like me, nor different from them in any essential way. I had my little tin-basin round of work and play, and I lived in it. I've spent half an hour, many a time, in a shop picking out the exactly right shade in a tie to wear with the socks that I had, perhaps, spent another half-hour in selecting."

"I'm getting you," said Starbuck, not without friendly sympathy. "Go on."

"Then, suddenly, as I have said, the house was looted. And, quite as suddenly, it grew and expanded and took on added rooms and spaces that I'd never dreamed of. I've had to fill it up as best I could, Billy: I couldn't put back any of the old things; they were so little and trivial and childish. And some of the things I've been putting in are fearfully raw and crude. I've just had to do the best I could—with an empty house. I found that I had a body that could stand man-sized hardship, and a kind of savage nerve that could give and take punishment, and a soul that could drive both body and nerve to the limit. Also, I've found out what it means to love a woman."

Starbuck checked the car's speed a little more to keep it well in the rear of the ambling cavalcade.

"That's your one best bet, John," he said soberly.

"It is. I've cleaned out another room since you called me down back yonder in the Little Creek road, Starbuck. I can't trust my own leadings any more; they are altogether too primitive and brutal; so I'm going to take hers. She'd send me into this fight that is just ahead of us, and all the other fights that are coming, with a heart big enough to take in the whole world. She said I'd understand, some day; that I'd know that the only great man is one who is too big to be little; who can fight without hating; who can die to make good, if that is the only way that offers."

"That's Corry Baldwin, every day in the week, John. They don't make 'em any finer than she is," was Starbuck's comment. And then: "I'm beginning to kick myself for not letting you go and have one more round-up with her. She's doing you good, right along."

"You didn't stop me," Smith affirmed; "you merely gave me a chance to stop myself. It's all over now, Billy, and my little race is about run. But whatever happens to me, either this night, or beyond it, I shall be a free man. You can't put handcuffs on a soul and send it to prison, you know. That is what Corona was trying to make me understand; and I couldn't—or wouldn't."

Harding had stopped to let the auto come up. Over a low hill just ahead the pole-bracketed lights at the dam were starring themselves against the sky, and the group of horsemen was halting at the head of the railroad trestle which marked the location of the north side unloading station.

From the halt at the trestle head, Harding sent two of his men forward to spy out the ground. Returning speedily, these two men reported that there were no guards on the north bank of the river, and that the stagings, which still remained in place on the downstream face of the dam, were also unguarded. Thereupon Harding made his dispositions. Half of the posse was to go up the northern bank, dismounted, and rush the camp by way of the stagings. The remaining half, also on foot, was to cross at once on the railroad trestle, and to make its approach by way of the wagon road skirting the mesa foot. At an agreed-upon signal, the two detachments were to close in upon the company buildings in the construction camp, trusting to the surprise and the attack from opposite directions to overcome any disparity in numbers.

At Smith's urgings, Starbuck went with the party which crossed by way of the railroad trestle, Smith himself accompanying the sheriff's detachment. With the horses left behind under guard at the trestle head, the up-river approach was made by both parties simultaneously, though in the darkness, and with the breadth of the river intervening, neither could see the movements of the other. Smith kept his place beside Harding, and to the sheriff's query he answered that he was unarmed.

"You've got a nerve," was all the comment Harding made, and at that they topped the slight elevation and came among the stone débris in the north-side quarries.

From the quarry cutting the view struck out by the camp mastheads was unobstructed. The dam and the uncompleted power-house, still figuring to the eye as skeleton masses of form timbering, lay just below them, and on the hither side the flooding torrent thundered through the spillway gates, which had been opened to their fullest capacity. Between the quarry and the northern dam-head ran the smooth concreted channel of the main ditch canal, with the water in the reservoir lake still lapping several feet below the level of its entrance to give assurance that, until the spillways should be closed, the charter-saving stream would never pour through the canal.

On the opposite side of the river the dam-head and the camp street were deserted, but there were lights in the commissary, in the office shack, and in Blue Pete Simms's canteen doggery. From the latter quarter sounds of revelry rose above the spillway thunderings, and now and again a drunken figure lurched through the open door to make its way uncertainly toward the rank of bunk-houses.

Harding was staring into the farther nimbus of the electric rays, trying to pick up some sign of the other half of his posse, when Smith made a suggestion.

"Both of your parties will have the workmen's bunk-houses in range, Mr. Harding, and we mustn't forget that Colonel Baldwin and Williams are prisoners in the timekeeper's shack. If the guns have to be used——"

"There won't be any wild shooting, of the kind you're thinking of," returned the sheriff grimly. "There ain't a single man in this posse that can't hit what he aims at, nine times out o' ten. But here's hopin' we can gather 'em in without the guns. If they ain't lookin' for us——"

The interruption was the whining song of a jacketed bullet passing overhead, followed by the crack of a rifle. "Down, boys!" said the sheriff softly, setting the example by sliding into the ready-made trench afforded by the dry ditch of the outlet canal; and as he said it a sharp fusillade broke out, with fire spurtings from the commissary building and others from the mesa beyond to show that the surprise was balked in both directions.

"They must have had scouts out," was Smith's word to the sheriff, who was cautiously reconnoitring the newly developed situation from the shelter of the canal trench. "They are evidently ready for us, and that knocks your plan in the head. Your men can't cross these stagings under fire."

"Your 'wops' are all right, anyway," said Harding. "They're pouring out of the bunk-houses and that saloon over there and taking to the hills like a flock o' scared chickens." Then to his men: "Scatter out, boys, and get the range on that commissary shed. That's where most of the rustlers are cached."

Two days earlier, two hours earlier, perhaps, Smith would have begged a weapon and flung himself into the fray with blood lust blinding him to everything save the battle demands of the moment. But now the final mile-stone in the long road of his metamorphosis had been passed and the darksome valley of elemental passions was left behind.

"Hold up a minute, for God's sake!" he pleaded hastily. "We've got to give them a show, Harding! The chances are that every man in that commissary believes that M'Graw has the law on his side—and we are not sure that he hasn't. Anyway, they don't know that they are trying to stand off a sheriff's posse!"

Harding's chuckle was sardonic. "You mean that we'd ought to go over yonder and read the riot act to 'em first? That might do back in the country where you came from. But the man that can get into that camp over there with the serving papers now 'd have to be armor-plated, I reckon."

"Just the same, we've got to give them their chance!" Smith insisted doggedly. "We can't stand for any unnecessary bloodshed—I won't stand for it!"

Harding shrugged his heavy shoulders. "One round into that sheet-iron commissary shack'll bring 'em to time—and nothing else will. I hain't got any men to throw away on the dew-dabs and furbelows."

Smith sprang up and held out his hand.

"You have at least one man that you can spare, Mr. Harding," he snapped. "Give me those papers. I'll go over and serve them."

At this the big sheriff promptly lost his temper.

"You blamed fool!" he burst out. "You'd be dog-meat before you could get ten feet away from this ditch!"

"Never mind: give me those papers. I'm not going to stand by quietly and see a lot of men shot down on the chance of a misunderstanding!"

"Take 'em, then!" rasped Harding, meaning nothing more than the calling of a foolish theorist's bluff.

Smith caught at the warrants, and before anybody could stop him he was down upon the stagings, swinging himself from bent to bent through a storm of bullets coming, not from the commissary, but from the saloon shack on the opposite bank—a whistling shower of lead that made every man in the sheriff's party duck to cover.

How the volunteer process-server ever lived to get across the bridge of death no man might know. Thrice in the half-minute dash he was hit; yet there was life enough left to carry him stumbling across the last of the staging bents; to send him reeling up the runway at the end and across the working yard to the door of the commissary, waving the folded papers like an inadequate flag of truce as he fell on the door-step.

After that, all things were curiously hazy and undefined for him; blind clamor coming and going as the noise of a train to a dozing traveller when the car doors are opened and closed. There was the tumult of a fierce battle being waged over him; a deafening rifle fire and the spat-spat of bullets puncturing the sheet-iron walls of the commissary. In the midst of it he lost his hold upon the realities, and when he got it again the warlike clamor was stilled and Starbuck was kneeling beside him, trying, apparently, to deprive him of his clothes with the reckless slashings of a knife.

Protesting feebly and trying to rise, he saw the working yard filled with armed men and the returning throng of laborers; saw Colonel Baldwin and Williams talking excitedly to the sheriff; then he caught the eye of the engineer and beckoned eagerly with his one available hand.

"Hold still, until I can find out how dead you are!" gritted the rough-and-ready surgeon who was plying the clothes-ripping knife. But when Williams came and bent down to listen, Smith found a voice, shrill and strident and so little like his own that he scarcely recognized it.

"Call 'em out—call the men out and start the gate machinery!" he panted in the queer, whistling voice which was, and was not, his own. "Possess—possession is nine points of the law—that's what Judge Warner said: the spillways, Bartley—shut 'em quick!"

"The men are on the job and the machinery is starting right now," said Williams gently. "Don't you hear it?" And then to

Starbuck: "For Heaven's sake, do something for him, Billy—anything to keep him with us until a doctor can get here!"

Smith felt himself smiling foolishly.

"I don't need any doctor, Bartley; what I need is a new ego: then I'd stand some sha—some chance of finding—" he looked up appealingly at Starbuck—"what is it that I'd stand some chance of finding, Billy? I—I can't seem to remember."

Williams turned his face away and Starbuck tightened his benumbing grip upon the severed artery in the bared arm from which he had cut the sleeve. Smith seemed to be going off again, but he suddenly opened his eyes and pointed frantically with a finger of the one serviceable hand. "Catch him! catch him!" he shrilled. "It's Boogerfield, and he's going to dy-dynamite the dam!"

Clinging to consciousness with a grip that not even the blood loss could break, Smith saw Williams spring to his feet and give the alarm; saw three or four of the sheriff's men drop their weapons and hurl themselves upon another man who was trying to make his way unnoticed to the stagings with a box of dynamite on his shoulder. Then he felt the foolish smile coming again when he looked up at Starbuck.

"Don't let them hurt him, Billy; him nor Simms nor Lanterby, nor that other one—the short-hand man—I—I can't remember his name. They're just poor tools; and we've got to—to fight without hating, and—and—" foolish witlessness was enveloping him again like a clinging garment and he made a masterful effort to throw it off. "Tell the little girl—tell her—you know what to tell her, Billy; about what I tried to do. Harding said I'd get killed, but I remembered what she said, and I didn't care. Tell her I said that that one minute was worth living for—worth all it cost."

The raucous blast of a freak auto horn ripped into the growling murmur of the gate machinery, and a dust-covered car pulled up in front of the commissary. Out of it sprang first the doctor with his instrument bag; and, closely following him, two plain-clothes men and a Brewster police captain in uniform. Smith looked up and understood.

"They're just—a little—too late, Billy, don't you think?" he quavered weakly. "I guess—I guess I've fooled them, after all." And therewith he closed his eyes wearily upon all his troubles and triumphings.

XXXIII
In Sunrise Gulch

William Starbuck drew the surgeon aside after the first aid had been rendered, and Smith, still unconscious, had been carried from the makeshift operating-table in the commissary to Williams's cot in the office shack.

"How about it, Doc?" asked the mine owner bluntly.

The surgeon shook his head doubtfully.

"I can't say. The arm and the shoulder won't kill him, but that one in the lung is pretty bad; and he has lost a lot of blood."

"Still, he may pull through?"

"He may—with good care and nursing. But if you want my honest opinion, I'm afraid he won't make it. He'll be rather lucky if he doesn't make it, won't he?"

Starbuck remembered that the doctor had come out in the auto with the police captain and the two plain-clothes men.

"Hackerman has been talking?" he queried.

The surgeon nodded. "He told me on the way out that Smith was a fugitive from justice; that he'd be likely to get ten years or more when they took him back East. If I were in Smith's place, I'd rather pass out with a bullet in my lung. Wouldn't you?"

Starbuck was frowning sourly. "Suppose you make it a case of suspended judgment, Doc," he suggested. "The few of us here who know anything about it are giving John the benefit of the doubt. I've got a few thousand dollars of my own money that says he isn't guilty; and if he makes a live of it, they'll have to show me, and half a dozen more of us, before they can send him over the road."

"He knew they were after him?"

"Sure thing; and he had all the chance he needed to make his get-away. He wouldn't take it; thought he owed a duty to the High Line stockholders. He's a man to tie to, Doc. He was shot while he was trying to get between and stop the war and keep others from getting killed."

"It's a pity," said the surgeon, glancing across at the police captain to whom Colonel Baldwin was appealing. "They'll put him in the hospital cell at the jail, and that will cost him whatever slender chance he might otherwise have to pull through."

Starbuck looked up quickly. "Tell 'em he can't be moved, Doc Dan," he urged suddenly. And then: "You're Dick Maxwell's family physician, and Colonel Dexter's, and mine. Surely you can do that much for us?"

"I can, and I will," said the surgeon promptly, and then he went to join Baldwin and the police captain, who were still arguing. What he said was brief and conclusive; and a little later, when the autos summoned from town by Sheriff Harding came for their lading of prisoners, Smith was left behind, with two of M'Graw's men who were also past moving. In the general clearing of the field Starbuck and Williams stayed behind to care for the wounded, and one of the plain-clothes men remained to stand guard.

Three days after the wholesale arrest at the dam, Brewster gossip had fairly outworn itself telling and retelling the story of how the High Line charter had been saved; of how Crawford Stanton's bold ruse of hiring an ex-train-robber to impersonate a federal-court officer had fallen through, leaving Stanton and his confederates, ruthlessly abandoned by their unnamed principals, languishing bailless in jail; of how Smith, the hero of all these occasions, was still lying at the point of death in the office shack at the construction camp, and David Kinzie, once more in keen pursuit of the loaves and fishes, was combing the market for odd shares of the stock which was now climbing swiftly out of reach. But at this climax of exhaustion—or satiety—came a distinctly new set of thrills, more titillating, if possible, than all the others combined.

It was on the morning of the third day that the Herald announced the return of Mr. Josiah Richlander from the Topaz; and in the marriage notices of the same issue the breakfast-table readers of the newspapers learned that the multimillionaire's daughter had been privately married the previous evening to Mr. Tucker Jibbey. Two mining speculators, who had already made Mr. Jibbey's acquaintance, were chuckling over the news in the Hophra House grill when a third late breakfaster, a man who had been sharing Stanton's office space as a broker in improved ranch lands, came in to join them.

"What's the joke?" inquired the newcomer; and when he was shown the marriage item he nodded gravely. "That's all right; but the Herald man didn't get the full flavor of it. It was a sort of runaway match, it seems; the fond parent wasn't invited or consulted. The boys in the lobby tell me that the old man had a fit when he came in this morning and a Herald reporter showed him that notice and asked for more dope on the subject."

"I don't see that the fond parent has any kick coming," said the one who had sold Jibbey a promising prospect hole on Topaz

Mountain two days earlier. "The young fellow's got all kinds of money."

"I know," the land broker put in. "But they're whispering it around that Mr. Richlander had other plans for his daughter. They also say that Jibbey wouldn't stay to face the music; that he left on the midnight train last night a few hours after the wedding, so as not to be among those present when the old man should blow in."

"What?"—in a chorus of two—"left his wife?"

"That's what they say. But that's only one of the new and startling things that isn't in the morning papers. Have you heard about Smith?—or haven't you been up long enough yet?"

"I heard yesterday that he was beginning to mend," replied the breakfaster on the left; the one who had ordered bacon and eggs, with the bacon cooked to a cinder.

"You're out of date," this from the dealer in ranches. "You know the story that was going around about his being an escaped convict, or something of that sort? It gets its 'local color' this morning. There's a sheriff here from back East somewhere—came in on the early train; name's Macauley, and he's got the requisition papers. But Smith's fooled him good and plenty."

Again the chorus united in an eager query.

"How?"

"He died last night—a little past midnight. They say they're going to bury him out at the dam—on the job that he pulled through and stood on its feet. One of Williams's quarrymen drifted in with the story just a little while ago. I'm here to bet you even money that the whole town goes to the funeral."

"Great gosh!" said the man who was crunching the burnt bacon. "Say, that's tough, Bixby! I don't care what he'd run away from back East; he was a man, right. Harding has been telling everybody how Smith wouldn't let the posse open fire on that gang of hold-ups last Friday night; how he chased across on the dam stagings alone and unarmed to try to serve the warrants on 'em and make 'em stop firing. It was glorious, but it wasn't war."

To this the other mining man added a hard word. "Dead," he gritted; "and only a few hours earlier the girl had taken snap judgment on him and married somebody else! That's the woman of it!"

"Oh, hold on, Stryker," the ranch broker protested. "Don't you get too fierce about that. There are two strings to that bow and the longest and sorriest one runs out to Colonel Baldwin's place on Little Creek, I'm thinking. The Richlander business was only an incident. Stanton told me that much."

As the event proved, the seller of ranch lands would have lost his bet on the funeral attendance. For some unknown reason the notice of Smith's death did not appear in the afternoon papers, and only a few people went out in autos to see the coffin lowered by Williams's workmen into a grave on the mesa behind the construction camp; a grave among others where the victims of an early industrial accident at the dam had been buried. Those who went out from town came back rather scandalized. There had been a most hard-hearted lack of the common formalities, they said; a cheap coffin, no minister, no mourners, not even the poor fellow's business associates in the company he had fought so hard to save from defeat and extinction. It was a shame!

With this report passing from lip to lip in Brewster, another bit of gossip to the effect that Starbuck and Stillings had gone East with the disappointed sheriff, "to clear Smith's memory," as the street-talk had it, called forth no little comment derogatory. As it chanced, the two mining speculators and Bixby, the ranch seller, met again in the Hophra House café at the dinner-table on the evening of the funeral day, and Stryker, the captious member of the trio, was loud in his criticisms of the High Line people.

"Yes!" he railed; "a couple of 'em will go on a junketing trip East to 'clear his memory,' after they've let their 'wops' at the dam bury him like a yellow dog! I thought better than that of Billy Starbuck, and a whole lot better of Colonel Dexter. And this Richlander woman; they say she'd known him ever since he and she were school kids together; she went down and took the train with her father just about the time they were planting the poor devil among the sagebrush roots up there on that bald mesa!"

"I'm disappointed, too," confessed the dealer in improved ranch lands. "I certainly thought that if nobody else went, the little girl from the Baldwin place would be out there to tell him good-by. But she wasn't."

Three weeks of the matchless August weather had slipped by without incident other than the indictment by the grand jury of Crawford Stanton, Barney M'Graw, and a number of others on a charge of conspiracy; and Williams, unmolested since the night of the grand battue in which Sheriff Harding had figured as the master of the hunt, had completed the great ditch system and was installing the machinery in the lately finished power-house.

Over the hills from the northern mountain boundary of the Timanyoni a wandering prospector had come with a vague tale of a new strike in Sunrise Gulch, a placer district worked out and abandoned twenty years earlier in the height of the Red Butte excitement. Questioned closely, the tale-bringer confessed that he had no proof positive of the strike; but in the hills he had found a well-worn trail, lately used, leading to the old camp, and from one of the deserted cabins in the gulch he had seen smoke arising.

As to the fact of the trail the wandering tale-bearer was not at fault. On the most perfect of the late-in-August mornings a young woman, clad in serviceable khaki, and keeping her cowboy Stetson and buff top-boots in good countenance by riding astride in a man's saddle, was pushing her mount up the trail toward Sunrise Gulch. From the top of a little rise the abandoned camp came into view, its heaps of worked-over gravel sprouting thickly with the wild growth of twenty years, and its crumbling shacks, only one of which seemed to have survived in habitable entirety, scattered among the firs of the gulch.

At the top of the rise the horsewoman drew rein and shaded her eyes with a gauntleted hand. On a bench beside the door of the single tenanted cabin a man was sitting, and she saw him stand to answer her hand-wave. A few minutes later the man, a gaunt young fellow with one arm in a sling and the pallor of a long confinement whitening his face and hands, was trying to help the horsewoman to dismount in the cabin dooryard, but she pushed him aside and swung out of the saddle unaided, laughing at him out of a pair of slate-gray eyes and saying: "How often have I got to tell you that you simply can't help a woman out of a man's saddle?"

The man smiled at that.

"It's automatic," he returned. "I shall never get over wanting to help you, I guess. Have you come to tell me that I can go?"

Flinging the bridle-reins over the head of the wiry little cow-pony which was thus left free to crop the short, sweet grass of the creek valley, the young woman led the man to the house bench and made him sit down.

"You are frightfully anxious to go and commit suicide, aren't you?" she teased, sitting beside him. "Every time I come it's always the same thing: 'When can I go?' You're not well yet."

"I'm well enough to do what I've got to do, Corona; and until it's done.... Besides, there is Jibbey."

"Where is Mr. Jibbey this morning?"

"He has gone up the creek, fishing. I made him go. If I didn't take a club to him now and then he'd hang over me all the time. There never was another man like him, Corona. And at home we used to call him 'the black sheep' and 'the failure,' and cross the street to dodge him when he'd been drinking too much!"

"He says you've made a man of him; that you saved his life when you had every reason not to. You never told me that, John."

"No; I didn't mean to tell any one. But to think of his coming out here to nurse me, leaving Verda on the very night he married her! A brother of my own blood wouldn't have done it."

The young woman was looking up with a shrewd little smile. "Maybe the blood brother would do even that, if you had just made it possible for him to marry the girl he'd set his heart on, John."

"Piffle!" growled the man. And then: "Hasn't the time come when you can tell me a little more about what happened to me after the doctor put me to sleep that night at the dam?"

"Yes. The only reason you haven't been told was because we didn't want you to worry; we wanted you to have a chance to get well and strong again."

The man's eyes filled suddenly, and he took no shame. He was still shaky enough in nerve and muscle to excuse it. "Nobody ever had such friends, Corona," he said. "You all knew I'd have to go back to Lawrenceville and fight it out, and you didn't want me to go handicapped and half-dead. But how did they come to let you take me away? I've known Macauley ever since I was in knickers. He is not the man to take any chances."

The young woman's laugh was soundless. "Mr. Macauley wasn't asked. He thinks you are dead," she said.

"What!"

"It's so. You were not the only one wounded in the fight at the dam. There were two others—two of M'Graw's men. Three days later, just as Colonel-daddy and Billy Starbuck were getting ready to steal you away, one of the others died. In some way the report got out that you were the one who died, and that made everything quite easy. The report has never been contradicted, and when Mr. Macauley reached Brewster the police people told him that he was too late."

"Good heavens! Does everybody in Brewster think I'm dead?"

"Nearly everybody. But you needn't look so horrified. You're not dead, you know; and there were no obituaries in the newspapers, or anything like that."

The man got upon his feet rather unsteadily.

"That's the limit," he said definitively. "I'm a man now, Corona; too much of a man, I hope, to hide behind another man's grave. I'm going back to Brewster, to-day!"

The young woman made a quaint little grimace at him. "How are you going to get there?" she asked. "It's twenty miles, and the walking is awfully bad—in spots."

"But I must go. Can't you see what everybody will say of me?—that I was too cowardly to face the music when my time came? Nobody will believe that I wasn't a consenting party to this hide-away!"

"Sit down," she commanded calmly; and when he obeyed: "From day to day, since I began coming out here, John, I've been trying to rediscover the man whom I met just once, one evening over a year ago, at Cousin Adda's house in Guthrieville: I can't find him—he's gone."

"Corona!" he said. "Then you recognized me?"

"Not at first. But after a while little things began to come back; and what you told me—about Miss Richlander, you know, and the hint you gave me of your trouble—did the rest."

"Then you knew—or you thought—I was a criminal?"

She nodded, and her gaze was resting upon the near-by gravel heaps. "Cousin Adda wrote me. But that made no difference. I didn't know whether you had done the things they said you had, or not. What I did know was that you had broken your shackles in some way and were trying to get free. You were, weren't you?"

"I suppose so; in some blind fashion. But it is you who have set me free, Corona. It began that night in Guthrieville when I stole one of your gloves; it wasn't anything you said; it was what you so evidently believed and lived. And out here: I was simply a raw savage when you first saw me. I had tumbled headlong into the abyss of the new and the elemental, and if I am trying to scramble out now on the side of honor and clean manhood, it is chiefly because you have shown me the way."

"When did I ever, John?"—with an up-glance of the gray eyes that was almost wistful.

"Always; and with a wisdom that makes me almost afraid of you. For example, there was the night when I was fairly on the edge of letting Jibbey stay in the mine and go mad if he wanted to: you lashed me with the one word that made me save his life instead of taking it. How did you know that was the one word to say?"

"How do we know anything?" she inquired softly. "The moment brings its own inspiration. It broke my heart to see what you could be, and to think that you might not be it, after all. But I came out here this morning to talk about something else. What are you going to do when you are able to leave Sunrise Gulch?"

"The one straightforward thing there is for me to do. I shall go back to Lawrenceville and take my medicine."

"And after that?"

"That is for you to say, Corona. Would you marry a convict?"

"You are not guilty."

"That is neither here nor there. They will probably send me to prison, just the same, and the stigma will be mine to wear for the remainder of my life. I can wear it now, thank God! But to pass it on to you—and to your children, Corona ... if I could get my own consent to that, you couldn't get yours."

"Yes, I could, John; I got it the first time Colonel-daddy brought me out here and let me see you. You were out of your head, and you thought you were talking to Billy Starbuck—in the automobile on the night when you were going with him to the fight at the dam. It made me go down on my two knees, John, and kiss your poor, hot hands."

He slipped his one good arm around her and drew her close.

"Now I can go back like a man and fight it through to the end," he exulted soberly. "Jibbey will take me; I know he is wearing himself out trying to make me believe that he can wait, and that Verda understands, though he won't admit it. And when it is all over, when they have done their worst to me——"

With a quick little twist she broke away from the encircling arm.

"John, dear," she said, and her voice was trembling between a laugh and a sob, "I'm the wickedest, wickedest woman that ever lived and breathed—and the happiest! I knew what you would do, but I couldn't resist the temptation to make you say it. Listen: this morning Colonel-daddy got a night-letter from Billy Starbuck. You have been wondering why Billy never came out here to see you—it was because he and Mr. Stillings have been in Lawrenceville, trying to clear you. They are there now, and the wire says that Watrous Dunham has been arrested and that he has broken down and confessed. You are a free man, John; you——"

The grass-cropping pony had widened its circle by a full yard, and the westward-pointing shadows of the firs were growing shorter and more clearly defined as the August sun swung higher over the summits of the eastern Timanyonis. For the two on the house bench, time, having all its interspaces filled with beatific silences, had no measure that was worth recording. In one of the more coherent intervals it was the man who said:

"Some things in this world are very wonderful, Corona. We call them happenings, and try to account for them as we may by the laws of chance. Was it chance that threw us together at your cousin's house in Guthrieville a year ago last June?"

She laughed happily. "I suppose it was—though I'd like to be romantic enough to believe that it wasn't."

"Debritt would say that it was the Absolute Ego," he said, half musingly.

"And who is Mr. Debritt?"

"He is the man I dined with on my last evening in Lawrenceville. He had been joking me about my various little smugnesses—good job, good clothes, easy life, and all that, and he wound up by warning me to watch out for the Absolute Ego."

"What is the Absolute Ego?" she asked dutifully.

John Montague Smith, with his curling yellow beard three weeks untrimmed, with his clothes dressing the part of a neglected camper, and with a steel-jacketed bullet trying to encyst itself under his right shoulder-blade, grinned exultantly.

"Debritt didn't know, himself; but I know now: it's the primitive man-soul; the 'I' that is able to refuse to be bound down and tied by environment or habit or petty conventions, or any of the things we misname 'limitations.' It's asleep in most of us; it was asleep in me. You made it sit up and rub its eyes for a minute or two that evening in Guthrieville, but it dozed off again, and there had to be an earthquake at the last to shake it alive. Do you know the first thing it did when it took hold and began to drive?"

"No."

"Here is where the law of chances falls to pieces, Corona. Without telling me anything about it, this newly emancipated man-soul of mine made a bee-line for the only Absolute Ego woman it had ever known. And it found her."

Again the young woman laughed happily. "If you are going to call me names, Ego-man, you'll have to make it up to me some other way," she said.

Whereupon, the moment being strictly elemental and sacred to demonstrations of the absolute, he did.

The End

CPSIA information can be obtained
at www.ICGtesting.com
Printed in the USA
LVHW030713200720
661094LV00031B/1328